The Jig Is Up

Also by Lisa Q. Mathews

The Ladies Smythe & Westin Mysteries

Fashionably Late
Permanently Booked
Cardiac Arrest

The Jig
Is Up

AN IRISH BED &
BREAKFAST MYSTERY

Lisa Q. Mathews

CROOKED
LANE

NEW YORK

Published in the United States by Crooked Lane Books, an imprint of The Quick Brown Fox & Company LLC.

Crooked Lane Books and its logo are trademarks of The Quick Brown Fox & Company LLC.

Library of Congress Catalog-in-Publication data available upon request.

ISBN (hardcover): 978-1-63910-851-0
ISBN (ebook): 978-1-63910-852-7

Cover design by Rob Fiore

Printed in the United States.

www.crookedlanebooks.com

Crooked Lane Books
34 West 27th St., 10th Floor
New York, NY 10001

First Edition: August 2024

10 9 8 7 6 5 4 3 2 1

With much love to my big sis, who isn't really a mystery fan—but maybe she'll read this one.

Chapter One

"Mommy, the shamrock's not smiling."

I took another swig of cold coffee from my travel mug and twisted toward the back seat, where my seven-year-old daughter, Bliz—aka Mary Elizabeth—looked confused in the semidarkness. "That means there's no vacancy, sweetie. The shamrock sign only smiles when there are hotel rooms left."

On cue, the interior of the Subaru turned neon green. Then black. Then green again. The crazy sign probably kept the Smiling Shamrock Bed & Breakfast guests awake all night. Or flashed in their nightmares.

My older daughter, Maeve, looked up from her phone and unslumped herself from her neck pillow in fourteen-year-old fashion. "Thought we were going to Gram's."

She sounded cranky, and I didn't blame her. The trip to Shamrock had taken double the usual time.

"We are. Just pulling over for a second."

Apparently, I needed the GPS to direct me through my own hometown. It was so foggy I couldn't see two feet past the windshield.

Neither rain, nor fog, nor gloom of night . . . Was that how the line went? I'd passed it engraved above the old General Post Office Building in Manhattan a million times on my way to work.

1

Nope, I'd forgotten the snow part. At least we hadn't dealt with that tonight. Just double the gloom, which had fittingly led us to the crunchy gravel driveway of the Smiling Shamrock.

I jumped at a sharp rap on the window. Instinctively, I hit the automatic door lock, managing to put down the window instead. Rain poured into the car.

A small elderly woman in a dark, shapeless trench coat peered in with beady, yellow bird eyes. The gnarled fingers of one hand clutched an umbrella patterned with Celtic knots. The other hand held a shopping bag from Kilpatrick's, the Irish import market off the square. Had she really gone out on a night like this?

"Why, Katie Buckley, all the way from the big city. Is it some kind of trouble you're having?"

I drew back. Una McShane ran the Smiling Shamrock with her sister Nuala, who was equally unpleasant. As a kid, I'd always avoided their house, even on Halloween. Bliz, I noticed, was clutching the sleeve of Maeve's hoodie.

"We're fine, thanks, Mrs. McShane. Just turning around."

"You shouldn't be out in this terrible storm with your young girls." She leaned in so close I caught a faint whiff of stale peppermint. "I'd offer you a room if we had one to spare. We're fully booked with Saint Patrick's Week coming up, of course."

"Appreciate the concern, but we're headed to the Buckley House." I was desperate to close the window. My whole left side was drenched, and she wasn't far enough away from the car for me to hit the gas.

"Your mother still has rooms available, then?" Una sounded pleased. "That's a shame."

"Sorry, we need to get going," I said. "'Bye now." With a wave, I put up the window and threw the Subaru in reverse, then carefully inched away from her. She still barely moved.

The Jig Is Up

When we reached the mailbox disguised as a tree-stump fairy home—don't ask—the fog cleared. Against my better judgment, I glanced back and spotted another green-flashing figure, much taller than Una, spying through the lace-curtained bay window.

The Irish Wicked Witches of Western Massachusetts.

Bliz pressed her nose against the back window as we headed toward the town square. "It looks like one of those little Christmas villages."

That was an accurate description of Shamrock, with its tidy shops and restaurants and old-fashioned lampposts with faux flicker flames. The library featured a bronze leprechaun out front, sitting cross-legged on a bench with a book. I doubted leprechauns were big readers, but the tourists loved it.

That was the important thing, wasn't it?

The whole idea behind the town revamp about ten years ago was to play up Shamrock's early Celtic history and make pots of gold by attracting new businesses, tourists, pub enthusiasts, crafters, and festival fans to the area. The "new" center of Shamrock was designed to resemble a charming village in Ireland.

My dad, who everyone still called the Chief even though he no longer officially headed the police department, was fond of claiming it didn't look like anything in the Emerald Isle at all, and that the diddly-idle details only fooled gullible city folk from Boston and New York. At the top of the square, the sign outside the Chamber of Commerce read, *Welcome to Shamrock: A Wee Bit o' Irish Heaven in New England*. The Chief muttered to himself every time he saw it.

I agreed with him. The whole project was a shade on the tacky side. Successful in a financial sense, yes, and as an accountant I appreciated that. The old woolen mills had reopened as a thriving made-in-the-USA Irish knitwear business, employing residents and selling online as well as locally. Many of the factory buildings on the outskirts of town had been repurposed into trendy dining and shopping areas, not to mention co-op apartments and communal workspaces. But Shamrock just wasn't the same anymore. We were a year-round, theme-town destination.

The place had its good points, though. Most of the residents, many of them small-business owners, loved the more exciting—and lucrative—Shamrock. And like the real Ireland, the town was much more diverse these days.

I tried to ignore my splitting headache, which wasn't helping my mood. I'd packed the Tylenol in one of our bags at the last minute. I couldn't remember whose.

"Don't miss the turn for Galway Court this time, Mom," Maeve piped up helpfully.

"Think I've got this, thanks." I hung a soggy right at Farrell's Pub and passed Our Lady of Angels Church and School. The Buckley House, my family's weathered white Victorian, was the fourth residence on the left. The green-and-gold awning above the door said *Céad míle fáilte*, which translated from Irish into "A hundred thousand welcomes." Or something like that. I'd never been able to pronounce it.

After unloading the car in another torrent of rain, we straggled up the steep, water-slicked steps to the house, with our ratty but beloved cat, Banshee, complaining all the way in his carrier. I leaned hard on the bell, exhausted. No one knew we were coming—well, maybe my twenty-four-year-old sister, Colleen, if she'd bothered to check her messages. Her urgent texts had arrived in quick succession while I was in a client meeting.

Need to talk. in person. Impt!
When can u get here?
Don't say anything to Mom.

I'd texted her back. I'd even tried to call her. Did she answer? No.

Colleen's last "emergency" had involved borrowing my new lavender tweed jacket for a crucial job interview. Not that it did much good, since she'd slept through her alarm and missed the appointment.

But this seemed different. Usually my sister offered full-blown details.

Lights blazed in the hallway, but no one answered the door. I jiggled the knob. Locked. After 8:00 PM, even the guests had to ring the bell.

"I hear the police scanner," Maeve said.

The entire neighborhood probably heard it. The Chief kept the volume at the highest setting and refused to let anyone touch it, even if the guests complained. He'd never wanted to turn the house into a bed-and-breakfast in the first place, to be honest, but he and Mom needed the money after his sudden retirement. Colleen helped run the place. That was her job, and my parents were happy to have her living safely at home.

"I'm getting all wet," Bliz said. "And so is Banshee."

"Hold on." Maeve pulled her sweatshirt hood over her head and ran back down the steps to the bushes alongside the house. She felt around in the mud and wet pachysandra until she found the old baby food jar with the spare key.

"Thanks, honey," I said when she returned, completely soaked. I did a double take. "Maeve, is that eyeliner running down your face?" I said as I shook out the key. "Get rid of it, please, so your grandfather doesn't see it."

"You look like a real, live zombie," Bliz said.

"Zombies are dead," Maeve told her, but she swiped at her eyes with her sleeve.

As I inserted the key in the lock, the door finally opened, and Colleen stuck out her towel-turbaned head. She wore a fuzzy, cow-print bathrobe thrown over a pair of black jeans, and her face was covered with a pink mud mask that reeked of vanilla. Her eyebrows were glopped over, but I could tell they were raised. "Hi, guys! Wow. What a surprise."

Surprise? "Didn't you see my texts and calls?" I said. "We got here as fast as we could. Is everything all right?"

"Oh, sure. I'll tell you later." My sister made a little zip-it gesture across her lips. Then she swooped down to give Bliz a hug. "Glad you're all here! Come on in."

I had to give Bliz a gentle push ahead of me over the threshold. She seemed transfixed by Colleen's blinding pink face and snow-owl eyes.

"Sorry about the glam getup, ladies." Colleen seemed perfectly cheerful, but her tone sounded nervous. "Thursday is self-care night."

Not for all of us. "Right." I kept my voice low and even. "So where are Mom and the Chief? They're okay?"

"I certainly hope so." My mom came down the hallway, tall and slim in gray flannel pants and a silver-threaded sweater that matched her hair. "Kate, girls, how lovely to see you. And unexpected too. What a terrible drive you must have had."

"Hi, Mom." I hugged her. Was it my imagination, or did she look slightly more tired than usual?

As I stepped away, she gathered the girls into her arms. "Welcome, all of you. The guest room situation may be a bit tight," she added, with a worried frown. "We're hoping to get more reservations for Paddy's Week, but—"

"Kate's bunking with me," Colleen said. "The girls can take the Nest."

"Yay!" Bliz gave an excited little clap.

The Nest was a cozy space under the eaves in the attic, with a trapdoor and folding ladder. I'd spent endless hours up there when I was younger, reading Nancy Drew and writing in my journal when spiders weren't in season. Too bad there wasn't room for three of us.

Mom seemed relieved. "Fine. Why don't you all troop in and say hello to the Chief? Colleen, take their bags upstairs. I'll put on the kettle for tea. It's lucky you didn't catch your death out there in that cold rain."

A feline yowl sounded from the carrier in Maeve's hand. "We, um, brought Banshee," she said.

"Oh." Colleen peered inside the crate. "Hey there, fella. Whoa, he's grown a lot. I can't pet him, though. I'm allergic, remember?"

"Sorry, I couldn't get a cat-sitter on such short notice," I said. "And you are not allergic."

She pointed to her face. "See? My eyes are already getting watery. But that's okay." Wiping her muddy-pink fingertips on her bathrobe, she grabbed the cat carrier along with Maeve's suitcase and lugged them toward the stairs. Banshee expressed his displeasure with another trademark wail.

I shepherded the girls toward the dimly lit living room. In my next life, I'd come back as a border collie. Maeve dabbed at her raccoon eyes again with her sweatshirt cuff.

Ensconced as usual in his wheelchair in the corner, the Chief rocked a heavy wool plaid robe and well-worn leather slippers. He was in his early seventies, but people sometimes took him for older. Not long after my ill-fated wedding, a guy my dad once helped put behind bars walked into the Shamrock PD—which the Chief had headed up for three decades—and shot him at his desk. My dad lost the use of his legs and, more importantly to him, the job he loved.

He looked the same as ever. Strong—and stubborn—as a mule. But looks could be deceiving when people were ill. Was he sick? In sudden mental decline? Is that why Colleen had summoned me?

Impossible. Not the Chief.

"Hi, Dad," I said.

Bliz ran forward and jumped straight into his lap.

If he was surprised to see us, he didn't show it. An ex-Marine as well as Shamrock's police chief emeritus, he never seemed surprised about much of anything. "Well, now, if it isn't the charming Miss Mary Elizabeth Buckley herself." He gave one of Bliz's blond braids a tug. "And her very wet sister, Maeve Patricia, with the dirt under her eyes."

Yep, still sharp. I breathed a secret sigh of relief and scratched "mental decline" off the possible disaster list.

"Lucky you made it, Katie. I've been following the scanner here. Plenty of wrecks out there tonight."

"Mmm." I tried to ignore the loud crackling over by the drapes. I couldn't decipher the dispatchers' mumbo jumbo, sprinkled with numbers. They could have been talking about the Red Sox, for all I knew.

As my dad and the girls traded new favorite jokes, I surreptitiously headed over to lower the volume. Much better. The guests—and my long-suffering mother—would thank me. The Chief raised a bushy eyebrow at me, but he didn't make a fuss.

I glanced around the faded living room. Same dark walnut furniture, fringed lamps, and gilt-framed paintings, the hutch jammed with Belleek pottery and Waterford crystal. The piano with one short leg I'd taught myself to play. Nothing looked out of place.

The Buckley House wasn't the fanciest bed-and-breakfast in town, but it was comfortable enough. Bliz was already helping herself to a handful of wrapped butterscotch candies from the cut-glass bowl on the coffee table. Maeve sat back on the well-stuffed, floral-patterned sofa and snapped her gum.

"Like a cow with her cud, you are," the Chief told her mildly. Maeve stopped mid-snap.

Mom walked in, wiping her hands on an embroidered dish towel. "Tea and drinking chocolate in the kitchen, girls. You'll be ready for bed soon, I'm sure."

Bliz tore for the kitchen.

"Gram, I'm almost in high school," Maeve said. "I stay up late now."

"Ah, of course," Mom said. "Your studies."

"Where are all the guests?" I asked, then wanted to kick myself. I hadn't seen any extra cars in the driveway. Just the vacancy sign hanging from the post out front. No shamrock, no smile. The Buckley House had cozy charm, but it was definitely no-frills.

"We aren't fully booked yet," Mom said, "but we've had inquiries. One elderly couple is already tucked in for the evening, and the other two ladies went out. Heaven help them in this rain, but they wanted to hear the music at the Barleycorn tonight. Your father drove them in the van."

"Guess they didn't want to stick around and listen to Crime Scan." Colleen waltzed into the living room and dropped down beside Maeve. She'd changed into houndstooth leggings and a curve-hugging black turtleneck. Her long blond curls were swept back with rhinestone barrettes.

"Don't be smart, missy," the Chief said. "Turn it up, will you?"

"Kate and I are going down to Farrell's," Colleen said. "It's still early, and there's nothing in the fridge."

"And whose fault is that?" our mom said.

My sister looked penitent. "Sorry, Mom. I totally ran out of time tonight. I'll hit the store first thing in the morning. Promise."

"No need to go out," I said. "We just got here, and there's practically a monsoon outside. We'll make sandwiches or something. And talk." I looked directly at my sister.

Colleen gave one curl a slow twist on her shoulder with her index finger. She'd been doing that nervous hair twirl ever since she was a toddler.

"I'm starving," Maeve piped up.

"Come with us, then," Colleen said.

"I don't like the idea of you girls taking Maeve into Farrell's at night." The Chief frowned.

"Oh, it'll be okay, Daddy." Colleen gave him a cute, dimpled smile. "We'll sit in the restaurant part."

"Humph."

My baby sister had our dad—and most people—wrapped in the tiny hands of her Claddagh ring. She could probably get away with murder if she wanted.

She turned to Maeve to seal the deal. "Hurry up if you want to change, okay? They shut down the grill at nine thirty."

I was too tired to argue, and Maeve was already halfway up the stairs. Fine. I'd talk to Colleen in private later. One advantage of sharing a bedroom.

Maybe it was oldest-sibling syndrome, or because I was a mom—but something *was* wrong. I could just tell, no matter how nonchalant my sister acted.

Nothing like beer and fried mozzarella sticks to take care of the weird churning in my stomach.

Chapter Two

The rain started lashing again the second Colleen, Maeve, and I stepped out of the house. "Want to take the Subaru?" I offered.

"It's only a couple of blocks," Colleen said. "We'll walk fast."

She and I shared the black golf umbrella I'd grabbed from the guest stand in the foyer, and Maeve had the mini tote to herself. Farrell's familiar wooden sign was barely visible in the distance, swinging in the wind. Bursts of laughter and loud music shot through the night, audible even over the rain, every time someone opened the door.

Maeve dragged behind us, trying to find more bars for her phone by holding it up under the umbrella in different directions. Cell service in Shamrock wasn't always the best. Kind of like the Buckley family communication system.

I needed to take advantage of this limited privacy window, since Colleen still wasn't saying much. Probably trying to find the right words to tell me the bad news I'd dreaded all day. Whatever it was, we'd deal with it together. That's what sisters did.

Or what we were supposed to do, anyway. I was the sister who usually bailed the other out. The older, responsible, less fun sibling. But Colleen had always looked up to me. And I always protected her, no questions asked.

Okay, maybe just one.

"Colleen, why did you want me to come home?"

She thrust her hands deeper into the pockets of her moto jacket. "You really didn't need to rush here like that. It wasn't, like, a huge emergency or anything."

That was a good thing, but my annoyance meter shot up anyway. "You implied it was something major," I pointed out. "You asked how soon I could get here."

"I didn't mean you had to drop everything and show up *tonight*."

If I completely lost it, she'd clam up even more. "Colleen, I have a job. And it's tax season."

"I know. It was sweet of you, and I totally appreciate it. But you always read into things too much, Katie."

"What? You're blaming *me*? Maybe if you'd bothered to answer my texts and calls after throwing out all the drama, I wouldn't—" I wanted to strangle her, but arguing wouldn't get us anywhere. "You said not to tell Mom. I thought she or Dad might be sick."

"No health stuff, I swear."

I practically collapsed on the sidewalk in relief. The worst catastrophe I could imagine—someone I loved being ill or even dying—wasn't something I wanted to face right now. Or ever, really.

Colleen fell quiet again. As the silence between us grew, so did the cold, creeping dread I'd felt earlier. I couldn't shake it.

I waited for a minute or two, hoping she'd jump in to fill the void. Detectives employed the same technique to get suspects to blurt out incriminating info. The Chief had used it on both of us for years. But it didn't work this time.

"Is it . . . a guy?" I asked finally. "Are you seeing someone?" I hesitated. "Getting married?"

"God, no." Colleen looked horrified. "None of the above. Jeez."

"Okay, so there's got to be some reason you're not coughing up details here." Maybe I was overreacting again, but I couldn't let it go. Something was very wrong in Colleen Land.

She glanced over her shoulder at Maeve, who was still oblivious. "There are two problems, actually. One is easier to fix, I guess, and the other is a little more complicated. I just wanted to talk to you in person."

"Well, okay, here I am. Do you need money?" I prayed that wasn't it, because I didn't have much to spare right now. Our landlord had jacked the rent last month, and I still owed the girls' spring tuition fees.

Before my sister could answer, another rush of wind blew up, and I fought to close the umbrella. The wind sent it sideways, snapping the ribs, and the top part bonked Colleen on the head.

"Ow!"

"Sorry, it got away from me. You okay?"

"I'm fine."

Maeve jogged toward us as I wrestled the umbrella into permanent submission. It was destined for the nearest trash container. We were soaked anyway.

Colleen started walking briskly again, then stopped at the front gate outside the church. "There's a light on in Angels Hall."

"Bingo night?" The faithful of Our Lady of Angels loved bingo, which included fifty-fifty raffles and miniature bottles of Baileys in crocheted baskets beside the coffee urn.

"Nah," Colleen said. "You remember Deirdre Donnelly, right? She teaches Irish dance classes there on Thursdays, but this week they're doing show rehearsals for Paddy's Day. She was going to stay after the kids left and work on choreography with some new music, but she should've been done by now. We'd planned to meet at Farrell's around eight thirty."

"As in, more than half an hour ago? Did you let her know you'd be late?" My sister operated on what people in Shamrock referred to as "Irish time."

"I texted her after you and the girls showed up. Let's go get her so she can walk over with us." Colleen turned into the church parking lot and splashed across it in her cute designer rain boots.

Maeve and I followed, heading toward the two-story brick building at the back. My suede work flats were already toast from earlier. Ditto the dress-code school shoes Maeve had worn during the house key fishing expedition in the bushes. Now her sneakers were ruined too. More expenses for the list.

We reached the parish hall steps just as Colleen pushed her way inside.

"They don't lock the door?" Maeve said.

"You've been living in the city too long, kiddo." Colleen grinned over her shoulder. "No one but the Chief locks anything here. Especially not at the church. Shamrock is super safe."

Maeve didn't remember much about living here, just our visits. She and I had moved to Brooklyn for good when she was Bliz's age. I wasn't sure the Chief and the hardworking women and men of the Shamrock PD would agree with my sister's "super safe" description, but okay.

When I'd moved to the city the first time to pursue my crazy, long-ago dream of becoming a professional musician, Dad told me the important thing was never to let your guard down. And I never did. Well, only once.

I should have heeded his other advice concerning the charming guy from Dublin who was no longer my husband. Colleen wasn't the only cop's daughter who tuned out what she didn't want to hear.

A lively jig played from an old-school boom box on a metal folding chair at the far end of the huge room. Blast from the way past.

Likewise, the hall itself still resembled practically every other one in the Northeast for the last hundred years.

Shiny wood floor doubling as a basketball court. Crucifix above the velvet-curtained stage. American and state flags in the corner. Athletic pennants displayed on painted concrete walls. Black roll-away piano. Buzzing, purplish, detention-hall lighting. Check. Check. Check.

Saint Anyone's of Anywhere.

"I'm freezing." Maeve rubbed her arms.

"Me too, honey." The hall was filled with little pockets of cold, like Emerald Lake in late August or a haunted house on a ghost-hunters show.

Colleen's friend was nowhere in sight.

"She must be in the bathroom," my sister said. "I'll let her know we're here."

I remembered Deirdre. A pale, serious girl with black hair and green eyes, she'd practically been Colleen's shadow since they'd met in the Babies class at the Donnelly School of Irish Dance, which Deirdre's parents owned. By the time they were Bliz's age, Deirdre was the best dancer in the class, followed by Colleen, who might have had some natural talent, but wasn't a fan of discipline and practice. Straight out of high school, after a successful competitive career, Deirdre joined Irish Steps, one of the major Irish dance shows. The move paid off big-time—financially, anyway. I had no idea why she'd left the show, but now here she was, back in Shamrock.

It was really hard to escape this town.

That infernal jig was still playing on endless loop. Or was it a reel? I couldn't remember. My step dancing career ended in second grade, the same as Maeve's. Colleen's lasted through high school. For a while she and Deirdre had big plans to tour with Irish Steps together, but that didn't work out for my sister.

Where *was* Colleen? It shouldn't take this long for her to find Deirdre, even if she took a minute or two to use the ladies' room herself. She'd headed toward the larger restroom, out in the hall. There was a smaller one backstage.

"Be right back," I told Maeve. Still clutching the dripping umbrella, I stabbed the Stop button on the boom box with the tip as I passed, smiling in satisfaction when the music abruptly died. Now the only sound was another round of rain pounding the roof.

The backstage ladies' room was closer, so I checked that one first. As I jogged up the stage steps, the curtain billowed in front of me, as if disturbed by a sudden breeze. I drew my trench coat closer and tightened the belt. I should have brought the zip-in winter lining from home, but I'd been in too much of a hurry to grab it.

It took another wave of wind and velvet before I noticed the thin, dark trail of red beneath the curtain, leading directly stage left.

Chapter Three

Adrenaline shot through me as if I'd been pulled over by a patrol cruiser. I gripped the handle of my dead umbrella tighter and closed my eyes to stop the dizziness.

The foreboding I'd felt since getting Colleen's text was back, stronger this time.

Not blood. Not blood. When I opened my eyes again, the floor below the stage curtain would be lemony-spray clean.

It wasn't. The blood—or whatever it was—still marked the shiny, polyurethaned wood like a dark plum lip pencil.

"Deirdre's not in the main bathroom," Colleen announced, coming up the stage steps behind me.

I didn't answer. I couldn't.

"What's the matter, Katie? Your face is the color of a Communion wafer." Colleen's gaze fell on the slightly smeared red line. "Oh. My. God." She pushed past me and grabbed at the curtain, trying to find the break.

"Colleen, wait!" I called, but she'd already disappeared.

I turned to confirm that Maeve was where I'd left her, in the middle of the main hall. Yes. My daughter frowned at me questioningly.

"Stay right where you are, honey," I said. "Don't move." I ducked under the heavy curtain and used my phone's flashlight app, which didn't help much. I half-felt my way toward the wings in the darkness, my arms outstretched in case I hit the wall—or anything else. Finally, I found a set of switches, and flipped them up.

Caught in the sudden glare of multicolored stage lights, Colleen whirled like a startled vampire.

"Shh." I placed a finger to my lips as I glanced around at the seemingly empty backstage area. A stepladder and a couple of cardboard boxes. A mop in a galvanized bucket. "What if someone's back here?"

"Hopefully Deirdre." Colleen's voice held a hint of trepidation.

"I need to get back to Maeve." I shivered as cold air blew up from the open stage door at the basement level. Beyond it, white-blue lightning cracked the sky, illuminating the backstage stairs.

In that split second, I glimpsed a glint of gold and a crumpled form at the bottom of the stairs. A pale young woman, long black hair swirled across her face, in a motionless heap.

Deirdre.

"Jayzus, Mary, and Joseph," Colleen breathed.

I hesitated, just for a second. What would be worse—my daughter seeing a person horribly injured, or being left by herself in the middle of Angels Hall?

"I'm getting Maeve." My words sounded strangled, even to my own ears.

Colleen had already rushed down the stairs, her boots barely grazing the steps.

I unsuccessfully tried to body-block Maeve's view as she came up. She gave a little gasp.

The Jig Is Up

My sister was huddled over her friend. "Is she . . . okay?" This time my voice cracked like an eighth-grade boy's. In my heart, I knew the answer.

Colleen gingerly placed two fingers at Deirdre's neck, beneath a delicate gold chain with two dangling charms. A tiny emerald adorned the center of one of them. "I don't feel any pulse. Maybe I'm looking in the wrong place."

"Mom. Stop." Maeve pushed away the broken-ribbed umbrella that I held in front of her, showering water droplets over both of us. "I'm not some little kid." She glanced down the stairs, then back at me, her expression oddly blank.

I slipped my phone from the pocket of my trench coat and tapped the screen. "I'm calling 911," I told Colleen.

"Maybe we should call Dad or Frank," Colleen said.

Seriously? If this wasn't an emergency, I didn't know what qualified as one. And even though Frank, our other sibling, was on the force, sometimes he could be a real pain.

My phone was taking forever to connect. "Is she breathing?"

Colleen leaned closer to Deirdre's face. "Not sure. I don't feel any air. And her chest isn't moving."

"At least she isn't bleeding anymore," Maeve said.

None of those were good things. Dead bodies didn't bleed. "Start CPR," I said.

Colleen bit her lip. "What if I break her ribs or something? That could happen, right?"

"Well, I'm no expert either," I said. "But we have to try until the first responders get here. Better broken ribs than . . ."

"Dead," Maeve finished.

I tapped my phone again. Still nothing.

Maeve ran over and dropped down next to Colleen. "I can help. We learned CPR at school. There's a song you use for

19

the rhythm. I forget the name, but it's from a John Travolta movie."

"*Grease*?"

"No. The disco one. At the beginning when he's walking down the—"

"'*Staying Alive*'!" Colleen called out, like a game show contestant. "Well, that's appropriate."

"Tilt her head back," Maeve said. "You have to open the airway first."

"Cloverhill County 911," a dispatcher's voice said in my ear. *Finally.* "What's the location of your emergency?"

"Angels Hall. Someone—Deirdre Donnelly—has been hurt. Really badly."

"Which city, please?"

"Shamrock." I tried to stay calm. Maeve and Colleen's CPR efforts didn't seem to be working, because Deirdre still wasn't moving. I turned my back to concentrate, my pulse pounding in my ears.

"Is that Our Lady of Angels Roman Catholic Church and School on Galway Court? Or the rectory?"

"Parish hall." I clutched my phone tighter. "In the back. Hurry, please."

The dispatcher fired more questions. What was the nature of the accident? Was the person conscious? Was she breathing? Could she speak?

I checked over my shoulder. Colleen was humming the song staccato-style as Maeve pushed down on Deirdre's chest with the beat.

"Come on, Dee," Colleen urged. "Breathe. Please. *Breathe*, for God's sake!"

"Hello? Ma'am, are you still on the line?"

"Yes."

"Emergency responders are on the way. What is your name, please? Are you related to the injured person? Is anyone else there with you?"

I answered the questions, then placed my phone next to Maeve and Colleen on speaker after the dispatcher offered to talk them through the CPR.

Following the dispatcher's directions, Colleen pinched Dierdre's nostrils shut and blew into her friend's mouth, working in tandem with Maeve.

Someone burst through the open stage door. Frank. "Mother of God, what happened?"

"Don't know," I said. "How'd you get here so quick?"

"Dad beeped me at Farrell's. He picked up the call on the scanner." Frank pulled off his dripping jacket and dropped it behind him on the floor as he jogged toward us.

"Whoa, Deirdre Donnelly?" He stopped short behind my sister.

"She's still not breathing." Colleen sat back on her heels, her eyes filling with tears. "This CPR stuff doesn't work."

"Move over. You girls don't know what you're doing." Frank took over for her and Maeve. Ordinarily, all three of us would have jumped on the "girls" reference, but this was hardly the time. "How long has she been like this?" he added, between compressions.

"No idea," I said. "We just found her here. About fifteen minutes ago."

"Oh my God." Colleen started to shake. "Deirdre can't die."

"It's going to be okay." I crouched to put my arms around my sister, and she sobbed into my shoulder. I glanced over at Maeve to see how she was holding up, but her eyes were laser-focused on Frank as he worked.

"What are you doing here, anyway, Kate?" he asked.

"We were on our way to Farrell's too, and Colleen saw the light on so—"

"No, I mean, why are you in Shamrock? You know. Home."

No idea. "Just a visit."

Frank grunted in reply. I put that down to the effort of keeping up the chest compressions. I was only three years older, but we'd never been super close. I loved him, of course. He was my brother. We just didn't always see eye to eye. Colleen had it worse. He treated her as if she were Bliz's age. Maybe we both did. Sometimes it seemed appropriate, to be honest.

I let the dispatcher know that an off-duty officer had arrived, and she assured me that the other responders would arrive any minute. A good thing, because I wanted to get my daughter out of here. She didn't need to be involved in any more of this. Neither did my sister. "Colleen, you should head back to the house with Maeve and me," I said.

She raised her head from the shoulder of my trench coat. "We can't leave. Deirdre needs us. Right, Frank?"

Our brother didn't answer. His neck was getting redder and redder as he continued CPR. I couldn't see Deirdre's face very well, but the hand sticking out from the sleeve of her black athletic top looked unearthly pale.

Deirdre's status hadn't changed. Eerily inert. From the way my sister started trembling again, she must have had the same realization.

"Is Deirdre . . . gone?" she said, in a smaller voice.

"Hope not," Frank muttered through his teeth, still pushing. "I'm sorry, Colleen."

My sister made a little choking sound.

"Maeve, go sit up at the top of the stairs," Frank ordered. "This isn't kid stuff."

My daughter complied without argument. I couldn't read her expression. Blank, almost. Probably in shock. She'd kept her head in an emergency, and I was proud of her, but she had to be traumatized by the sight of a likely dead body. Who knew what she saw these days on TV or online, or even in the news, when I wasn't monitoring things. But in person it was much worse.

"Maybe they can do something for Deirdre at the hospital," I said to Colleen. "We'll just be in the way here. Come back with us." I offered my hand, and she let me pull her to her feet.

"Are you crazy?" Frank said. "This might not have been an accident, okay? There could be a freaking psychopath out there."

"Oh." Colleen glanced nervously toward the open stage door. "Right."

No. This had to have been a terrible accident. Deirdre fell down the stairs and hit her head. She'd had a fainting spell, or gotten dehydrated, or stressed after dealing with a show rehearsal full of out-of-control kids. She could have had a seizure, or a brain aneurysm, or gone into a low-blood-sugar coma.

Frank always carried a gun, even when he was off duty. Would we be safer staying here with him, just in case?

The Chief would pick us up. I sent him a text, a little shocked he wasn't here already.

"I'm not going," Colleen said. "I'm staying here with Deirdre."

"Okay," I said. "Totally up to you. Maeve, we're going back to Gram's."

"I'm f-fine." Maeve's teeth chattered slightly as she hugged herself at the top of the stairs. "Just cold."

From somewhere not far off, a siren wailed. Finally.

"The detectives will want to talk to you and Maeve when they get here. You're witnesses." Frank was still furiously doing CPR. I could tell from his expression he didn't think there was much point, but a cop's first job was to try to save the person, no matter what.

"They can ask their questions later," I said. "It's not like they don't know where the Buckleys live." I patted my sister on the shoulder. "Everything's going to be okay, sweetie."

Colleen nodded, rocking from the heels to the toes of her rain boots and back. One of her rhinestone barrettes had slipped to the end of a long blond curl. She looked like an older Bliz.

"Come on, Maeve," I called. "We'll go out this door."

Probably safest to stay in Frank's sight for as long as possible, rather than retracing our steps past the stage and through Angels Hall to the front entrance. We'd cut through the side parking lot and meet the Chief out on Galway Court, down a ways, to avoid the emergency vehicles.

Now that the lightning had stopped, there was only a small semicircle of light outside the open door. Beyond that, blackness.

My cell phone flashlight faded. Before I could get it back on, Maeve stumbled over something dark and plastic-sounding, but I quickly caught her. "Ow!" she said, reaching for her ankle. "What was that?"

"I don't know, honey," I said. "A stage prop, maybe. Keep moving, okay? We'll ice your foot when we get home."

As we stepped out into the misting rain, an emergency van and a police cruiser squealed up in front of the parish hall. A fire truck screamed in from the other direction.

Two paramedics carrying equipment jumped from the van, and a radio crackled as a cop threw open the cruiser door. All three sprinted toward the building.

None of them noticed us. Where was the Chief? It usually took him a few extra minutes to get into his custom van, but he had it down to a science.

"Mom," Maeve whispered. "Don't look, but there's a guy back there in the bushes."

Of course I looked. Through the mist, just beyond the flood-light at the corner of Angels Hall, I made out a shadowy figure crouched behind the boxwood hedge. His attention seemed glued to the open stage door.

We'd walked right past him.

The person was slight—gangly, like a grasshopper. Maybe a teen. Knit cap drawn over shaggy, dark hair, dressed entirely in black except for the silver zigzag logo on his sneakers.

What was he doing there, lurking in the rain? Did he know what had happened to Deirdre? Had he been responsible somehow for her accident?

My body went into cryogenic freeze as the figure suddenly turned his head. I couldn't make out his expression, but I knew two things for sure.

He'd definitely seen us. And he knew we'd seen him.

Chapter Four

The Chief pulled up just as Maeve and I reached the street. He zoomed away almost as soon as we got in the van, before we'd even said hello or he'd asked us if we were okay.

I quickly told him about the person we'd seen lurking outside Angels Hall, but almost the second I finished we'd reached the Buckley House. "You girls go in. I'll make some calls here on the radio," he said.

Mom tsk-tsked loudly as she held the side door open for us under the dripping awning. "Get in, get in, both of you. You'll catch pneumonia out there. And just that wee umbrella. No wonder you're soaked."

"We had another one," I said as Maeve and I took off our wet coats and hung them in the laundry room. "That's the least of it, Mom."

"Your father told me. Are you girls all right?"

"Fine."

"Where's Colleen?" She gazed out into the night and frowned. "With Frank, I hope?"

"Yes. They're still at the hall with Deirdre. She's . . . Things don't look good, Mom."

She pursed her lips. "I'll give her mother a call, in case she needs a ride to the hospital. Maeve, you should go right to bed."

"But I still haven't eaten anything yet," Maeve said.

"Well, go on up to the Nest, and I'll bring you a toasted cheese sandwich," Mom said.

"Oh, that sounds wonderful," I said brightly. "Doesn't it, Maeve?" Really, anything would be better than either of us getting grilled in the kitchen, along with the cheese, by my mother. "Why don't you have a nice hot shower, and I'll tuck you in?"

Maeve did seem exhausted. She nodded and headed for the stairs, limping a little.

"We'll take a look at that ankle too," I called.

She turned, one hand on the banister. "My foot is fine. I just want to be alone for a while, okay?"

"Let her go," Mom said in a low voice. "She'll come to you when she's ready to talk. Just say a prayer that Frank or Colleen will ring us soon to tell us Deirdre will be fine."

"I don't think so, Mom."

She cocked her head, then gave a short nod. "Come get a bite before you talk to your father. I need to call Bernie Donnelly."

I trailed Mom down the hall, feeling as if I were Maeve's age again. To be honest, that didn't seem like such a bad thing. But I couldn't imagine what my sister was going through right now.

I checked my cell. No missed texts.

Mom dialed Bernie—no one in Shamrock ever called Deirdre's mom Bernadette—while I took a hunk of cheddar cheese from the fridge and sparked the burner under the fry pan.

"No answer," she said, replacing the receiver of the moss-green corded wall phone. Most people in Shamrock still had backup landlines, and the guests found the old-school phones charming.

"I'm going over there. I don't want Bernie driving herself around if she hasn't left already. I'm sure she's in a state."

"I'll hold the fort," I said.

"Don't forget to check in with your father," she added over her shoulder, grabbing a rain poncho from a peg next to the kitchen door.

"I won't," I said, dreading the debrief of the scene in Angels Hall. As I dropped the first pieces of bread into the cast iron pan and they hit the sizzling butter with a hiss, Deirdre's pale face wavered in my mind, hauntingly beautiful. How could such a talented, vibrant young woman suddenly be . . . gone?

Accidents happen, I reminded myself. Life was never predictable, even if we thought so.

I flipped the bread with Mom's well-worn spatula. There was still hope. They could do amazing things now to bring people back from the brink of mortality.

I said a Hail Mary under my breath and added an insurance appeal to St. Jude, the patron saint of hopeless causes. I hadn't been to Mass much lately, but I was sure he would understand.

After a mindless stab at cleaning up my cooking mess, I brought the sandwiches up to the Nest. By the night-light glowing from the base of the bedside lamp, I saw Maeve already asleep beside Bliz in the antique iron bed.

Should I wake her? The two of them looked so peaceful. Maeve's shoulder-length dark hair streamed across her pillow, strands lightly entwined with Bliz's much longer blond curls. My younger daughter was a bed hogger, just like my sister.

Gently, I set the sandwich plate on the nightstand in case Maeve woke up, then tiptoed down the folding ladder. Hopefully she'd sleep until morning and be greeted by bright sunshine streaming through the round window below the eaves.

The Jig Is Up

I headed back downstairs to find the Chief, but he was on his cell phone in the living room, listening intently to the person on the other end. I could grab a quick shower. My dad was a night owl anyway, so chances were good he'd still be up when I was done. He hardly ever slept more than five hours at a time, especially since The Accident. That was how we Buckleys referred to the shooting incident that had left him in a wheelchair for life.

It was easier that way. Fewer questions from strangers and disturbing memories. Maybe less anger too.

When I flipped on the light in Colleen's room, the first thing I saw was my suitcase. She'd dumped it on top of the unmade queen bed. Not near the pillows, thank the Lord, but still. Gross. I tried not to imagine the germs.

I rummaged under a motley collection of Bliz's frizzy-haired fashion dolls—she'd dropped them in as I was closing my suitcase—for my flannel jammies and fleece robe. Then, grabbing my toothbrush from one side pocket and my drugstore-bargain moisturizer from the other, I padded down the hall in my bare feet. I'd forgotten to pack slippers, so I'd need to save those two pairs of clean socks.

The bathroom was still steamy from Maeve's shower, but the warmth felt heavenly as I carefully adjusted the faucets. The hot and cold were switched, a fact I usually failed to remember until too late. A sudden hiss from the old-fashioned radiator made me jump, but I finally started to relax as I stepped into the claw-footed tub, pulled the round shower curtain closed, and let the hot water spray over my head.

In some ways, there was no place like home. In others, not so much.

"Kate, are you in there?" Colleen pounded on the bathroom door.

She was back already. Was that a good sign? I hoped so.

"The cops are here. They want to talk to you."

The water turned ice cold. I twisted off the faucet.

"No need for all that now," I heard another voice say, over the squeak of wheelchair brakes. "They'll talk to your sister and Maeve in the morning. It's already arranged."

"Frank said—"

"I know what he said," the Chief broke in firmly. "I told them Kathleen is wrecked and Maeve is sleeping, so there will be no disturbing them tonight."

Wrecked? I thought I'd been holding up pretty well, under the circumstances.

"But I had to talk to the cops." I could practically see Colleen pouting through the door.

"If anyone has questions for your sister or Maeve, they can deal with me. There's been enough damage for one night." The wheelchair creaked off down the hall.

Well. No offense to Bob Ryan, the current chief of police, but Dermot Buckley still called the shots for the Shamrock PD. Or thought he did.

A moment later, I heard the little ding that meant my dad had pressed the button for his private elevator. It went straight to his office on the top floor he shared with Mom.

I silently thanked him for the brief reprieve. The Chief always went by the book as far as police matters were concerned. In his personal book, though, things were sometimes different.

What had he meant by "enough damage"? Was he talking about Deirdre?

Shivering, I groped for a dry towel from the rack at the end of the tub and held it to my face. The fluffy white cotton became a damp, cloying mask.

Suddenly I couldn't breathe, and not because of the towel. My heart skipped a beat or two, then three, as vivid images from backstage at the parish hall swirled in my mind. The dark red line. The billowing velvet curtain. Colleen's best friend lying in a silent heap on the floor. The guy in black lurking in the bushes.

A person hiding outside Angels Hall in the rain at an accident scene had to mean whatever happened to Deirdre wasn't an accident. And her attacker knew Maeve and I could identify him.

My heartbeat was completely out of whack now. Tears stung my eyes. *Don't panic. Stay calm. Breathe.*

Through the drop-spattered, clear shower curtain, I saw the glass doorknob turn.

"Hey!" I called. "I'm in here."

"Sorry." Colleen again. Her voice sounded muffled.

"Let me get my robe on," I said, but the sound of creaking floorboards clued me in that she'd already left.

At least the interruption had abated my panic attack. My heartbeat was almost back to normal. I stepped out of the tub and rubbed the steam off the mirror above the marble-topped sink. My hands felt like dried apricots and the hue of my skin resembled the lobsters Mom boiled for the guests in a giant pot every Fourth of July.

I averted my eyes from my reflection and tried to yank a wide comb through my tangled hair. The wind had created monster snarls no conditioner could tame. I made a cursory check for the hair dryer under the sink. Nope. Maeve must have taken it back with her to the Nest.

I pushed up on the window to get rid of the steam. The cold air was a shock, but I stood there for a minute, staring out at the rain-soaked street below. A handful of blocks away, I saw Farrell's and the steeple of Our Lady of Angels, lit by the blue and red glow of police and emergency vehicles. I closed the window so hard the glass pane rattled.

When I stepped out into the hall, muffled voices drifted up from downstairs. A Buckley conversation, since the guest rooms were on the other side of the house.

Mom and Colleen. Neither sounded happy.

Belting my robe tighter, I moved quietly toward the stairwell and perched on the top step. When Frank and I were kids, we used to slide down the stairs on our butts, braving carpet burn and our mother's wrath. We set a bad example for Colleen, who'd managed to break her arm.

I slid a little by mistake now as I leaned forward to hear the convo more clearly. I didn't want to walk into the middle of any family discussion cold.

Colleen wasn't crying, at least. That was good.

". . . out of your mind," our mother was saying.

"You don't need to give me another one of your *(murmur)* lectures, Mom," Colleen said. "How was I supposed to know *(murmur, murmur)*? But I'm still *(murmur, murmur)*."

"You don't need to remind anyone about that," Mom said.

"A-*hem.*"

I grabbed the railing to keep myself from falling farther. Why did everyone in this house always sneak up on people?

The Chief hadn't stayed upstairs for long. He could be very stealthy with that wheelchair when he wanted. "Contemplating things from the top of the world, are we?"

"Sort of."

"A wee bit of surveillance, then." He looked oddly pleased.

"Mom said you wanted to talk to me?"

"No need for that right now," he said. "It's been a long night. Maybe you should check on the girls and move along to bed yourself. You'll want to be on your toes tomorrow."

"On my toes? Why?"

He waved. "Ah, nothing much. They're sending out a Statie detective in the morning, and we'll have someone from Shamrock PD as well. Just a few routine questions for you and Maeve. They've already had a chat with your sister."

"Dad, wait," I said as he turned his chair to go. "Is Deirdre . . . gone?"

He nodded sharply, just once. "May she rest in peace. Very sorry, Kathleen."

"Oh my God." I hugged my knees, my teeth chattering like a wind-up denture toy.

"A terrible shame." My dad shook his head. "Deirdre was a nice, sensible girl. Never let all that dancing fame go to her head, always took care of her mother. This will devastate Bernie. Poor woman is all on her own now."

"Colleen must be in bits." I pulled myself to my feet, with a little extra help from the banister. "I'll go talk to her."

A second after the words were out of my mouth, I realized there were no more voices coming from downstairs. Just the revving of Colleen's car in the driveway.

It was after midnight. Where was she headed?

"Ah, let her go," the Chief said.

"But she's upset. What if she gets in an accident or something? I can—"

My dad reached up to place a firm hand on my arm. "Your sister has done enough talking for tonight."

"What do you mean? What did she say?"

His expression was unreadable in the dim hall light. "She's not herself right now, is all."

I rubbed my temples, trying to lessen the throbbing. This whole nightmare had happened so fast. Colleen's best friend was dead. And my sister obviously didn't want to talk to me now about whatever had seemed so important. Had she been worried that something might happen to Deirdre?

No. She would have gone to the Chief. Colleen's life was an endless wheel of colorful drama, but never anything dangerous. As far as I knew, anyway.

"Investigators are still at the scene," the Chief said. "They'll be there a while longer, I'm sure. We should have a preliminary report from the medical examiner sometime tomorrow. Hopefully we'll get some answers before the Staties come in."

I loved the way my dad used "we," as if he were still running the show. Technically, the state police investigated cases that involved suspicious deaths, working with the local PD. But the Chief had always prided himself on his department solving every case themselves. "So you don't think Deirdre's death was an accident?" I said slowly.

"Doesn't look like it."

I sighed. "I knew it."

My dad's eyebrows twitched slightly, like an overly alert rabbit's. "How's that, Kathleen?"

"The blood under the curtain," I said. "We found Deirdre downstairs. And that rustling before we left and the guy in the bushes. But if he'd been involved somehow, wouldn't he have run, instead of hanging around like that in the rain?"

"You never know." The Chief popped a wheelie toward his elevator. "Get some sleep," he said over his shoulder. "Downstairs, 0900 sharp."

The Jig Is Up

"Yes, sir." Nothing else to do but wait for Colleen to get home. I headed back to the Nest to check on the girls again.

Still fast asleep. In the rosy glow of the night-light, I saw that Maeve had woken up at some point, because she'd eaten her grilled cheese sandwich. At least she still had her appetite.

I sat on the braided rug next to the bed for a while, comforted by the sounds of my daughters' slow, steady breathing.

I stared through the round window at a sliver of moon visible among the clouds. It was terrifying to face the fact that, somewhere below it, a killer was on the loose in my hometown.

I wasn't naive. Evil lurked everywhere. But as a cop's daughter—even a cop who'd been shot in the line of duty—I'd always felt protected in Shamrock. Until now.

Chapter Five

The first thing I saw when I opened my eyes was Colleen's hot-pink laptop, surrounded by cosmetics on the vintage vanity. 8:33 AM.

My sister's side of the bed was empty, still faintly warm.

I'd tried to wait up for her last night, but I'd managed to miss Colleen and doze through both the family and guest breakfasts. Mom hadn't even woken me up to help.

That was thoughtful of her. I'd clean up and volunteer to handle teatime this afternoon. The Buckley House didn't serve lunch or dinner, just continental breakfast at seven and tea at four. And usually a late evening snack.

Throwing on a pair of jeans and a snug ladies' Bruins jersey from Colleen's closet, I ran a brush through my hair in a futile attempt to tame the frizz, then ran down to the kitchen. It was a house rule that no family member—other than the Chief, apparently—could appear in any part of the B and B in their pajamas. No one had ever said anything about looking like a model.

I found Bliz and the Chief settled around the long oak kitchen table. My dad was absorbed in the *Shamrock Sentinel* over a steaming mug of coffee.

"Morning, Mommy." Bliz was drawing on a yellow legal pad.

"Glad you could join us." The Chief glanced pointedly at the rooster clock.

"Good morning to you too," I said, my voice croaking a little from sleep. I grabbed a fork from the crammed, mismatched silverware drawer and speared the last sausage from the platter on the table. Cold and slightly dried up, but still delicious, especially dipped in Mom's homemade raspberry jam. Well, it used to be homemade. Now she bought it from Kilpatrick's, praying no one but the Irish import market's owners would be on to her little shortcut. The online reviews for the Buckley House raved about that jam.

"Gram says she left the dishes for us," Bliz said.

"Absolutely," I said. "Where's everybody else?"

Bliz twirled her pencil around to the eraser end and expertly shaded her portrait of Banshee, who was posted directly under the table to catch wayward crumbs. "Maeve's helping Gram make beds. Aunt Colleen went to the store. Then she came back and then she went out again."

The Chief rattled his paper before wetting the tip of his thumb with his tongue to turn the page. The habit drove me crazy—right up there with his occasional cigar. "How are we feeling today, Kate?"

"Okay, I guess." I blasted a mug of water in the microwave and dropped in a Barry's tea bag. The mug said, *May you be in Heaven an hour before the Devil knows you're dead.* I shuddered, thinking of Deirdre, and turned the cup around before I picked it up.

My dad looked unconvinced, but we couldn't talk about last night in front of Bliz. I'd need to get myself together before the detectives got here.

I turned my attention to the weather guy on the countertop TV.

Sunny and seasonably warm, he promised. Nice. Shamrock usually offered two choices this time of year: cloudy or raining, with a chance of winds. During extended wet spells, the Chamber of Commerce website and brochures boasted about Shamrock's authentic "soft" Irish weather.

I spotted a bright orange-and-pink box of donut holes beside the TV. Colleen loved them, and our dad never turned them down either. My hand closed on the last powdered sugar treat just as the doorbell rang.

"Get that, would you, Katie?" the Chief said.

The cops had arrived to interview me and Maeve. "Bliz, honey, will you go find your sister and ask her to come down? While you're up there, I bet Gram will let you help her with the rest of the beds."

"Okay. Then can we go for ice cream?"

"Ice cream? It's way too cold outside," I said. "And we just finished breakfast, for heaven's sake."

"Aunt Colleen said we could when she got back."

The doorbell rang again. "We'll see," I said.

When I peeked through one of the narrow windows on either side of the door, two detectives stood on the porch, looking unusually formal and official for a visit to the former chief's house. One was Shirley Walker, a large, tight-lipped woman with short salt-and-pepper curls who'd worked with my dad for years before joining the State Police detective unit assigned to the Cloverhill County DA's office. The other was Shamrock PD. Tall, with auburn hair like mine, a gold badge at his hip, and familiar broad shoulders.

Of all people, how had Garrett McGavin become a cop? A detective, no less. And why hadn't anyone in my family casually mentioned that piece of news to me?

Not that it mattered, really. We'd dated for two minutes in high school, then again for longer after my ex returned home to

Ireland. Garrett and I had drifted apart when I moved back to New York.

But still.

Shirley, looking impatient, pressed the bell again, and I jumped back from the door. Smoothing my jersey, which held a slight scent of Colleen's perfume, I counted to three and forced a smile as I answered.

"Kathleen Buckley?" The woman didn't smile back, and I avoided glancing Garrett's way. "You may remember me. I'm Detective Sergeant Walker, and this is Detective McGavin."

"We've met." Behind her back, Garrett grinned and gave me a little wave.

"I'm sure you've been expecting us," the lead detective went on. "We're here to talk to you and your daughter about the incident at Our Lady of Angels Hall last night."

"Right," I said.

She gestured beyond the door. "May we come in, please?"

"Oh. Sure. Sorry." I opened the door wider and stepped aside to let them pass.

"Well, hello there, Shirley. And Garrett, my boy." The Chief whirled into the hallway like a plaid tornado, still in his bathrobe. "Always glad to see you. Excellent work on the Rukan case, both of you."

"Thank you, sir."

"And how is your mother, Shirley? I hope Louise is enjoying that well-earned pension of hers." The Chief was laying the pleasantries on a little thick.

"She is, thank you."

"Glad to hear it. Haven't seen her around the gym much lately."

Probably because he hadn't been going himself. Last I'd heard, Louise was bugging him to join a wheelchair basketball team.

"So, you're here to speak with my lovely daughter and grand-daughter." My dad beamed at us.

"Correct, Chief. We waited until this morning, as you . . . suggested." Sergeant Walker gazed at me as if silently judging my rolled-out-of-bed look.

Who cared? This was a police matter, not a supermodel go-see.

"Let's head into the living room, shall we?" the Chief said. "We'll be more comfortable there."

Also, less visible to any guests. Two more ladies had checked in, and Mom was settling them upstairs. They didn't need to see members of law enforcement at the door. I wondered if they knew yet about the possible murder down the block.

At least detectives wore suits and drove unmarked cars. But you could always tell when someone was a cop. Even Garrett's posture had improved.

Maeve came running down the stairs as I was about to step into the living rom. No hobble left at all. She wore her navy school uniform sweater, a light-blue button-up shirt, and a clean pair of jeans. Much more put together than her mom. "Morning, sweetie," I said. "You doing okay?"

"Yup."

My dad was already parked in his wheelchair near the fire-place, which was cheerfully blazing to ward off the morning chill. Garrett took the oversized, scratched leather chair, and the sergeant perched on the edge of the striped armchair across from him, tablet in hand.

Colleen wouldn't be joining us. Was she too upset, or had the Chief arranged that too? He hadn't sounded happy about whatever she'd told the investigators last night. But it wasn't as if Colleen herself had killed her best friend. We'd discovered Deirdre's body. Together.

"Make yourselves comfortable, girls," the Chief said. "Maeve, you come sit by me." He threw her a winning smile.

I settled on the love seat. Obviously, my dad thought this was his show.

"We'll start with Maeve." Sergeant Walker angled herself toward my daughter. "Just some questions about last night. No right or wrong answers. We're looking for as many details as possible, whatever you remember. Nothing to worry about."

"That's right," the Chief said heartily. "Maeve will be happy to help in any way she can." When she nodded, he turned back to the lead detective. "I'm sure this won't take much time. Wouldn't want to overly upset a vulnerable child, would we?"

He was really overdoing it now. My eyes unintentionally met Garrett's, and his lips twitched slightly in amusement.

"No, sir." Sergeant Walker sounded annoyed. She was one tough cookie, I knew, whose grandmother had been the first Black female officer on the force in the late '60s. To my relief, she asked Maeve very easy questions: age, address, what school she attended in New York, what grade she was in, if she had known her aunt's friend Deirdre Donnelly. And finally, exactly what she'd seen in Angels Hall.

"You mean, the dead body?"

My daughter, the delicate flower. Guess I didn't need to confirm for her that Deirdre was no longer with us.

She seemed fascinated by the whole interview process. No surprise—she streamed every police procedural, cold case, and forensics show on the planet. I'd given up trying to monitor them, but she and her grandfather enjoyed discussing the details over the phone. The Chief always impressed on her that most of the storylines and cop procedures she saw on TV were completely unrealistic, but that never dampened her enthusiasm. Lately she'd been considering a career as a forensics specialist.

I got puffball questions too, and the Chief kept everything moving at light speed. Occasionally he jumped in to rephrase or redirect, but Sergeant Walker stayed on course. She refrained from telling my dad to butt out, but I'm sure she wanted to.

Sergeant Walker tapped her tablet. "So what brought you out here yesterday, Kate?"

"What do you mean?"

She smiled, more pleasantly than earlier. "Why are you here in town?"

"Just a visit. Family stuff. It's Paddy's Week, almost."

"Aunt Colleen wanted us to come," Maeve spoke up. "She said it was super important, so we got here right away."

I felt, rather than heard, my dad's tiny sigh.

"I see," Sergeant Walker said. "So, Kate, why did your sister say she wanted you to come home? A problem of some kind?"

"Colleen said there wasn't any problem." That was the truth. "She sent me a text. I read it wrong. Just a little miscommunication."

"Mm-hmm." Sergeant Walker made a note on her tablet.

What did any of this have to do with what happened to Deirdre? Was it related to whatever Colleen told the cops last night?

My sister was going to cough up everything the minute I saw her.

"Last night you saw someone in the bushes as you were leaving the parish hall," Sergeant Walker said. "Can you describe this person, please?"

"I didn't get a really good look at him," I said. "He was hunched, so I couldn't tell how tall he was. Definitely skinny."

"He was pale," Maeve said. "About my age. Dark hair, all black clothes. And a black beanie." For someone who'd nearly been face-to-face with a possible killer, she sounded nonplussed.

"So how was the guy acting?" Garrett asked. "Did he seem scared, or . . .?"

Maeve considered that. "More nervous than scared. Alert, maybe? And, oh yeah, he had those cool sneakers with the silver lightning bolt logo. Everyone has them. Except me." Her eyes slid in my direction. "My mom is kind of cheap."

I preferred the term "thrifty."

"Thank you, Maeve," Sergeant Walker said. "Kate, anything you'd like to add?"

"I don't think so. It was dark . . ." My voice trailed away at Surly Shirley's withering look. I knew I sounded lame. I needed to get my act together, or I wouldn't be of use to anyone. Especially my sister.

"Maybe you ladies can give more details to our forensics artist to help us find this young man. We'll be in touch." Sergeant Walker rose to her feet. So did Garrett.

"Of course," I said. "Sorry we couldn't be more helpful."

"I think we have enough to go on for now," Garrett said. "We'll add everything into the report."

"Thank you." The Chief nodded at Sergeant Walker. "Appreciate you coming out to the house. Be sure to give your mom and grandmother my regards."

She nodded back. "I'll give you ladies my card," she said to Maeve and me. "Call if you remember any other details, no matter how small. Even if you don't think they're important."

"Nice to see you, Katie." Garrett also handed me a card. "You too, Maeve. You probably don't remember me."

"Sure I do." My daughter smiled. "From when I was a little kid. You used to buy me and Mom Italian ices."

"That's right, I did. You have a pretty good memory."

"She does." The Chief sounded pleased with both of them. He'd always been a big Garrett McGavin fan, for some reason.

Sergeant Walker stood at the front door. "Is Colleen here, Chief?" she asked, craning her neck slightly for a better view of the stairs. "I have just a few more questions for her."

Who was she, Columbo?

"She's doing errands for her mother, I believe," the Chief said.

"I haven't seen Colleen this morning," I said. One hundred percent true.

When the detectives were safely out the door, Maeve and I headed back into the kitchen, where Bliz had moved on to sketching Banshee action pieces. The Chief had disappeared via his private elevator. Probably getting dressed for the day in another plaid bathrobe.

"Mommy, can we go for my ice cream now?" Bliz asked. "Aunt Colleen said she'd take me to PJ Scoops if I ate all my breakfast, and I did, but she's taking forever."

"I'll go," Maeve said.

I checked the rooster clock. Still too early for ice cream, but the idea of getting outdoors sounded great to me. The plates, pans, and bowls I'd seen stacked in the sink and on the counters earlier had disappeared, thanks to either the house fairies or Mom.

After a shot or two of PJ's espresso, I'd ask her what the girls and I could do to help. And maybe check in with the office too. I mostly worked from home, and I'd taken the day off anyway, but my clients' tax documents were multiplying faster than Buckley House dishes. "Get your jacket," I told Bliz.

When my daughter returned, she was wearing her purple slicker and pink polka dot boots.

"It's not raining, honey," I said. "The weatherman said it'll be nice all day. Don't you want your princess jacket?"

"No."

"The Chief told her the weatherman is a liar," Maeve said.

I almost defended the poor weather guy, but I let it go. Plenty of people in this town had a complicated relationship with the truth.

* * *

It felt good to breathe some non-Buckley air as we headed the few blocks to PJ Scoops. Bliz skipped along, stopping every now and then to pick up a tiny pine cone or a glinting piece of mica from someone's driveway. Maeve trudged beside me, hands stuffed into her hoodie pocket. She'd already told me to stop asking if she was okay.

This street, Windsor Terrace, was nearly identical to Galway Court, with the same large Victorians and narrow multifamily houses—known throughout New England as "triple-deckers." A sprinkling of Craftsman-style bungalows too, with lovely, inviting porches. Each front door was painted a different color, like the ones in the Doors of Dublin poster sold in every gift store downtown.

I'd never really noticed before, but the still-leafless branches of the huge maple trees along the sidewalks were twisted and vaguely creepy. Occasional pines interspersed among them lent the appearance of silent watchmen, and the sky had filled with dark, nasty-looking clouds. There was no one else in sight.

Today Shamrock felt like the perfect place for a murder—and the ideal town for a murderer to hide.

"Ooh, a raindrop!" Bliz held her palm up to the sky. "Look, there's another one. The weatherman *was* lying."

"Race you to PJ's," Maeve said. They reached the gold-scrolled door of PJ Scoops just as the rain began to come down sideways. I was right behind them.

"I want a bubble gum cone with rainbow sprinkles," Bliz announced as we walked in. After a two-second delay, a door chime played the first few bars of "When Irish Eyes Are Smiling."

"You always get bubble gum, honey," I said. "Don't you want to try something else this time?" I looked around for the flavor list, but my eyes lit on the giant, gleaming espresso machine at the end of the counter.

Behind it, wearing a black PJ Scoops T-shirt and black jeans, stood the shaggy-haired kid Maeve and I had seen last night outside Angels Hall.

Chapter Six

The boy behind the counter definitely recognized us. His eyes darted toward the door.

Maybe he hoped someone else would come in. Or else he planned to make a break for it.

Maeve, perusing the specialty coffee menu, showed zero reaction. Either she didn't recognize the kid from last night, or she was playing it cool.

Bliz peered through the display glass at the colorful tubs of ice cream. "I don't see any bubble gum."

The kid in black moved down to the ice-cream section. As he placed his elbows on the glass case, I noticed his coffee cup-shaped name tag. *Conor.*

"We've got rainbow ice cream. It's almost the same thing."

"But there's no bubble gum in it," Bliz pointed out.

How could I get the girls out of here without calling attention to our hasty exit? Bliz would pitch a fit.

Conor shrugged. "I can put Gel Stars over the top. They're kinda chewy."

"Okay," Bliz said. "Deal."

He knew how to negotiate successfully with a picky seven-year-old. But he was a sales guy. That was his job. And murderers could sometimes be oddly charming to lure their victims and elude suspicion. He seemed like a regular kid, though, to be honest.

"What does she want?" he asked Bliz, jerking his head toward Maeve. His voice cracked slightly, in an almost endearing way.

"Her name is Maeve," Bliz told him helpfully. "Maeve Buckley."

Great. Now he could find out everything about us.

"I know who she is," Conor said.

What? Even worse.

"She likes peanut butter fudge and black raspberry and cookie dough. With whipped cream."

"Thanks, Blizzie B." Maeve was clearly mortified. Did she really not recognize this kid? She'd been full of details for the detectives this morning, and now the guy was standing right in front of her.

Conor began to scoop the rainbow cone. "We went to grade school together."

Now he had her attention. "We did?"

"Till third grade." He shrugged. "I sat behind you in Sister Valeria's class."

I gave an inaudible sigh of relief. If he'd gone to elementary school with Maeve at Our Lady of Angels, he and his family couldn't be complete strangers, right?

On the other hand, didn't neighbors always say the alleged axe murderer was quiet and polite, the last person they'd consider capable of evil? And it wasn't like the school ran criminal background checks on families. They needed the tuition.

"You're Conor Murphy?" Maeve said. "You look, like, totally different now." She blushed. "I mean . . . taller."

"I hope so." He reached to get the Gel Stars jar from the toppings shelf.

"I thought you looked familiar." I paused, very slightly. "From much more recently."

"Don't forget to press the stars down into the ice cream with a spoon, okay?" Bliz said. "Otherwise they'll fall off."

"Got it," Conor said, apparently ignoring my comment.

Maybe if I gained his trust, I could ask him some questions. He wasn't a threat to us right now, here at his job. An ice cream and coffee shop, for heaven's sake.

That's probably what Deirdre had thought—and look what had happened to her, on church property, no less. But he didn't seem worried about hiding his identity.

"You're pretty good with kids," I said as Bliz wandered off to look at a decorative display of antique ice-cream scoops interspersed with stuffed animals for sale.

"I have three little sisters around her age."

I tried to imagine Bliz in triplicate and failed.

"Worked here long?" I asked casually. Maeve gave me a withering Mom-please-shut-up look.

"Not really."

"Wait, aren't we the same age?" Maeve said. "How did you get a job?"

He shrugged. "Nothing official. My mom's cousin owns the place, so I help out. Cone's ready," he called to Bliz.

She ran back, and Conor handed her the colorful ice cream. In about two minutes, she'd have a rainbow-hued tongue and start bouncing off the walls on a massive sugar high. "It's scrumptiously delicious," she said after her first huge bite.

"So do you two want anything?" The kid sounded slightly impatient now as his eyes shot back toward the door. It hadn't been my imagination. He was nervous.

Maeve requested a double shot mocha with extra whipped cream, and I ordered espresso. Then we joined Bliz at a marble-topped table in the corner to wait.

I tried not to look at the framed map of Ireland behind Bliz's shoulder as she went to town on the Gel Stars. My ex-husband, Ian Forde, lived in some trendy section of Dublin. His whole life now was his music and his Irish indie rock band, Peat.

Eight years of my life wasted. Well, not exactly. We were happy for a while, before he left and I changed my name back to Buckley, along with the girls'. He'd barely blinked. But I couldn't think about my failure of a marriage right now. I had other things to deal with. Like a murder.

Conor set the drinks down on the table. Maeve's whipped cream had burst through the lid and poured over the side of the cup like fake lava from a science fair volcano. "Sorry," he said.

I grabbed extra napkins from the dispenser. "Conor, I need to ask you something."

His shoulders stiffened. Either he knew what I was about to say, or he thought an adult talking to him so much was weird.

I spoke fast. "We saw you last night. You know that, right?"

"Hold on, I need to get a mop," Conor said.

"No need, we're fine here," I said quickly. "Bliz, go get the newspaper someone left on that table over there. We can use that." She dashed off.

The kid took a step back. He knew he was trapped.

"Angels Hall?" I pressed. "Deirdre Donnelly? Any of that ring a bell?"

"Yeah."

That was it? One word? "You know Deirdre is dead, don't you? The police think she might have been murdered."

Officially, the case wasn't a homicide yet. But that status would likely change soon. I waited for some kind of reaction.

Nada.

"My grandfather used to be the police chief here," Maeve said.

Well, that was another approach. Not exactly subtle.

"Did he make you and your mom detectives or something?"

My daughter was rarely deterred by sarcasm. She was used to it, in our family. "We saw you hiding out in the bushes last night," she told him. "And we're not gonna cover for you, okay?"

Bliz dashed back to our flooded table with the Sports section and jumped into her chair as the rest of us tried to sop up the mocha spill, which by now had waterfalled onto the floor. She daintily raised her boots to avoid the mess.

"Well?" I whispered to Conor as he diligently scrubbed beside me.

He was about to answer when we were all treated to a reprise of "When Irish Eyes Are Smiling." The cheerful tune didn't match the dour expression of the person who strode through the door: Detective Sergeant Shirley Walker.

I doubted she was much of an ice cream fan, but PJ Scoops did serve extra bitter black coffee.

The detective didn't strike me as someone desperate for a midday caffeine fix. She was here to talk to Conor.

Or us.

Would it seem strange to Surly Shirley that my daughter and I were casually chatting with this kid in an empty ice cream shop, right after mentioning we'd seen a person of the same description at a probable crime scene?

Bet on it.

Chapter Seven

Conor beat Sergeant Walker to the counter. Barely. Before I could stop her, Maeve was up there too. What was she doing?

"Maeve!" I called. "Time to go. Gram wants us back right now."

Bliz looked confused. "But Mommy—"

As the detective watched my older daughter with narrowed eyes, Conor reached over next to the cash register and scrawled something on the back of an old receipt. He pushed it toward Maeve under his hand. "Text me," I saw him mouth.

She nodded and palmed the receipt as she turned away.

Nope, not happening. This kid was not talking to my daughter again, for any reason. If he wanted to say something, he could deal with me. Or the cops. And right now he had the perfect opportunity.

"Uh, can I help you?" Conor asked the detective.

I swiped a last stray, wet napkin off the table and tossed it into a nearby trash can painted with shamrocks as I hustled both girls out the door, to yet another round of "When Irish Eyes Are Smiling." How could anyone stand listening to that over and over?

"What did Conor say in that note?" I asked Maeve when we were halfway down the rain-soaked block. The cloudburst was over, thank heavens.

Reluctantly, she took out the crumpled receipt from her pocket. He'd scrawled his number. And below it: *Luckys @7.*

Lucky's was an arcade off the square where a lot of kids hung out. The place had been there forever, even before the town's Great Irish Invasion. Frank used to play Whac-a-Mole there for hours.

"I don't think you should be friends with that boy," I said.

"Is he going to be your boyfriend?" Bliz looked hopeful.

"Absolutely not." The words were out of my mouth before I could stop them. Maeve scowled.

"Hey, he seems like an okay kid," I said. "And I get that you used to know him. But it's been years." *Also, he may be a murderer,* I wanted to add.

All three of us jumped when a tall woman in a zebra-print coat stepped out in front of us from a Shamrock trolley stop. Despite the overcast sky, she wore oversized designer sunglasses, and her frizzy, bright red hair was pulled up high and tight off her forehead with a bedazzled headband.

"Well, hello there!" She directed her greeting to my daughters, summoning a huge, false smile the way some people did when they talked to kids. Her lipstick was a distracting dark shade. She reminded me of the Cheshire Cat from *Alice's Adventures in Wonderland*, whose grin remained in the air after the rest of its body disappeared. There was something familiar about this woman, but I couldn't place her.

Cruella de Vil? The Joker?

"You girls are Irish dancers, am I right?"

For most girls in Shamrock, that would be a decent guess—and back in our Brooklyn neighborhood too.

"Nope, they're not," I said. "Sorry."

The woman ignored me and bent down to face Bliz at eye level. "Aren't you adorable? I bet you'd love to perform on a big stage in front of lots and lots of people."

Bliz blinked nervously.

Obviously, this one wasn't good at reading kids. She didn't seem to understand that approaching them directly, even with a parent present, wasn't appropriate either. "Excuse me," I said, taking Bliz's hand. "I don't think we know you, but we're late for something, so if you don't mind . . ." I hustled both girls down the sidewalk.

The woman clicked after us in astonishingly high red heels. "Oh, but you must know me. I'm Moira McShane Kelly."

"Sorry, no recollection." I quickened our pace. Bliz kept looking over her shoulder, strangely fascinated with the Zebra Lady. Or maybe more of a giraffe, with those long legs. "Please stop following us."

Moira McNutcase rushed ahead on the wet grass along the sidewalk and almost literally blocked our path. When she lowered her giant sunglasses, I realized she had to be related to the elderly McShane sisters at the Smiling Shamrock. Not her hair—Una and Nuala wore theirs in severe silver buns—but her eyes held that same reptilian look. No wonder she covered them up with those dark glasses.

"You're visitors, then? Always lovely to meet fellow Irish culture enthusiasts," Moira gushed as I tried to step around her with Bliz. "I grew up here. My great-aunts run the Smiling Shamrock."

Bingo.

"I'm sure you've heard of their award-winning B and B. Five-star reviews on every travel site. Or maybe you're staying there?"

I didn't bother to reply. She didn't give me a chance.

"Anyway, I am an international dance professional, and I started a fabulous school for exceptionally talented girls and boys in New York City. I'm opening another one right here in Shamrock." She gave Bliz and Maeve another Cheshire smile. "You can call me Miss Moira." Then she reached into her faux Givenchy bag and handed each of them a colorful brochure.

For once, Maeve was without words. Probably not a bad thing.

"We don't live here," Bliz said. "We're from Brooklyn."

The woman was unfazed. "Well, whenever you visit Shamrock, you can join a class here." She turned her garish smile to me. "Like a gym membership, but better."

No thanks. The last time I'd been suckered into a health club membership, they'd refused to let me cancel.

"We're planning amazing recitals with authentic, handcrafted costumes from Ireland, and we hope to bring an award-winning choreographer on board. He's so famous I can't even reveal his name yet."

Obviously, this woman wasn't going to quit. "We'll think about it," I lied.

"Fabulous!" Miss Moira adjusted her sunglasses back into place. "And do me a favor, girls. Please take more flyers and let all your friends know too. See you soon!"

"Are we really going to take Irish dance?" Bliz asked as Miss Moira swept back toward her trolley stop lair. "Aunt Colleen used to, and she promised she'd teach me someday."

I didn't have the heart to tell her that Aunt Colleen made a lot of promises and didn't always get around to keeping them.

"So will all of Miss Deirdre's students go to Miss Moira's school? Because she died?" Bliz looked up at me, her blue eyes wide.

I stopped short, still holding her hand. "Ow," she said.

"Sorry, sweetie. What did you hear about Deirdre?"

"Her picture was on the news this morning. Aunt Colleen explained it all to me. Deirdre was her bestest friend, and a very bad person may have killed her, but now she's in heaven."

My heart hurt. "That's right, she's with the angels." I started walking again, wishing Colleen had let me tell Bliz. At least she'd delivered the news gently.

Maeve must have read my mind. "She was going to find out anyway," she said to me, in a low voice. "Don't worry, Blizzie B, Uncle Frank and the police will find the bad guy right away and put him straight in jail."

"That's what the Chief said." Bliz stopped to pick up another tiny pine cone for her growing collection. "But Aunt Colleen said he's still out there somewhere, probably right here in Shamrock, and no one has any idea who he is."

I bit my lip. Sometimes my sister had the good judgment of a rock. Who would tell a kid something like that? Especially extra-sensitive ones, like Bliz. "Come on, honey, no more pine cones," I said. "Gram's going to wonder where we are."

Colleen had to be home by now. If she wasn't, I was heading straight out to find her.

As we passed another row of identical triple-decker homes, I spotted one of Miss Moira's flyers posted to a telephone pole. Another was taped to a blue USPS mailbox—a federal offense, I was pretty sure—and a third blew across someone's lawn. She'd killed a lot of trees with all that paper.

Bliz was right, though. With Bernie Donnelly's health declining, Deirdre's students might enroll at the new dance school now. And Miss Moira had put plans in place to open the Moira McShane Kelly Academy of Irish Dance at almost the exact time Deirdre was murdered. Coincidence?

Regardless, the woman was beyond pushy. At the very least, anyone who ran around advertising a sparkly new dance studio when her prospective business rival's body was barely cold had to be missing an empathy chip.

The Jig Is Up

Plus, she had the extreme misfortune of being related to Una and Nuala McShane. The poison apple probably didn't fall far from the family tree. I could totally imagine an unglued Moira McShane Kelly killing off her competition.

Chapter Eight

"Don't bother taking off your coats, kids," Colleen said as the girls and I let ourselves in to the Buckley House. "We're going out."

My sister wore her black leather jacket, along with black boots and a short, pleated skirt. Had she been waiting for us, or had she just been ready to run away from me again?

"Sorry, we already went for ice cream," I said.

"No, no, I'm just stopping by a friend's house, and I told her you were all coming too," Colleen said. "Mom's really busy right now, so she won't mind. We won't be gone long anyway."

"I have to go to the bathroom," Bliz announced.

"Me too," Maeve added.

"No problem," Colleen said. "Make it quick, okay?"

The girls raced toward the downstairs powder room, the fancier one reserved for visitors and guests.

"Why are you in such a hurry to get us all out of the house?" I said.

"I'm not," my sister said. "I told Bernie Donnelly we'd be there half an hour ago. Mom thought you'd be back sooner."

"Wait, Bernie? As in, Deirdre's mother?"

"There's only one Bernie Donnelly." Frown lines materialized through the layers of Colleen's caked foundation. I could tell she'd made an extra effort to conceal dark circles and puffiness. She'd been crying. "We need to pay our respects. Mom already went over there last night."

"Isn't it kind of soon for her to have so many visitors? I mean, the kids and all . . ."

"No, it's fine. Bernie loves kids."

I didn't know if that was entirely the case, but as a dance studio owner for so many years, she'd certainly been surrounded by a lot of them.

"Plus, Bernie said she wanted to talk to me about something important."

About Deirdre? I wondered. Did her mother also have questions about what had happened last night? That would be a tough conversation for Colleen.

And it wouldn't be the only one. "Okay, but as soon as we get back, the two of us need to sit down and talk," I said. "For real."

My sister sucked in her dimple slightly. "Sorry, Katie. I don't mean to keep blowing you off. It's just . . . there's so much going on. Everything's changed now. I don't know what to do. Deirdre's gone, and that detective thinks I killed her. Everything is so messed up."

"Wait, Sergeant Walker really thinks *you* killed Deirdre? That's crazy. Why?"

"I don't know." Colleen's eyes filled with tears. "Dee and I had a teensy fight last week, and the cops checked her phone and saw the texts."

"What was the fight about?" Deirdre and my sister rarely argued, as far as I knew.

"It was stupid. I borrowed some money from her, and she needed me to pay her back and I couldn't yet."

"Why didn't you ask me, if you needed a loan?"

Colleen sniffled. "I always ask you."

True. "It's okay, Colleen Queen." I reached out to give her a hug, and she put her head on my shoulder. "Everything will be fine," I added, gently smoothing her hair.

"You said that when we found Deirdre," Colleen said.

Also true. "Look, I understand things are super hard right now, but I'm here for you," I said. "You'll get through this. We all will."

Poor Colleen. She was obviously still in shock. Her emotions zigzagged like the Chief navigating Boston traffic. How often did anyone find their best friend dead?

And poor Bernie too. Colleen was right. No reason to put off a condolence call. We could deal with everything else later. Just one more teensy question for my sister for now. An easy one.

"Colleen, do you know Moira McShane Kelly?"

She swiped at her eyes. "Sure. Everyone knows Moira."

"Are you friends?"

"Not exactly. I try to avoid her whenever she's in town."

"Was Deirdre friends with her?"

"More like frenemies. Why?"

"You know she's starting a dance school here," I said.

"She thinks she is." Colleen's expression clouded. "Never going to happen."

"Does Moira know that?"

My sister shrugged. "Deirdre and I made it pretty clear. Well, I did, mostly, because Dee was too chicken. Moira came to talk to her, and I happened to be there and pointed out, very nicely, that she had a terrible business plan. Shamrock isn't big enough for two dance schools."

"But now, with Bernie retiring and Deirdre . . ." I let my voice trail away.

Colleen lifted her chin. "Doesn't matter. I can't believe you don't remember Moira. No one liked her much, to be honest, because she's such a one-upper. But her parents were killed in a car crash when she was a kid, and she had to go live with her great-aunts at the Shamrock. So then people felt really sorry for her. I told her she should focus on her dance school back in New York. It can't be that hot, because Bernie's never heard of it."

Ouch. Usually I was the judgy one. Moira's timing was incredibly inappropriate, but she couldn't have appreciated being discouraged from opening a business.

"You don't think she could have taken things to extremes and killed Deirdre, do you?" I said slowly. "Because she was mad? Or jealous? Or just wanted her out of the way?"

"Moira, a murderer?" My sister snorted. "She's harmless. All talk and no action."

I wasn't as sure about Deirdre's frenzied frenemy. "You have to admit, though, she does have an actual motive."

"Nope, not possible." Colleen patted her jacket pocket. "Whoops, I left my phone in my room. I'll be right back, okay?"

"Sure." I dropped onto the spindled bench in the foyer. As I waited, I gazed at the familiar framed photo directly across the hallway. Mom had hung it there in a place of honor, under the Sacred Heart painting and beside a portrait of John F. Kennedy. The photo was taken on Fourth of July when Colleen was sixteen and Maeve about six. They were eating ice cream on the steps of the gazebo on the square. That was the year Colleen was crowned Miss Shamrock and Maeve somehow ended up as the junior version, Little Miss Shamrock—I suspected due to a bit of secret lobbying around town by the Chief. Both girls wore tiaras and matching gold-and-green sashes. That photo made the front page of the *Shamrock Sentinel*.

What was taking everyone so long? I got up and walked down the hall, then peeked around the corner. The girls were still standing outside the powder room door, with Maeve absorbed in her phone and Bliz doing an anxious little hop from boot to boot. When a large guest in a badly fitted polyester pantsuit finally stepped out, Bliz zipped in like a pink-and-purple hornet.

Since I had another couple of minutes, I went to check in with Mom, in case she'd been wondering what happened to us. I could use the brownie points too, after being less than helpful with the housework earlier.

"Mom?" I stuck my head through the kitchen doorway.

She sat at the table in front of her laptop, surrounded by spreadsheets, notepads, envelopes, and torn slips of paper.

"Hi," I said. "What are you working on?"

"Accounts," she said, rubbing her forehead. She sounded as overtired and out of sorts as the old dishwasher cranking away beside the double sink. "If you can call them that." She tossed her reading glasses on the table in frustration. "Did I hear Colleen out in the hall?"

"Yes," I said. "We're going to visit Bernie Donnelly and taking the girls. But, hey, do you want some help with these while I'm home, Mom? You have a professional accountant standing right here. Why not let me take a look at the books?"

I'd offered in the past, of course—every time I visited—but she'd never taken me up on it. She always told me I already had a job.

"Thank you, honey," Mom said. "Maybe later, after I've gone through the records one more time. Colleen has been taking all of this over for me, but . . ."

Alarm bells went off in my mind, but I shut them down. I knew my parents hoped my sister might take over the B and B someday, to keep it in the family and give her a steady job. Numbers weren't really Colleen's thing, but she was amazing with people. It might work out if she had a little help on the business side. Whether she wanted to run the Buckley House, though, I wasn't sure. "Do you, um, want me to get her for you?"

"No, you all go ahead," Mom said. "Bernie is keeping a stiff upper lip, but she's completely devastated. She always enjoys seeing you girls."

By "girls," my mom meant Colleen. Bernie didn't know me as well because I was so much older than Deirdre. "I'll be home to help with tea," I said. "What's the dinner plan?"

"We can order pizza and eat early," Mom said. "All the guests are having happy hour at Molly's before the Cockles and Mussels special, so we'll have the house to ourselves."

Ugh. Molly's Fish and Ale House stank like rotten seafood, stale beer, and general unpleasantness year-round, but tourists seemed driven to the place like Saint Patrick's snakes. We couldn't tell the guests that, though. There was a mutual understanding in town that businesses would recommend each other—or at least avoid throwing shade.

Not all of them followed that unspoken rule, but the Buckley House held to the code. We gently guided our guests elsewhere if directly asked.

Colleen and the girls were waiting for me by the front door, finally ready to go. "Mommy, Aunt Colleen says Maeve used to take Irish dance when she was my age," Bliz said. "That means I can too, right?"

"I wasn't any good," Maeve told her. "So it doesn't count."

"You didn't practice enough, that's all," Colleen said. "You made Miss Bernie cry every week."

Bliz gazed at her older sister in awe. "Not true, Blizzie B," Maeve assured her as we all trooped down the steps and started up the street in the opposite direction from Angels Hall.

Bernie Donnelly was no crier. The woman was as tough as the jellied candies in Mom's Easter coffee cake. I didn't remember Deirdre ever crying either. Off the dance stage, she'd been a quiet girl, which might explain why she and Colleen had gotten along so well. Colleen loved attention, and she'd talked enough for both of them. Deirdre was the shy one who had gone on to become a star.

A Shamrock PD cruiser pulled over and stopped across the street. "Uh-oh," Colleen said. "Just what we need."

The driver lowered his window. "Hey, where are you girls headed?"

"Hi, Uncle Frank!" Bliz broke free of my grasp and rushed toward the cruiser. Luckily, my street-smart city child remembered to check both ways first for traffic.

He smiled and handed her a Tootsie Roll out the window. My brother had a definite sweet tooth. Exhibit A: the open family pack and trail of empty wrappers across the passenger seat. "How's my little princess?"

"Good." Her mouth was already full of candy.

Frank looked at Colleen. "So you're going where?"

"Just the Donnellys'."

"Are you freaking kidding me?" Frank banged his hand on the steering wheel. It probably had plenty of dents in it already. "What did I tell you?"

"Bernie wants to see me," Colleen said. "What was I supposed to say? We need to go over there anyway. Deirdre was my best friend." Her eyes filled with tears.

Frank sighed. "Get in, all of you. I'll drive you."

Colleen didn't look happy about the offer, but she crossed the street and slid into the passenger seat. "You're a piggy, Frank," she said, tossing the candy bag to the floor. Tootsie Rolls scattered everywhere.

When he hit the unlock button for the back door, the girls and I clambered into the low, cramped seat, designed to discourage a passenger from escaping or trying to attack the driver. The seat was covered in some type of easy-to-clean vinyl. Who knew what kind of stuff got spilled on it. "Try not to touch anything, girls," I whispered.

Bliz clasped her hands in her lap, but her eyes were on a lone Tootsie Roll that had rolled toward us from the front seat.

Technically, I doubted Frank was supposed to be driving his family around in a cruiser, but no one at the PD ever complained about him breaking any rules.

"You don't get it, Colleen." Our brother kept his eyes on the road as he drove. "A lot of people are asking questions, okay? The last thing you want to do right now is talk to the vic's family."

I leaned forward, trying to hear better. The back of the cruiser was sealed off at the top by a plastic partition, like a New York City cab. Didn't Frank realize his nieces and I could still hear everything he said up there? Well, almost.

Luckily, Maeve was looking at her phone again, and Bliz hummed to herself as she drew smudged smiley faces with her finger on the filthy rear window. She was bathing in hand sanitizer tonight.

"Stop calling Deirdre 'the vic,'" Colleen said. "It makes her sound . . . dead."

"Sorry, but that's exactly what she is. It sounds cold, I get that, but the sooner you face that fact, the better." He glanced Colleen's way. "Are you in some kind of denial or something?"

"I am not in denial." She crossed her arms defensively.

"Look, I knew Deirdre too," Frank said. "Not as well as you did, but she was a nice girl and all. You just can't make any more dumb moves right now, okay?"

More dumb moves? Our sister had definitely messed up somehow. Probably the same mistake the Chief had been muttering about last night. She'd blabbed something to the cops, given them some kind of info she shouldn't have.

But wasn't more information—of any kind—better in a murder investigation? Especially if you were innocent. What had Colleen told them that was so damaging for her?

She looked out the passenger window, and I spotted a tear starting down her right cheek. She quickly brushed it away.

"They know about the money, Colleen," Frank said, in a lower voice.

Did he mean the loan from Deirdre? Clearly, my sister was dealing with some major financial issue. By now my nose was practically flattened against the partition. I'd have to submerge myself in sanitizer later too.

"I told you and the detectives last night, that was all a coincidence," Colleen said. "I was going to pay it back, I swear. And I had nothing to do with *(mumble, mumble)*."

I didn't get it. If Colleen needed money that badly, and she didn't want to ask me, our parents would have loaned her emergency cash.

Not that they had much to spare, even with the Chief's pension and disability checks. His ongoing medical bills and the house upkeep were both serious drains on the finances. And Mom had seemed really discouraged about those B and B accounts.

The hospitality business was big in Shamrock, but that meant there was plenty of competition, especially from vacation rentals. The house needed constant repairs, but the Chief would never give the place up. The perpetual Buckley money pit.

Colleen had been doing the books lately, Mom had said. Maybe she'd made some simple mistake. Whatever it was, I was sure I could salvage things with a little rejiggering. Or at least help my parents negotiate with the IRS.

"Why don't I take all of you home?" Frank was saying as I refocused on the conversation up front. "Maybe later—"

"No thanks," Colleen said. "Pull over, please." She turned and rapped on the partition, jolting me backward. "Come on, everybody. We can walk the rest of the way."

"Fine." Frank stopped along the curb. Our brother was as stubborn as she was. "Don't say I didn't warn you, okay?"

The girls and I couldn't let ourselves out since the back doors of the squad car didn't unlock from the back seat. Colleen jumped onto the sidewalk and opened the door on Bliz's side. "It's only one more block," she said.

"'Bye, Uncle Frank," Bliz said.

"Thanks for the ride," I added. Frank meant well, but he always tried to play the big protector. Like me, I guess—but he was even worse. It annoyed me and my sister to no end.

He nodded, but he didn't look happy. As he peeled away, I saw him reach down to the floor to grab another Tootsie Roll.

The four of us finally pushed through the Donnellys' spindly iron gate and trudged up the concrete steps of the two-story brick home. Bright red flowers—plastic—filled the window boxes. One of the flowers had fallen to the porch, and Bliz scooped it up as Colleen leaned on the bell.

Deirdre wasn't inside, of course, but I felt strangely overwhelmed by her presence. My logical mind told me the poor girl's cold, still body was lying on a slab in a morgue somewhere, or maybe at the funeral home by now. I didn't believe in ghosts, but somehow the whole place felt like death.

Chapter Nine

Bernie Donnelly looked exactly as I remembered: unhealthy. Hard to imagine she'd once been the Irish champion step dancer Bernadette McFadden.

Startlingly thin, with overteased black hair that looked as if it had been dyed with shoe polish, Deirdre's mother came to the door in a burgundy velvet tracksuit and fleece-lined black clogs. A silver cross dangled over the top edge of her white ribbed turtleneck. Like her daughter, she had always been scary-pale, but today her face was splotched with red. Overdone blush or too much sherry. Maybe both.

"Hello, girls," she said, with a hint of brogue. "Good of you to come."

Even if Bernie had looked completely different now, I would have recognized that gravelly voice. She'd been a chain smoker for years—even when she'd taught her dance classes—and she never bothered to hide it. The house reeked of stale smoke from all the way outside on the porch.

I caught myself and felt ashamed. How petty could I be? Bernie was going through a terrible ordeal right now, and here I was, criticizing her. I hadn't lost a daughter last night—who could imagine the horror of that experience? I'd been a mess answering basic questions for the Shamrock PD. Bernie Donnelly was a strong, no-nonsense woman. Steely, even.

"We're so sorry for your loss, Bernie," Colleen said as we stepped inside. "How are you holding up?"

Deirdre's mother stood straighter. "As well as can be expected, I suppose." She nodded to me and raised one thin, penciled brow at Maeve. "Such the grown-up young lady now."

Maeve offered an awkward smile.

Bernie glanced down at Bliz, then back at Colleen. "A wee angel. She looks just like you, Colleen."

"I get that a lot," Colleen said.

We all did. Bliz was a miniature Colleen, right down to the cute dimple. I tried not to let that bother me, but I'll admit it did sometimes.

"Why don't we go into the kitchen, then?" Bernie said. "The police have turned most of the house upside down, I'm afraid."

The place was a mess all right, almost on par with one of those reality hoarding shows. I doubted it was entirely the work of the Shamrock PD. The living room couch was piled with dance magazines and old newspapers. A crumpled bag of Tayto crisps and empty bottles of cheap diet soda littered the coffee table. Ashtrays, most of them dirty, were set near the recliner and TV. A small folding table held a half-eaten frozen dinner tray and a glass of melting ice.

So sad. Bernie and Deirdre were well known in Shamrock. Hopefully their neighbors and many friends planned to send Bernie casseroles, at least. She needed to eat better to keep her strength up. I made a mental note to talk to Colleen and Mom about what we could do. Bernie would never admit she needed help.

"Ooo, look." Bliz peered into a room crammed with silver, gold, and crystal trophies and bowls. Framed photos and certificates and felt banners with medals pinned to them plastered the walls. Even Maeve seemed impressed.

"That's nothing, honey." Bernie gave a dismissive wave. "You want to see more? Follow me."

She stopped in what was once the dining room. Three glass cases with recessed lighting, like Mom's china cabinet back at the Buckley House, were jammed with even more trophies. "I had to store my mother's Donegal China in the basement." Bernie shrugged. "Deirdre wanted to buy me a bigger house, but I always said no. Never needed anything fancy."

Bliz turned slowly in a circle, staring at all the shiny awards. Then she spotted a photo of Deirdre in high school, wearing an elaborate black dance dress covered with embroidered Celtic designs and multicolored rhinestones. Her hair was piled in long, tight curls, set with a tiara. "She's so pretty," Bliz breathed.

"Yes." Bernie pulled a handkerchief embroidered with shamrocks from the pocket of her tracksuit and blew her nose. "She was."

I felt a new rush of sadness. I'd been wrong about Bernie being too tough to cry. My heart hurt for her, and I didn't dare look at Colleen. This had to be killing my sister too. I knew she was trying to be extra strong for Deirdre's mom. Colleen went over and gave Bernie a hug.

"Come on, sweetie," I said to Bliz, touching her raincoat sleeve.

"Oh, it's all right." Bernie stuffed the handkerchief back into her pocket. "She can look at anything she wants. I don't mind. Look at this one, honey." She pointed toward another wall, where Maeve stood.

Maeve quickly stepped aside. Behind her, an Irish Steps promotional poster about four feet high and illuminated by a museum-style spotlight showed Deirdre onstage, wearing another fancy show costume. A tall, handsome young man, his hair as blond as Deirdre's was black, had one arm around her waist. He wore a silky, V-necked green shirt and black pants with an embroidered cummerbund.

"Is that her boyfriend?" Bliz asked.

Maeve rolled her eyes, and once again I didn't dare glance at Colleen. Bliz was in that romance-and-princesses stage right now, but her question seemed legit, the way the pair gazed raptly into each other's eyes. They were professional performers, and couples in love sold tickets.

A strange expression flashed across Bernie's face. She glanced at Colleen, who gave a little shrug. "Nah," Bernie said, with something like a grunt. Or maybe a lingering cough from all those cigarettes. "That's Aidan O'Hearne, Deirdre's old partner. They danced the leads together in Irish Steps for years."

She stared at the portrait for a long moment or two, seemingly forgetting we were there.

Colleen cleared her throat. "Bernie, why don't we go into the kitchen and sit down? You said you needed to talk to me about something."

Deirdre's mom snapped out of her private thoughts. "Right, of course. This way, girls. I must have some chocolate biscuits hidden away somewhere."

I wasn't sure I wanted them to eat anything in that house, but I swallowed hard and dismissed my germ paranoia. "Thanks, that sounds perfect, Bernie."

We headed toward the tiny kitchen, with Bliz a ways behind us. She made up little dance steps and twirls as she moved down the hall, pointing her toes and keeping her fists at her sides like an Irish dancer.

Bernie turned at the doorway as if she were about to say something else, but when she saw Bliz, she stopped short. "Aren't you quite the little dancer?" she said, with a catch in her voice. This time, I was sure it wasn't due to half a carton a day of cigs.

"Oh, she's just pretending," Colleen said quickly. "You can mess around when we get home, okay, Bliz?"

I frowned at my sister. Pretend Irish dance steps wouldn't make Bernie feel any worse. This whole house was filled with memories of Deirdre. They seemed to bring her comfort.

"She didn't mean any harm, now," Bernie said, with a sad smile. "It does my heart good to see a child's joy in dancing. She's a natural, like her mother."

I didn't correct her, even when Maeve looked at me in surprise. I just smiled.

"I'm going to take lessons soon," Bliz announced.

I concentrated on the swirled-paisley pattern in the forest-green wallpaper, silently willing my daughter not to mention the galactically famous Moira McShane Kelly and her new dance school. Correction: dance *academy*. Deirdre's mom didn't need to learn right now that someone planned to put the Donnelly School of Dance out of business—if she didn't know already. She had plenty of other things to deal with.

"Isn't that nice." Bernie sounded pleased. "You're off to a fine start."

Bliz beamed.

"You know," Bernie went on, "I have some old dance tapes you and your sister could watch in the living room. Would you girls like that?"

I tried not to think about Maeve and Bliz sitting in that dark, claustrophobic living room, bingeing videos of Deirdre's old performances. It would be like watching a ghost.

But Bliz looked completely thrilled. Maeve nodded politely. Bernie went over to a hall closet and removed a large, green plastic tub overflowing with old VHS tapes and DVDs. "Be right back," she told me and Colleen before she retraced our steps to the living room.

"Thanks, sweetie," I whispered to Maeve as she passed. She nodded, already retrieving her phone from her jacket pocket. At least she'd keep Bliz company.

"Don't look so nervous, Kate," Colleen said as the girls disappeared down the hall behind Bernie. "It'll give them something to do while we're talking. Bliz will love all that show stuff. There must be some clips of me in there somewhere too."

When she and I sat down with Deirdre's mom at her burn-marked kitchen table, I was glad to see two floral arrangement deliveries on the counter. "Very pretty," I said.

"Aren't they?" Bernie reached across the table for a pack of cigarettes and a retro ashtray bearing the name of a long-gone Boston hotel in flowy, painted script. "The gorgeous lilies are from Aidan— he's in town for Paddy's Week, of course. Came in last night. Staying at the Smiling Shamrock."

For free, no doubt. The McShane witches never missed a publicity opportunity.

Deirdre's former dance partner did have excellent taste, though. The flowers he'd sent were stunning, artfully arranged in a black ceramic vase tied with a purple-and-gold mourning ribbon.

"And that other one is from Ray Flanagan," Bernie added.

Mayor Flanagan—or, more likely, his assistant—had chosen green-tinged carnations and white baby's breath set in a shiny green plastic top hat. Probably on sale for Saint Patrick's Day. The carnations were already brown around the edges, and they smelled awful.

Bernie brought out the shamrock handkerchief again. "I've always been allergic to baby's breath. Be a dear and throw those in the bin under the sink, will you, Colleen?"

My sister dutifully removed the delicate sprigs of baby's breath without dispersing the dried white blossoms all over the kitchen. She stuffed as much of the arrangement as she could into the trash, stabbing herself with the tiny plastic card holder, which snapped in half.

"Ow! Sorry." Colleen handed the card to Bernie. In green ink, it read, *With most sincere condolences, Honorable Raymond F. Flanagan, Mayor of Shamrock.*

"Honorable" wasn't the title that jumped to my mind. The Chief referred to him as a pompous windbag. Or worse.

Bernie waved away the card. "You can toss that too, thanks. Can you believe that man had the nerve to call to ask me how the Saint Patrick's Day show preparations were coming along?"

"You're kidding," Colleen said.

Zero surprise on my end. The Irish dancers from the Donnelly School were the highlight of Shamrock's annual Saint Patrick's Day festivities. Paddy's Week, as the locals called it, brought considerable money into the town, and the big dance show at Great Shamrock Hall sold out every year.

Bernie tapped her cigarette pack, then offered it to me and Colleen. We both shook our heads. "Good girls," she said. "A dirty habit."

"So how did Mayor Flanagan take the news that the show was off?" I asked. "Everyone will understand, I'm sure."

Bernie leaned back in her chair and drummed her nails on the table. I tried not to notice the tar stains visible where the bright red polish had chipped off. "That's what I want to talk to Colleen about. I need your help, honey."

Colleen nodded. "Anything."

"Thank you," Bernie said. "I have so much to do right now. Hopefully the police investigation will end soon. They're saying my baby was murdered, can you believe that?"

"No," Colleen said. "That's crazy, Bernie." She gently patted the woman's hand.

"I can't imagine anyone wanting to hurt my Deirdre." Bernie's voice broke. "But she's gone, and I need to plan a wake and funeral and—"

"Oh, I plan parties all the time," Colleen broke in. "Say no more. I'd be happy to handle the details, Bernie."

"Mom and I can help too," I said quickly.

Bernie held up one hand. "No, nothing to do for the funeral. I want you to take over the dance show, Colleen."

"Me?" Colleen seemed floored. I was too.

"You're the perfect person for the job," Bernie said. "You know all the dances, everyone in town loves you, and you'll be wonderful with the kids. The younger girls all looked up to you when you were dancing. And Deirdre mentioned you were thinking of taking it up again."

"Um, I don't . . . I mean, how would I do . . . everything?" My sister could hardly get the words out.

"Oh no, I forgot those biscuits for the children." Bernie looked at me. "The tin is in the living room somewhere, I think. Could you take a look-see, Kate?"

"Sure." I couldn't help feeling dismissed as I rose from the table. It was pretty clear Bernie wanted to speak to Colleen alone.

That made perfect sense. Maybe she wanted to talk about Deirdre and what had happened, as well as the show. I should check up on the girls anyway.

I found them both curled up in the dark on the plaid couch. Maeve was asleep at one end, clutching a crocheted pillow and snoring slightly. Bliz, petting a scrawny gray cat in her lap, was glued to the TV screen, which lent the room a faint, flickering glow. A lively jig played on the tape, the same one that had provided the opening soundtrack to the disturbing scene in Angels Hall. But this time the beats were punctuated by the pounding of dancers' hard shoes.

One-two-three-four. Two-two-three-four. Three-two-three-four.

I pushed Maeve's feet aside and squeezed onto the couch. She mumbled something and returned to her nap.

I didn't see Deirdre in the line of girls dancing furiously on the screen. They moved in perfect unison, faster and faster, their toes perfectly pointed and their kicks identically high.

Then the line parted and another girl, maybe a year or two older than Maeve, danced lightly to the front of the stage, her chin held high and her dark curls bouncing. I didn't know a lot about Irish dance, but the girl's steps were crisp and polished.

"There she is, Mommy!" Bliz edged so far forward, she almost fell off the couch. Even the scraggly cat paid strict attention, ears pricked forward. "That's Deirdre."

I felt another wave of sadness as I watched the raven-haired girl twirl and leap across the stage. It was obvious how much she loved to dance, and she exuded confidence. In spite of her gracefulness, though, I sensed her determination, as if she felt she had something to prove. Onstage, Deirdre Donnelly was no shrinking violet.

It was hard to believe she would never dance again.

The backup dancers formed a circle around her. "See, she's the Faerie Queene," Bliz said.

In the dim light, I glanced at the top of the pile of DVD cases on the coffee table. The handwritten label read, *Deirdre—Faerie Queene, Philadelphia, 20XX.* The last two numbers of the year were smudged.

"And look, there's Miss Moira too!" Bliz hugged Bernie's cat tighter, and he gave a muffled protest.

How could I have missed Moira? There she was, all right, the tallest dancer of the bunch. Her hair was a more subtle shade of red back then, but she wore that same striking lipstick.

The other girls' faces stayed expressionless as they stepped faster and faster to the beat, their feet and legs starting to blur. But Moira was different.

She didn't seem entirely focused on the dance, and there was no hint of the ditziness she'd displayed outside the trolley stop. Moira's gaze was pure steel—and aimed straight at the Faerie Queene.

Chapter Ten

"So what happened?" I asked Colleen as we left Deirdre's mother's house. "Did you tell Bernie you'd take over the Saint Patrick's Day show?"

"Of course. How could I say no? It's the least I can do."

"Well, I think that's fantastic," I said. "I'm happy to help, if you need me for anything."

"Oh, I will for sure." Colleen didn't look up from the sidewalk. "Thanks, Katie."

"Hey, you'll do an amazing job," I said in the cheerleader tone I used for things like the girls' art projects and impressive report cards. It would be a load of work, but the show was the perfect thing to help distract Colleen—a tiny bit, anyway—from Deirdre's death and her other troubles. She might even earn brownie points with the Shamrock PD. Murderers didn't take over dance show productions. "The girls will pitch in too," I added. "That's what families do, right?"

"Mm-hmm." Colleen seemed lost in thought, but she shook herself to attention. "I mean, yeah, thanks, that'll be awesome."

"It would have meant so much to Deirdre for you to take her place," I said. "Plus, you'll be taking a ton of stress off Bernie and saving the show for the kids and the Donnelly School and probably the whole Paddy's Week extravaganza for Shamrock. It might even be fun."

"Right." She smiled, but there was no sign of the dimple.

Maybe I was pushing it with the "fun" part, but all we had to do was not screw this up. Otherwise Mayor Flanagan would probably send a hit squad out for us.

"You'll be in charge of all the Irish dancers, Aunt Colleen!" Bliz spun ahead of us on the sidewalk like a top, waving a rolled-up dance magazine Bernie had given her. Then she rushed back. "Can Maeve and I watch all the practices?"

Maeve gave me the side-eye, but I pretended not to notice. School was out next week for the kids, so that was one problem avoided, at least.

"You bet," Colleen said. "And you'll be front and center at the show too."

"I can't wait to tell Gram," Bliz said.

"Maybe you should let me tell everyone," Colleen said. "It'll be a surprise, okay?"

Bliz looked disappointed. "I'm not good at keeping secrets."

True. The Buckley secrecy gene had skipped my younger daughter.

"I'll announce it tonight," Colleen promised.

* * *

When we got home from the Donnellys' there was a note on the kitchen table from Mom letting us know she'd gone to a hair appointment at the Curly Q. Colleen and I made lunch, and as soon as the four of us finished eating, I sent the girls upstairs with an extra-thick ham sandwich for the Chief. "Keep your grandfather company for a while, okay?" I added, grabbing three Flake bars from the brown candy jug and dropping them onto the tray.

"So do you want to talk now?" Colleen said, dropping into a kitchen chair when the girls were gone.

"Absolutely." I scurried over to the table and sat across from her. This was great. She'd actually brought it up. I'd start with the easiest issue first. "Remember the other night, when we were walking to Farrell's, and I asked if you needed money?"

"Yeah. Hold on a sec, okay?" Colleen jumped up again and started rummaging in the pantry.

"What are you doing?"

She reemerged with a package of dark-green paper napkins and a tray of clean, fancy-looking flatware we used for the guests. "We can roll up the forks and spoons for tea at the same time."

"Oh. Good idea." I separated out a stack of napkins for myself.

"It's more sanitary for serving buffet-style. Mom wants to start doing guest dinners too, but that'd be a lot of work. And expensive."

"Right," I said. "Back to the money. Do you still need some?"

"I always need money." Colleen sighed.

"Who doesn't?"

"I don't need to borrow any from you, if that's what you're asking," Colleen said. "But thank you. It might've helped before, but it's water under the bridge now."

"What did you need money for?"

"Doesn't matter," she answered. "It was something personal, nothing bad, and I really don't want to talk about it yet. I think I have another solution."

"Well, okay," I said reluctantly, but now I had even more questions. I tried another tack. "What did Frank mean when he said the cops knew about the money? Was he talking about the loan from Deirdre?"

Colleen wadded up a piece of napkin she'd ripped. "Oh, you know Frank. He's always talking about stuff he doesn't have a clue about."

This time I didn't respond, just tapped the teaspoon I'd been about to wrap on the table. She'd spill in four, three, two . . .

"I really messed up," she blurted. "But Deirdre knew I'd pay it back."

"How much?"

"Five thousand."

"Ouch," I said. "That's a lot."

"The problem was, I spent Deirdre's money, and some other money too. She asked me if I could pay it back sooner because she wanted to take Bernie on a vacation to Ireland this summer, because she's been sick. I mean, it's not like Deirdre didn't have the money or anything. She said she was just asking. But the texts sounded a little suspicious to the cops. I told her I was working on it."

"Mom mentioned you've taken on more responsibilities here at the B and B," I said. "Did you get a raise?"

"Not exactly." Colleen added another utensil bundle to the pile between us. "I, um, may have taken another loan. Kind of like an advance on my paycheck."

I suddenly realized what was coming next, and it wasn't good. I should have thought of it earlier. Maybe I just hadn't wanted to. "Colleen, did you take money from the Buckley House accounts?"

"I borrowed it." Colleen lifted her chin. "Only five thousand dollars, the same as I owed Deirdre. I needed ten in total, so . . ."

Ten *thousand*? No wonder the detectives were interested. I kept my voice calm and steady. "Colleen, where is all that money now?"

"I'm trying to get it back," she said. "But there was a contract, and I couldn't get out of it."

My throat went dry. What kind of contract? "What did you do?" I asked softly.

Colleen stared at the table. "I just wanted my own place, that's all. I put down the money for first and last month's rent, plus a separate security deposit and a broker's fee and . . . other stuff, I dunno."

"But why?" I asked. "You have free room and board right here. I get that you want your own place, but you could've saved up and then gotten one. How high are rents here now in Shamrock, anyway?"

She looked away.

I closed my eyes, gathering what was left of my sanity. "Okay, Colleen," I said finally. "We're going to work on budgeting and financial planning. Together. You can't throw money around you don't have and make major decisions without a plan. You know that, don't you?"

"Yes," Colleen said, drawing out the word. She put her elbows on the table and covered her face with her hands.

"But first we have to figure out this current situation," I went on. "You have to pay back Mom and Dad. And Bernie too, since Deirdre's gone. I don't have ten thousand dollars right now. We'll work things out."

"Thanks, Katie," she said, in a small voice. "But how?"

"I don't know yet," I said.

"Are you going to rat me out to Mom?"

What was she, ten? No, she sounded even younger. "I think she already suspects," I said. "You need to tell her yourself. Soon, so we can figure out how to fix this."

"Okay." Her voice was almost a whisper. "I'll talk to her. Maybe we won't have to tell Dad."

Doubtful, but I was determined to stay out of that part. "Can you finish up the tea prep?" I said, standing up from the table. "I need to clear my brain."

"Sure," Colleen said. "But there's, um, one more thing."

Of course there was. I sat down again, bracing myself. Did it ever end with her?

"The cops think I stole the money for the Donnelly School scholarship Deirdre was starting. You know, for kids who couldn't afford lessons, or the fancy dresses or traveling to competitions."

For a second or two, I was speechless. *"What?"* I finally managed. "Is that what Frank meant when he was talking about the money? Not the loan from Deirdre?"

"Well . . . both, I guess," Colleen said. "But, Kate, I didn't steal the donation money. I swear." She looked at me pleadingly, her eyes clear blue. "No one even knows how much money it was exactly. It hadn't been counted yet. But the kids and Deirdre had a table outside the church and the library each week, and people gave money, and we consolidated all of it into this big plastic jug. I offered to take it over to the Donnellys' one afternoon, because it was heavy and I had my car, but then I went back into Angels Hall for something, and someone stole it from the back seat. No one knows who. It was there, and then it wasn't."

Now it was my turn to cover my face. "Colleen," I said, "why didn't you tell me this?"

"Bernie wanted to keep it quiet," my sister said. "She and Deirdre knew I didn't steal it. They didn't even file a police report; they just asked for whoever took it to come forward. But no one did. And when Dee and I had that teensy text fight, she said I was careless about money, like with the scholarship donations that disappeared. So when the cops took my phone, they saw it and . . ." Her voice trailed away.

I stood up again, very carefully. No wonder the cops were interested in my sister. She looked desperate for money—especially Deirdre's. "Excuse me. I need to go throw up."

* * *

I dashed to the downstairs powder room, where I did not officially hurl. But I sure felt like it.

I wanted to leave the house and keep on walking. Anywhere. But I couldn't risk running into anyone I knew right now. And I needed to help Mom with family dinner.

There weren't any guests in the living room yet. I curled up on the couch, hedgehog style, and considered pulling a pillow over my head to block out the world. Colleen had finally driven me over the edge.

It took a minute for me to realize that someone had left the TV on, without sound. A banner along the bottom of the screen scrolled breaking news, courtesy of WSCK, right here in Shamrock.

Not live, just a replay of a press conference that had ended a few minutes ago. *Suspicious death under investigation in Shamrock ruled a homicide.*

Finally, official info on Deirdre's case. I fumbled for the remote on the coffee table without taking my eyes from the screen.

In the light rain, His Dishonor was speaking from a podium on the steps of the town hall, surrounded by a sea of reporters and cameras. Beside him stood Chief Ryan, with Detective Sergeant Walker visible just behind his wide shoulders. Bernie Donnelly was there on the steps also, apart from the others, holding a framed picture of Deirdre. Her eyes stared straight ahead at the cameras.

I still couldn't get the volume to work. One of the guests must have been confused by the remote. When the sound finally came on, the mayor's voice blasted through the living room. I quickly readjusted, but I'd missed half the announcement.

"So I'll wish a very happy Saint Patrick's Week to you all and hand this press conference over to our very capable Chief Ryan for more details," Mayor Flanagan concluded. "He'll be delighted to answer your questions."

Bob Ryan did not look delighted in the least. Unlike the Chief, he didn't enjoy the spotlight. I literally felt sick to my stomach again. Happy Saint Patrick's week? This would be Shamrock's saddest Paddy's celebration ever.

Chief Ryan stepped to the podium and cleared his throat. "Good afternoon," he said. "As many of you know, a suspicious death is under investigation. An unconscious adult female was found in the backstage area of Our Lady of Angels Hall on Galway Court on Thursday at 9:17 PM. That woman was identified as Deirdre Anne Donnelly, 24, of Shamrock. First responders attempted to provide medical treatment, and Ms. Donnelly was transported to Cloverhill Hospital, where she was pronounced dead. The autopsy has revealed Ms. Donnelly's cause of death was blunt impact injuries to the head. The manner of death has just been determined by the chief medical examiner to be homicide."

He paused, and there was a long moment of dead air.

My sister needed to hear this. I lowered the volume and rose from the couch, remote still in hand. I backed toward the doorway, still glued to the screen. "Colleen!" I yelled.

"At this time, we have multiple persons of interest, whom we will not be naming at this time. We do not believe there is currently any danger to members of the public. Anyone with information is asked to call 911 or the Shamrock Police Department's anonymous tip line."

The number flashed in the banner as Chief Ryan fumbled with something at the podium. Was he reading his statement from a cheat sheet? Yes.

"Additional information will be released as it becomes available while protecting the integrity of the investigation," he added. "We will not take questions at this time."

So much for being delighted to provide further details. Mayor Flanagan stood smiling and nodding under the black umbrella held over his head by a shivering aide. As Chief Ryan stepped away from the podium amid a storm of reporters' demands for details, the mayor leaned in toward the microphone. "Again, no anticipated danger to the general public," he said. "All is well, and we'll keep you posted, folks."

Sure, Ray.

At least Colleen Buckley's name hadn't been mentioned. A huge relief, but not really a surprise. It was still early in the investigation, and the police needed as much ironclad evidence as possible before turning things over to the DA. Dermot Buckley was probably impressing that importance on his former colleagues. Hourly.

My sister showed up in the hall holding a knife. "What's up? Everything okay, Kate?"

"What are you doing?" I asked, eyeing the knife.

"You called me." Colleen looked down at her hand. "Oh. I was slicing up cake for the tea platter."

We both realized there was someone at the door at the same time. I spotted Sergeant Walker through one of the side panel windows.

"Don't answer—" I began. Too late.

I ducked back through the living room doorway but peeked out as Colleen stepped forward and opened the front door. The detective raised an eyebrow at the knife.

Colleen gave a tiny chortle as if carrying a knife around the Buckley House was completely normal. "Oh, hey, Detective," she said. "Here to talk to me?"

I leaned back against the living room wall and rolled my eyes to no one. My sister was beyond help.

Maybe I was the one Surly Shirley wanted to grill. She'd seen Maeve and me chatting this morning at PJ's with another person of interest. I'd meant to call, or at least text, her. I hadn't.

"No, ma'am," Surly Shirley said. "I'm here to see the Chief."

"I think he's taking a nap."

"He asked me to meet with him. He's expecting me in his office."

"Oh. I'll take you up, then, because the elevator has a code."

"The stairs aren't a problem, thanks. I know the way."

"Detective, would you like a piece of cake?" Colleen called after her.

"No, thank you." As Shirley lumbered up the stairs—creaking under her weight—I silently stepped into the hall and followed my sister back to the kitchen.

She dropped the knife onto the table next to Mom's lemon pound cake and blew out an exaggerated breath. "I swear, I'm going to lose it. Like, for real. That woman makes me so nervous. Did you see the way she was looking at me?"

"Don't say anything, sweetie. Let the Chief handle it." I picked up the knife and started slicing the rest of the cake. I didn't have to tell Colleen about the press conference right away. Even if Chief Ryan hadn't named any persons of interest in the Donnelly investigation, we both knew who one of them was.

Chapter Eleven

D inner was fairly quiet, by Buckley standards. Even the Chief, who'd gotten dressed for the occasion, was busy digging into his pizza. I gave him my black olives, which he loved.

Outside of working teatime, Colleen and I had spent the rest of the afternoon doom-scrolling on our phones. She found the press conference clip, and there was plenty of chattering about Deirdre's murder on social media. I saw a reference or two to my sister, but she had plenty of defenders. Mostly, there were glowing memories of Deirdre, tributes from past students and famous Irish dancers, clips of her and Aidan, condolences for Bernie, and the official announcement from Irish Steps. WSCK interviewed the McShanes outside the Smiling Shamrock—literally, in front of the neon shamrock sign—where both sisters offered their thoughts and prayers. Una slid in how honored they were that Deirdre's world-famous dance partner, Aidan O'Hearne, was a guest in their humble home for Saint Patrick's Week, but was understandably unavailable for comment.

Surprisingly, no reporters were camped out on our lawn, staking out my sister, but I did notice a watchful police presence parked outside the Buckley House. Frank, in his cruiser. And in the unmarked vehicle not-so-discreetly circling the block: Garrett. The Chief's request, no doubt.

Our dad said nothing during dinner about his conversation with Sergeant Walker, and neither Colleen nor I brought it up. We both knew better. He usually told the family things on a need-to-know basis. In this case, probably no news was good news.

"Can I please be excused?" Maeve dumped her pizza crusts into the disposal as everyone else was still eating. "I have some vacation homework to do."

"What about dessert?" Mom looked disappointed. "I made oatmeal cookies. There's shortbread too."

"We can have them later," Colleen said. "They're even better with frosting. Bliz will help me make it."

"We should send a tin to Bernie." I filled Mom in on the dismal food situation at the Donnelly house.

"Good heavens," she said. "That poor woman needs to keep up her strength. I'll up the portions on dinners this week, and we'll run them over."

With Bliz covered in confectioner's sugar, happily whipping up frosting beside Colleen, I headed upstairs to email my boss. I dreaded telling Kashmira I'd need to adjust my client schedule for the next week. She wouldn't be thrilled, but emergencies were emergencies. When I got back to New York, I'd triple my in-office hours until Tax Day.

A guest stood talking animatedly on her phone halfway up the stairs, surrounded by shopping bags full of Celtic treasures, so I took the Chief's private elevator. I had no problem plugging in his top-secret code, SPCNU1, which stood for Shamrock Police Chief Numero Uno One. I'd figured it out by watching him press the buttons when I was younger than Bliz. Another one of his extra security measures.

The Nest's ladder was pulled up. Maeve was probably doing that homework or chatting with her friends.

As I continued down the hall, I figured I should text Sergeant Walker about the talking-to-Conor deal. Better late than never. I hadn't seen her leave after her meeting with the Chief.

I reached for Surly Shirley's card in my back jeans pocket and pulled out Garrett's instead. Even better. I could speak with him in person, even if things were a little awkward between us.

He didn't answer his cell, so I left a quick message. Good. My obligations were complete as far as the cops were concerned.

Time to send that email to Kashmira. But as I stepped inside the dimly lit bedroom, I spotted the bathroom hair dryer hanging from one of the scarf hooks in Colleen's closet. Maeve must have thought that was a good place to leave it last night. Luckily, she hadn't started a chiffon and silk-fueled fire.

I'd return it now in case anyone else was looking for it. Grabbing the hair dryer by the nozzle end, I wound up the cord as I made my way back toward the door. As I passed the nightstand, I heard something crunch under my foot.

Uh-oh. I reached down and ran my hand through the shag carpet, until my fingers closed on something fragile, cold, and metal. A necklace.

Hoping I hadn't crushed it, I carefully reached up to pull the little chain on the mid-century bedside lamp. The sudden light blinded me for a second or two before I gazed down at my open palm. Entwined in a delicate, coiled gold chain were two gold charms: a Celtic cross and a half-heart set with a tiny emerald.

The necklace looked familiar. Had Colleen worn it in high school? They'd sold them in a gift shop on the square.

But the jagged heart? A couples or friendship necklace, the kind where someone else had the matching half. But the heart charm on Colleen's necklace had a ruby in the center. For July, her birthstone. This one held an emerald.

I suddenly realized I'd seen this necklace very recently: around Deirdre's neck in Angels Hall. I distinctly remembered the tiny emerald, and the flash of gold.

The now-familiar feeling of dread rose in my chest as I slowly turned over the heart. Sure enough, it was engraved in tiny script: *DD & CB. Best Friends.*

I lifted the chain from my palm and let it uncoil. Frowning, I peered at the tiny links more closely. The chain was broken, as if it had been torn somehow. Not crushed, so the damage hadn't happened when I'd stepped on it.

What was my sister doing with Deirdre's necklace? Had she nicked it from a crime scene?

Maybe Bernie had given it to her as a keepsake, I told myself hopefully. Or a thank-you for taking over the show.

No. My sister hadn't been upstairs since we'd gotten home. We'd all gone straight to the kitchen, and then gotten the tea ready.

Not only had she tampered with a crime scene, but she'd stolen a possibly key piece of evidence. How could she be that stupid?

Was Colleen that desperate for money? I couldn't believe she'd rip it straight off her dead friend's neck. Plus, her DNA—and now mine—was all over the necklace. Maybe even mixed up with a killer's.

One thing was for sure: My sister's little stunt would not go down well with Sergeant Walker.

I grabbed a Kleenex from the nightstand, wrapped it around Deirdre's necklace, and pushed it as far down as possible in my back pocket. That scheduling email to Kashmira would have to wait. Again.

Should I march straight downstairs and confront Colleen? Or tell the Chief and get his advice?

No, that would be snitching—maybe for no reason. I had to hear Colleen's explanation first. She'd gaze back at me with those big blue eyes, all innocence, and offer some explanation so crazy it would be completely believable.

I really hoped she'd come up with a good excuse, because I sure couldn't think of one myself.

Instead, another terrible possibility sprang to my mind. What if Colleen removed the necklace from the crime scene because she was afraid it might incriminate her somehow, and she'd wanted to hide the evidence?

Even with the sharp edges of Deirdre's necklace charms threatening to slash my butt straight through my jeans, my gut screamed that my sister hadn't murdered her best friend. Yes, Colleen acted without thinking things through, and she wasn't so hot with rules and money and keeping jobs. She probably held the all-time Town of Shamrock records for parking tickets, library fines, and who knew what else. She went through guys like last week's lipstick, and true, she sometimes made bad choices. Who didn't, including me? But murder? That was a hard no.

Plus, she had an alibi, I reminded myself. My sister had been home, steaming up a bathroom for her spa night at the time Deirdre was murdered.

I didn't believe my sister was a murderer. Not for a second. But without that alibi, confirmed by the former chief of police and his wife, I could see how a detective might build that case.

On my way to find Colleen, I pulled on the chain with the green tassel to let down the folding ladder from the Nest, taking care to avoid the stairs dropping on my head. "Maeve?" I called, climbing up partway. "You doing okay up there? Just saying hi."

No answer. I tried again. "Maeve?"

The lamp beside the bed was on, and I spotted a large, odd lump under the quilt. Could she breathe sleeping like that?

I hurried up the rest of the stairs and sat on my butt at the top to pull myself into the room. When I rose, I carefully ducked to avoid the low, pine-beamed ceiling. I strode over to the bed and threw back the covers.

Pillows. Nothing but pillows and a couple of wadded-up bath towels. It was 6:50 PM by the moonbeam clock on the dresser, and I knew exactly where Maeve was headed: to meet Conor Murphy at Lucky's.

My pulse pounding with fury and fear, I rushed back down the ladder, skipping the last two steps.

"Hold on now, Kathleen." The doors of my dad's elevator closed behind him as he wheeled down the hall and rolled his chair up in front of me. "Where's the fire? You'll break your neck."

"Sorry, Dad. Gotta go."

He nodded toward the Nest. "She's upset, is she?"

"No. She's gone." I sucked in my breath. "To meet . . . a boy. The one we told you about outside Angels Hall last night. At Lucky's."

The Chief's bushy brows had already shot up at the word *boy*. "We'll take my van."

"Dad, I think—"

"You think too much, missy. Just do."

Usually my dad reserved the "missy" for Colleen. But it meant any argument was futile. I nodded.

"Not a word to the others. No sense in adding more troubles to their shoulders. Meet me at the garage in five minutes. Sharp."

"Thanks, Dad." I headed toward the guest elevator at the other end of the hall, where I'd be less likely to run into any other family members. Hopefully Colleen and Mom were having that discussion about the accounts right now. That ought to occupy them both for a while. And when I got home with Maeve safely in tow, Colleen and I would have our own little talk—about Deirdre's necklace.

Chapter Twelve

The garage was cold, leaky, and packed with all kinds of junk from the guest rooms: cardboard boxes, broken lampshades, old mattresses wrapped in plastic, and at least three dinosaur TVs. There was barely any room left for the Chief's van or Mom's ancient Camry. Colleen parked her Mini under the rusty carport out back.

If the Buckley House needed quick cash, I had a hot tip for Mom: eBay.

As my dad eased his wheelchair into the driver's side of the custom van, I hit the button for the automatic garage door. The rain was coming down in king-size sheets.

Maeve was out there somewhere, probably soaking wet and oblivious to the dangerous situation she could be walking into. This wasn't the city, where she was used to going places she knew by herself and feeling safe. After Deirdre's murder, didn't she understand she was taking her chances in Shamrock right now?

"Tell me more about this young man my granddaughter is meeting."

I focused my gaze through the raindrops on the passenger window, searching for Maeve. "It's the boy from Angels Hall last night. He works at PJ Scoops, so we saw him there this morning. His name is Conor Murphy, and he and Maeve knew each other years ago at Angels. He asked her to meet him tonight, and I told her no."

Even if I'd had any other details, I wouldn't have mentioned them to my dad. In his book, the boy factor was sufficient to require action.

"Oh, and Sergeant Walker came in right after us," I added. "Maybe to speak with him, I'm not sure. I got the girls out of there."

"Shirley mentioned that," my dad said. "But back to the boy thing. I don't care who he is, I don't want my granddaughter traipsing all over town at night. Especially now. Keep a sharp eye on that one, Kathleen. Remember: Stay alert, no one gets hurt."

There'd been a time when I'd given the eye roll to my dad's favorite motto. Maybe all parents warned their progeny like that, but it was extra tough being a cop's kid. We couldn't be careful enough, in his view. Of course, as far as parenting skills went, the Chief loved all of us dearly, but he'd spent a considerable amount of our childhoods either at the station house or debriefing with the "lads" at Farrell's. Mom was always the hammer.

"So, how's the investigation going?" I asked, changing the subject. "What did Sergeant Walker want to talk to you about this afternoon?"

"Sorry, Kathleen. I can't share that."

His craggy profile didn't change as we passed Our Lady of Angels. The parish hall was dark, other than that same lone floodlight, but the doors were still shrink-wrapped in fluorescent yellow crime tape. Wilted bunches of grocery store flowers, along with equally saggy Mylar balloons and a soggy stuffed teddy bear, were piled in front of the door. Memorial candles that hadn't already been extinguished by the rain flickered bravely under the awning.

We were halfway to the square by now, with no sign of Maeve. Hopefully she'd already arrived safely at Lucky's.

Who knew how Conor had been involved in Deirdre's death? I still didn't think the kid was a killer. But if he'd been a witness, the killer might be after him—and anyone he talked to—to shut him up.

The Chief frowned in concentration. Not on his driving, because he almost hit the curb as he took a hard right turn onto Donegal Drive. "Dad, can't you tell me *anything*? I'm trying to help here. We're on the same side."

"Not much to tell yet," he said. "They're still conducting interviews. Waiting on forensics. Lab's backed up, so it may be a while."

"But they have persons of interest."

"They do." My dad was as tight-lipped as Bob Ryan at the press conference.

"Like Colleen?"

He kept his eyes on the road. Luckily. "You and your sister need to go about your business like I told you both. Stay under the radar. No talking to anyone about the case. The investigation's already in fine hands. We need to keep everyone safe, especially Colleen."

"She's in danger?" I tried to keep the instant panic from my voice.

"No, no, don't worry your head, Kathleen. Standard precautions," he said. "We don't know who we're dealing with."

I yanked on the shoulder strap of my seat belt, which suddenly felt tighter. My dad was a lot more close-lipped than usual tonight. And he was lecturing the wrong missy. What would he say if he knew Colleen might have swiped her dead friend's necklace right off her neck? Or that I had said necklace in my jeans pocket right now? "Can you drive a little faster, Dad?"

He obliged with a sharp left turn and a spray of water at the corner before Lucky's. Only a block left. Still no Maeve.

"So what happens to a victim's jewelry and stuff from a crime scene?" I asked. "You know, like their wallet or watch?"

This time my dad gave me a sideways look.

"I'm just . . . interested."

"Well, everything is photographed first, of course. Any personal effects stay with the body until the autopsy. Then the ME bags up anything needed for evidence and turns it over to us."

"When does the person's family get the things back?"

"Depends. We keep the evidence in storage for however long it's needed."

"Is Frank working Deirdre's case?"

"Negative."

"Why not?" Cops couldn't work cases involving family members.

The van gave a sudden lurch. I'd pressed too far.

"Enough, Kathleen," my dad said. "PD will solve this. Before the Staties, to be sure. We've got the local ground game."

"Yes, sir." I resisted the temptation to salute. The necklace in my pocket would burst into flames any second. But I wanted to hear what Colleen had to say before I handed it over to anyone. Maybe she had a decent explanation. If anyone could provide one, it was my sister.

With a squeal of wet brakes, the Chief brought the van to a stop in front of a one-story building with green and orange light bulbs that spelled out "Lucky's" on the roof. In the front window, a black plastic cauldron left over from Halloween overflowed with crumpled gold-foil streamers. Another tangle of multicolored streamers was taped in a large rainbow arc over the fake pot of gold. An explosion of tacky from the Party Hearty store outside of town.

"You go in for the recon," the Chief said. "Ten minutes. If you spot Maeve, come to the door and give me the thumbs-up."

"Or I could text," I said.

"Fine. Any problem, or if she's not there, I'm calling it in."

I nodded and jumped down from the van, slinking into Lucky's past all the kids hanging outside under the dripping awning. Maeve wasn't among them. They'd be thrilled to see the Chief parked directly in front of the building, even if they weren't doing anything wrong. Back when he was on the force, my dad had a well-earned rep for sniffing out troublemakers.

The cavernous front room was crowded, even for a Friday night, with dim green lights overhead and a mini-Vegas worth of flashing arcade games. A small boy ran straight into my knees.

"Mikey, get back here!" a voice shouted over the ping-ping of a nearby pinball machine. A long buzzer and a string of alarm bells sounded as someone's game went down in flames.

"Are you Mikey?" I asked. He shook his head no.

"Sorry." A slim girl about Maeve's age grabbed the little gremlin and swung him up on her hip. She wore a green T-shirt with "Donnelly School of Irish Dance" screened across it in gold, the D's designed in large, swirling Celtic font.

A younger girl with glasses and perfect cornrow braids came up beside her, carrying a plastic bucket. "Zoe, did you ask her yet?"

"Nope." Zoe detangled Mikey's slimy fingers from the tight bun of jet-black hair on top of her head. "We're taking up a collection for Deirdre Donnelly's funeral," she said to me over the noise. "We want to get some really nice flowers. Any money left over goes to her memorial scholarship fund."

So the fund Colleen was accused of stealing from was now dedicated to Deirdre. "That's a lovely idea." My hand brushed

Deirdre's necklace as I fished in my back pocket for bills. I handed Zoe a crumpled ten.

"Thanks." She set Mikey down and turned to leave. The other girl had already disappeared into the crowd with her bucket.

"Zoe, wait," I said. "I'm very sorry about your teacher. I'm looking for my daughter. Do you know a guy named Conor Murphy?"

Her thin, penciled eyebrows shot up. "Conor? Sure. He's a good friend of mine. He's talking with a girl named Maeve in the back. Is that her?"

I nodded, giving a silent sigh of relief.

"Want me to get him?"

"No, thank you. I'll just follow you, if that's okay."

Mikey squirmed out of his sister's grasp and tore gleefully through the crowd like a greased pig at the Great Shamrock Fair. "Hold on," Zoe said.

She gracefully retrieved both her own cash bucket and Mikey from the top of a nearby arcade game. I tried not to notice the stares as we cut through the crowd. Moms didn't show up here often.

Maeve would be livid. Even more so when I grounded her for sneaking out.

Lucky's back room was quieter and brighter. It held pool tables with chalk scoreboards and a bar that served nonalcoholic drinks. In one corner, a bunch of kids played darts. Another group was gathered around an intense game of Ping-Pong.

I spotted Maeve standing behind Conor as he lined up a shot at the farthest pool table. I refused to be impressed when the kid expertly sent two striped balls into a corner pocket, leaving the cue ball in the center of the table.

Should I march over and drag my daughter out? Or take another opportunity to grill him about Thursday night?

The Chief's ten minutes had to be up. In no time, a SWAT team would arrive.

"Thanks, Zoe. I'll be right back," I said, sending my dad a quick text. Hopefully he'd see it, but I had to make sure. "I need to hit the ATM. So I can give Maeve some cash."

Ha. She could finance her own shenanigans, the little sneak.

I plowed back through the crowd and out Lucky's front door. The Chief's van was still at the curb. He had his cell phone in hand.

I rapped on the passenger-side window, shielding myself from the rain with one arm. "She's here," I said when my dad put it down. "Everything's fine."

"Glad to hear it."

"I'll go back and get her." Unless she'd ducked out the back door when she heard I'd shown up.

He leaned toward me across the seat. "Kate, why don't you girls stay here for a half hour or so? I need to head over to Farrell's to talk to someone. Maybe you can get something out of the boy."

Fine. The decision had been made for me. "Okay, Dad."

"I'll pick you up here at half past eight. Don't be late, or your mother will be looking for all of us."

Now we three were coconspirators. I nodded and ducked back under the awning.

"I got you some backup, just in case," my dad called before he put up the window and the van peeled away.

Backup? I didn't need any help managing my own daughter and some zit-faced kid. I had a good mind to rat the Chief out to Mom when we got home.

"Hey, Katie," a cheerful voice said behind me. "Reporting for duty."

Please no. I turned to find myself face-to-shoulders with Garrett McGavin, dressed in jeans and a plaid flannel shirt with a black windbreaker thrown casually over it against the rain. He grinned as he took in my soaked coat, least favorite jeans, and oversized Notre Dame sweatshirt with the fighting leprechaun I'd grabbed in the garage at the last minute. Oh, and Mom's muddy wellies for a finishing touch. "You really haven't changed," he said.

"Thanks," I said, not sure that was a compliment. "Listen, I appreciate you showing up, but you don't need to be here. Really. I've got this."

"Yeah, I know that." The sea of kids parted to let us through, and Garrett reached past me to get the door. "But when the Chief calls with a personal request, you can't exactly turn him down."

"He's not the chief anymore." I squinted in the green-tinged darkness as we entered Lucky's kiddie cave.

"Right. So your wayward daughter is patronizing this fine establishment?"

"She is not wayward," I said. "For some reason, she decided to come here to meet that kid I left you the message about earlier. You got my voicemail?"

"Yup." He didn't sound concerned.

"Maeve'll freak when she sees me. Accompanied by a cop, no less."

"Not just any cop," Garrett said cheerfully. "Conor Murphy's uncle."

"What?"

He shrugged. "Yeah, Conor is my sister Siobhan's kid."

"Oh. Then they'll both freak." I hesitated. "Are you off the Donnelly case since you're related?"

"Pretty much, until he's a hundred percent cleared of any involvement," Garrett said. "But I know Conor. He wouldn't kill a mosquito."

"You've talked with him?"

"Yeah, he came to me first, and then Walker took over. Kid was just in the wrong place at the wrong time."

"Like Colleen," I said. Garrett didn't answer. "I'd still like to talk to him again."

"Good luck. He's not a big talker." Garrett dropped a crisply folded twenty into a Deirdre Donnelly fundraiser bucket on a table as we passed. "Look, this is a covert operation, okay? I'll hang out near the back door, beside that stupid blow-up harp over there. This place could probably use a little extra security anyway."

"Sounds like a plan." I threw him a small smile before I peeked through the entrance to the back room. "There they are, at the table in the corner with Conor's friend Zoe. I'm going in."

Garrett nodded, his windbreaker brushing my sleeve slightly as he motioned me past him. "Everyone is safe if they're with Zoe Koo. Just give a signal if you need me, though. You know, the old thumbs-up." He demonstrated, with a grin. He was enjoying this.

No wedding ring, I noticed. I was pretty sure he'd been engaged at some point. "Okay. See you around, then. And thanks."

He didn't hear me over the arcade games and driving pop music. He was already on his way toward the giant harp, with that jaunty cop stride my dad used to have.

When I reached the table, Maeve and her new buddies were so absorbed in conversation they didn't notice me right away.

"Hi, guys!" I said brightly. "I'm Kate Buckley, Maeve's mom. Conor, we met at PJ's this morning. And Zoe, we just spoke back in the other room. Mind if I join you?"

Maeve froze, her face horrified. Zoe must not have mentioned my fib that I wanted to bring her money. Conor sank back in his chair. "Whatever," he mumbled.

The Jig Is Up

Zoe dumped a squirming Mikey off her lap. "We're talking about Miss Deirdre. Want a slice?" She pointed down at the Lucky's Special Charm pizza advertised on the chalkboard behind the snack bar: cheese dotted with pepperoni, green peppers, and broccoli. And a sprinkling of tiny green marshmallows.

"No thanks," I said, with a mental gag. "We had pizza for dinner. I might take some of that, though." Trying to be social, I nodded toward the stack of extra cups beside a half-full pitcher of some unidentifiable, neon-green drink. I didn't dare look Maeve's way. I knew she was glowering.

I got that I didn't belong here, but a little embarrassment served her right. Zoe extracted a plastic cup and poured me a hearty amount of the noxious green liquid, which proved fizzy and slimy at the same time. I pretended to sip it.

"Once you get used to it, it's not that bad." Zoe sounded apologetic. She tried to shoo Mikey's chubby hand away from the pizza, but he managed to grab half the cheese off a slice and stuff it into his mouth. "That's disgusting. Just wait till we get home," she scolded. "Kids," she said to me, rolling her eyes.

I hid a smile at Zoe's ease in conversing with adults, as opposed to Maeve's sullen silence and Conor's clear ambivalence. He stared toward the action at the pool tables, arms crossed. I'd really busted up this little party.

"Maeve said she has a younger sister," Zoe added into the void.

I nodded. "Yes, she's seven, and her real name is Mary Elizabeth, but Maeve couldn't pronounce it when Bliz was born. She'd just lost her two front teeth."

Maeve's face went nearly purple.

Now it was my turn to break the continuing silence. "Bliz wants to be an Irish dancer now."

105

"Well, she came to the right place," Zoe said. "Except now Miss Deirdre's gone." Her eyes teared up, and she blinked hard. "I still can't believe it. She was the best dance teacher ever, and I've been dancing since I was three. I took ballet and jazz before my mom moved us here to Shamrock a couple years ago. But I dropped those for Irish dance. Miss Deirdre really cared about her students."

Hmm. I could get a lot more info out of Zoe than Conor. He was studying his trendy zigzag-bolted sneakers now. "You must have known her well."

"Not really," Zoe said. "She just quit Irish Steps last year, but she was the best."

"Wonder why Deirdre left the show," I said, still fishing. "She was the star."

"Miss Deirdre didn't care about being famous or money or anything. She came back to Shamrock when Miss Bernie got sick, to help her run the school," Zoe said. "She tried to keep costs low for all us students. Like, we pass down our dresses and hard shoes to the younger girls when we outgrow them. We only wear the fancy costumes and wigs for shows and *feiseanna*."

"Fesh-na?" Maeve finally spoke. In fairness, it was hard to get a word in edgewise anyway. Zoe was a talker.

"Irish dance competitions," Zoe explained. "If it's just one, it's called a *feis*."

She pronounced the word "fesh." I made a mental note, in the unlikely event I ever needed to sound like an Irish dance expert.

"Miss Deirdre even started a scholarship fund for dancers who couldn't afford classes and stuff. She was going to announce the first winner at the Paddy's Day show." Zoe sighed. "But now she's gone, and so is all the money we collected before she died."

"What happened to it?" I asked.

"Some jerk stole it. No one knows who."

Luckily, Zoe didn't know my sister was the suspected jerk.

Even in the greenish darkness, I sensed Garrett's eyes on us from across the room. I couldn't see him, though—just that ridiculous inflatable harp. A cardboard arrow beside it pointed toward a pulsating bouncy castle, where happy screams and squeals rose over the music and arcade buzzers and bells.

I was racking my brain for a way to get Conor to talk when he suddenly leaned across the table. "Okay, so here's the deal."

His eyes held the same odd intensity I'd seen outside the parish hall. I braced myself. Was Garrett's nephew about to confess to murder?

"I didn't kill Deirdre. But I think I saw who did."

Chapter Thirteen

"Who was it?" My voice came out in a croak. *Please, not Colleen.* "Conor, were you there when . . . it happened?"

"If I was, you think I'd be sitting here, telling you this?"

"I don't know, would you?" I shot back, then bit my lip. *He's fourteen,* I reminded myself. And I was relieved he hadn't actually witnessed a murder, even if that meant he couldn't a hundred percent identify Deirdre's killer. That experience would be traumatic for anyone, but especially a kid. I glanced at Maeve, who sat very still.

"I helped Deirdre out sometimes with the music for the school," Conor began.

I could see him as a music guy. A techie, or maybe playing in some underground teen band. I also pictured him writing music alone in his room. A lot.

"I, uh, play the accordion."

"For real?" Maeve said.

Conor looked away, and a deep flush filled his face. I frowned at my daughter.

"I inherited it from my grandpa," he said. "He died a couple years ago. I play for the Irish dancers sometimes, that's all. Shows, and practices sometimes. My sisters dance. It's a job."

Now Maeve seemed embarrassed. "That's totally cool. I'm sorry about your grandpa."

He nodded. "I don't even have my accordion right now. The police took it."

"Why?" Maeve beat me to the question.

"They wouldn't tell me," he said. "It was backstage. Not far from . . . Miss Deirdre. They said I could have it back when they were done."

Well, that didn't sound good. Could the accordion have caused the blunt force trauma that killed Deirdre? Hard to imagine such an instrument proving fatal to anyone.

Zoe ducked to drag her little brother out from under the table, where he was scraping old gum off the floor. He rolled to his feet and made a beeline for the girl with the braids I'd seen earlier. "Natalieeeeee!!" he shouted.

"I have to take him home soon," Zoe said. "Talk faster, Murphy."

"Okay, okay." He leaned back and crossed his arms again. "So after practice yesterday, everyone was leaving, and Deirdre asked if I could stay longer. She wanted to try some different music for a new number she was working on."

"Someone else was supposed to come in last night to play the piano while he played accordion," Zoe added. "But they never showed up."

"Who was it?" I asked.

"Don't know," Conor said. "Didn't ask. I was getting overtime, anyway."

"Then you went to get a sub from Hogan's Hoagies." Zoe made a let's-speed-this-up gesture.

Conor nodded. "Deirdre was hungry too. She asked me to bring her back a salad."

"What time did you leave for the sub place?" I asked. Colleen and Deirdre planned to meet at Farrell's around eight thirty. Was the salad Deirdre's dinner, or had she planned to eat twice?

"Around seven, maybe," Conor said. "I was gone for a while because Hogan's only had one guy working, and he kept screwing everything up."

I could stop by Hogan's and verify that. If he'd shared this part of the story with the police, they'd probably already checked. But why would Deirdre order something right before she had to meet up with Colleen? She would have had zero time to eat it.

On the other hand, the two of them had been best friends forever. Deirdre could have guessed—correctly—that Colleen would be later than she promised.

"So then—" Zoe began.

Conor threw up his hands. "Let me tell this, would you? You'll mess me up. Anyway, as I was on my way out, Colleen Buckley and some other lady came by to see Deirdre."

Oh no. Had this kid just placed Colleen at the scene—and time—of the crime? My heart dropped, and Maeve shot me a mixed look. Confusion? Disbelief? Fear?

Ridiculous. Conor was flat-out lying. Unless . . .

My mind swirled. I could still see my sister in her pink-vanilla face mask when the girls and I arrived, her wet hair in a towel, the cow-print robe over her jeans.

But when she'd rejoined us later downstairs, she was wearing leggings. Maybe it wasn't weird that she'd changed her mind on what to wear. Still . . . she must have had the fastest spa treatment ever if she'd been at Angels Hall with Moira minutes before. She could have run back home, dumped her head under the shower faucet, thrown on the robe over her jeans, smeared her face in goop, and rushed downstairs to greet us at the front door. Then she could have orchestrated the trip to Farrell's and suggested we stop at Angels Hall to pick up Deirdre on the way—knowing her best friend was dead.

Impossible. Colleen wouldn't have set up Maeve and me to find a body. And she'd adored Deirdre. Only a truly desperate person would stage a scenario like that to shift blame from herself.

"It couldn't have been Aunt Colleen," Maeve said. "No way."

"I'm sure there's a good explanation," I told her. "Or maybe Conor was mistaken." I looked at him hopefully.

"Nope," he said. "Everyone knows Colleen Buckley."

"Who was the other woman?" I asked.

"I've seen her around a few times lately," he said. "She had these big dark glasses on indoors, and she seemed kind of . . . weird."

Dark glasses? Weird?

"Was she tall, with bright red hair?" I asked. "Zebra print coat?"

"I don't remember the coat. It was ugly, though. Made me kinda dizzy."

"It had to be Miss Moira," Maeve said.

"Wait, Moira McShane Kelly?" Zoe's eyes widened. "She's here in Shamrock again?"

"You know her?" Maeve asked. "She's putting up flyers everywhere around our neighborhood. For her new Irish dance academy. She practically jumped my little sister and me on our way home from PJ's this morning. She wouldn't leave us alone."

"I can't believe she's starting a dance school here after she got dumped from Irish Steps." Zoe shook her head.

Moira was *fired*? "Do you know why she . . . left?" I asked.

"*Ceili Daily* said there were artistic differences. That's show speak for no one could stand her. She wanted to take Miss

Deirdre's place when Miss Deirdre quit, but they said no. I heard Aidan O'Hearne refused to dance with her."

Aidan. The guy we'd seen in the poster today at the Donnellys'. Bernie had mentioned he was in town, staying at the Smiling Shamrock. Had he been angry that his partner—possibly his better half—had left him high and dry? I made a mental note to talk to him ASAP. I'd met him a few times, but Colleen knew him.

"I don't remember seeing this Miss Moira person around here until a week or so ago," Conor said. "I would have noticed her."

"She competed at the same time as Miss Deirdre and Colleen, but she was never as good," Zoe said. "I've seen the videos."

"But Moira was in Irish Steps," I said.

Zoe shrugged. "Miss Deirdre beat her at every *feis* but one, and that was only because she had a sprained ankle. Everyone in Shamrock knows that."

"Oh." I guess I'd missed some drama living in the city.

I turned to Conor. "You told the cops about Moira and Colleen coming to see Deirdre last night, right?"

"I told my uncle Garrett. And he told Sergeant Walker, so she came to talk to me at work today. She said people saw me hanging around in the bushes outside where Deirdre got killed."

"Those people were us," Maeve said.

"Yeah, you mentioned that this morning." Conor spun his empty plastic cup.

"When you came back with the food from Hogan's Hoagies, did you hear what the three of them were talking about?" I pressed. "Did Moira and Colleen just stop by to visit Deirdre, or . . . ?"

"I didn't really hear anything they said," Conor replied. "But I think maybe they were having some kind of argument. I walked in, and Deirdre asked me if I'd give them a few minutes. She took the salad, though."

"Where did you go?" I asked.

"Into one of the rooms downstairs, in the way back, where they keep props and lights and stuff. There's a table in there, so I was eating my sandwich and listening to music with my earbuds in. Then I realized Deirdre might be looking for me to go over the music stuff, so I took the earbuds out and went into the hall."

"Had Moira and Colleen left?" I held my breath. *Yes. Please say yes.*

"Dunno."

"Did the piano player ever show up?"

"Don't know that either. All the lights were off downstairs when I came out of the prop room, which was weird. They'd been on earlier, so someone turned them off. But I heard music playing out in the main room, on the other side of the curtain, so I figured Deirdre was just working out steps or something." He hesitated. "And someone else was there too."

Part of me didn't want to hear the rest. But I had to know the truth to find Deirdre's killer—and clear Colleen.

"I heard a really loud scream over the music," Conor continued. "And then a thud. I kinda froze and ducked back into the prop room for a minute or two. When I came out, someone ran past me in the dark and out the side door. They almost knocked me over."

The hair rose on my neck like Banshee's when he saw our neighbor's pit bull from our apartment window. "Who was it?" *Please don't say Colleen,* I silently willed him again.

"I just saw, well, the shape of the person when they opened the door. They had a dark raincoat on, with the hood up. They had their back to me."

"There's a light at the side of the building," I said, thinking aloud. "They must have gone past it on their way out. Or near it, anyway." Hopefully there was a security camera too. But the cops would have looked into that first thing.

"Yeah, but there was a big flash of lightning when the person opened the door. It totally blinded me. Everything was so bright. Anyway, I figured the person would head to the back gate, so I ran toward the fence. I didn't want them to get away. But they just . . . disappeared. Like, into thin air."

"Why didn't you go help the person who screamed instead?" Maeve sounded indignant.

"Probably Miss Deirdre." Zoe frowned.

"I know." Conor stared at his sneakers again. "I should have."

"Could you tell if the person was a man or a woman?" I asked. Whoever they were, it couldn't have been Colleen. She'd been with Maeve and me at that point.

Conor shook his head. "They seemed tall, but the person was kind of hunched over and wearing that big coat."

"After they disappeared, you didn't go back to help Deirdre, assuming she was the one who screamed?" I asked gently.

"I started to." He squeezed his eyes shut for a moment. "I went back inside the building, and the music was still going on that boom box. But then it stopped, and I heard people talking on the other side of the curtain."

"That was us," I said.

"Yeah." His voice gave a little shudder. "Then the lights came back on, and I saw Deirdre lying there backstage. It freaked me out, and then you ran down the stairs. And then Colleen was there, and Maeve, and you all found her. I just sort of hid outside in the bushes, watching."

Zoe's mouth formed a tight line. "I still can't believe you didn't help. You could have called 911."

"People were already helping her. And I was afraid maybe they'd think I was the one who hurt her," Conor said. "They did anyway."

"Uh-oh, time for me to go," Zoe said suddenly.

We all followed her gaze. Across the room, Mikey was pulling a long string of bubble gum out of Natalie's braids as she collected fundraiser money from a couple of older boys. She hadn't noticed yet.

"'Bye, everybody," Zoe said. "Nice to meet more of the famous Buckleys. Conor's got my number—give it to Maeve, will you, Murphy? And I want to hear the rest of the story later."

"There is no more story," Conor said, but Zoe had already rushed off to rescue Natalie from the sticky clutches of her mischievous admirer.

Famous Buckleys? I didn't even want to know.

Conor unfolded his lanky self from the table. "I've gotta get home too."

"We all do," I said. The Chief was waiting. Hopefully. "Thanks for talking with us about all this. It was really helpful. Let's go, Maeve."

"I'm working tomorrow morning." Conor addressed my daughter. "If you want, you can stop by PJ's again. I'll be busy most of the time, but I usually take a break around ten thirty."

"Okay." Maeve avoided my gaze. "I'll be there."

Maybe. I hadn't decided yet whether she was grounded.

"Maeve, sweetie, not a word to anyone about anything Conor told us, okay?" I said as we headed toward the front room. "Especially Aunt Colleen."

"But—"

"Chief's orders," I said. "Nothing to worry about. Let me handle it." Not quite what my dad had directed, but I knew what I had to do.

And yes, now I sounded exactly like him.

I stole a glance toward the harp balloon as we headed toward the front room through the tight gaggle of kids. Garrett was still at his post, swigging a bottle of water. I threw him a small smile in thanks as I brushed through the beaded green curtain. He raised the bottle in a mock cheers but didn't follow.

Not that it mattered. I wasn't a person of interest to Garrett McGavin anymore. Just the sister of one.

Chapter Fourteen

"Hop in, girls!" the Chief called through the van's open passenger window. "No time to dally!"

Maeve hid her face with her hoodie as we pushed through the kids still huddled under Lucky's awning. An extra-cold drop of water hit the back of my neck and rolled under my sweatshirt.

"Have a nice time with your young fella?" the Chief asked Maeve pleasantly as she clambered into the back seat.

"Dad." I threw him a warning look. "Did you have fun yourself?"

"Ah yes. Fine *craic* with the lads."

That was Irish-speak for "a good time." I'd already figured he wouldn't tell me about his little meeting, even in private.

The Chief didn't drink much, just a nightly nip or two, but he loved hanging out with his old cop buddies at Farrell's. The firefighters frequented Gallagher's Tavern on the square. Both pubs were the true headquarters where all important business was discussed off-duty, usually over pints.

None of us said much else until we pulled into the Buckley House driveway, where the van headlights fell on Frank emerging from his newly leased Lexus. My brother didn't make a big salary, but he lived in a condo on the trendier side of town. He saved money by dropping by our parents' house on a regular basis to mooch free food and do his laundry.

He held up one hand in a "stop" motion, as if the Chief might run him over. Our dad was probably tempted sometimes. He and Frank often disagreed, especially in the area of law enforcement practices and procedures. Frank was even more old-school than the Chief.

My brother went in the side door, and the rest of us entered the house through the garage after dumping our wet things. It took a little extra effort for the Chief to get back in his wheelchair tonight, even with my help. He looked tired.

We all gathered in the kitchen, as usual. Colleen and Mom had already prepared late-evening snacks for the guests. I set out a tray with the frosted shortbread cookies and reserved a few for us. After taking the teapot into the living room, Colleen busied herself applying a coat of aqua nail polish at the table.

Ms. Nonchalance. Or just an amazing actress.

No. I had to stop thinking like that. This was my sister.

Bliz perched on a stool in the corner, fidgeting as if she were trying to keep some huge secret—which she was.

"And where were you three tonight?" Mom asked.

"Ah, just on a message," the Chief replied. More post-Farrell's Irish speak. A "message" meant an errand.

"I'm sure." Mom gave the cord of the hot water kettle a little extra yank as she unplugged it. "You should be resting more, Dermot, like the doctor said."

Frank helped himself to three pieces of leftover pizza and a Leprechaun Lager from the fridge. He held up the can, frowning. "This all we got?"

"It was on sale," Colleen said.

He popped the top. "That nail stuff reeks, Colleen. Can't you do that somewhere else?"

She delicately blew on each nail. "I would, Frankie dearest, but since everyone is here now, I have news."

"Good or bad?" Frank seemed wary, and Mom braced herself slightly against the counter. The Chief perked right up. He loved news of any kind. Well, almost any.

"You're looking at the new director of the Saint Patrick's Day dance show extravaganza," Colleen announced. "Ta-da!" She flung a blue-tipped hand in the air with an exaggerated flourish.

"Yay!" Freed from having to keep the big secret, Bliz jumped down from her stool and started dancing all over the kitchen.

"That's wonderful, dear." Mom looked confused. "You mean . . . the Donnelly School show?"

"Yup."

"Really happy for you, sis," I said, as if I hadn't already been privy to the information. She seemed much less nervous now.

Hopefully this whole show deal would be a good distraction for her from Deirdre's death and the investigation. Unless Sergeant Walker showed up at the door with a pair of handcuffs.

No, I reminded myself. That wasn't going to happen. Conor saw someone else run out of Angels Hall just before Colleen, Maeve, and I had arrived.

"Congrats, Aunt Colleen," Maeve said. "That's amazing."

"Good girl, you are!" Beaming, the Chief rolled over in his chair to give Colleen a meaty clap on the back. "You'll do a fine job. Make the Buckley clan proud."

"Well done, Colleen." Frank set his beer down on the butcher's block. "How did that happen? You haven't danced in years."

Colleen looked hurt. "Bernie Donnelly asked me to take over for her so the kids would still have a show. That's why she wanted to see me today. And FYI, I can dance just fine. I've been getting in shape lately. I'll only be demonstrating stuff for the kids anyway. And Bernie gave me Deirdre's notes."

"Paddy's Day is coming up fast," Frank said. "Good luck."

"Thank you ever so much." Colleen edged the open nail polish bottle closer to him.

"We'll all be cheering you from the front row." I took a big bite of cookie.

"Actually, Kate . . ." Colleen flashed her winning dimple. "I had this great idea while you were out. Bliz and Maeve can dance in the show, since they'll be here anyway. Isn't that brilliant? I already figured everything out with Bernie. We'll showcase beginners as well as the stars. You know, to show other kids and their parents in the audience how fast they can learn the basics if they sign up. We could even add an adult number if you—"

"Not necessary," I said quickly.

Maeve muttered something under her breath I didn't quite make out.

Bliz jumped and twirled even more around the kitchen. "I'm going to be an Irish dancer, I'm going to be an Irish dancer," she sang.

"Bernie really needs to sign up some new students, especially with all the negative vibes swirling around about the school right now," Colleen went on. "Some of the kids are scared to come back, and parents are freaking out too."

Another reason to find Deirdre's murderer ASAP.

"That's a wonderful idea, Colleen," Mom said. "Kate, can you manage the extra time with your work schedule?"

I'd have to. Somehow. "Happy to help." I smiled at my daughters. "Aren't we?"

Bliz nodded energetically.

"Sure," Maeve said.

"You don't have to dance if you don't want to, honey," I told her.

"I haven't danced since second grade," Maeve said. "And I sucked at it then, remember?"

"Hey, we can get back into it together," Colleen said.

"Okay." Maeve sighed.

"Fine then, it's settled." The Chief beamed.

Frank stuck his fist into the extra cookie jar labeled "Fool's Gold" and fished for the last of Mom's cookies. She always kept the biggest ones for him. "It's good you're sticking around town this week, anyway, Kate," he said, his mouth stuffed. "In case anyone has more questions for you and Maeve on the investigation."

"Cops can't ask anyone to stay in town because of a case," I said. "That's only for TV shows."

Frank shrugged. "Doesn't matter. You girls found the body. Like I said before, you're witnesses. And Colleen here—"

"Zip it, Frank," I muttered through my teeth, giving Bliz a reassuring smile at the same time. She'd stopped her dancing, listening with wide eyes.

Colleen focused on tightening the cap of her nail polish bottle.

Mom handed Frank a plate of green after-dinner mints. "Francis, make yourself useful and take these into the parlor, would you? The guests will appreciate something to settle their stomachs after Molly's."

"I have to get back to my homework," Maeve announced.

"What is this big project over Saint Patrick's Week?" the Chief asked.

"We're supposed to keep a journal and write it in the style of our favorite author. What we're doing over break. Sister Josephine said she'd choose some to read in class."

I tried to imagine Sister Josephine reading Maeve's journal entries about finding a dead body in a church hall and a local murder investigation that involved members of her immediate family. She and Maeve's classmates would be riveted.

"Interesting," I said. "Which author did you choose?"

"Robert B. Parker."

Yup, Sister Josephine was in for an intriguing read.

"Oh, that's a fine project. Be sure to put me in it, now." The Chief didn't bother to suppress a chuckle as he wheeled his chair away from the table. "I'm retiring for the evening," he added, with a wave over his shoulder. "Maybe after a wee nightcap in my office."

By that he meant a nip from the bottle in the bottom drawer of his desk, like Lou Grant in the old *Mary Tyler Moore Show* reruns I used to watch with Mom. She rolled her eyes at his departing back. "I'll go have a chat with the guests," she said. "Girls, can you finish up in here?"

"Absolutely, Mom," I said. "You should have a nightcap too. You deserve one."

"Thank you, dear." She gave me a quick wink before she left.

Maeve headed upstairs with Bliz, who was starting to droop. "I'll be up soon," I called.

After Colleen and I had a serious conversation. Where to start? The necklace? Or that little matter of her being at Angels Hall with Moira right before Deirdre was killed—and lying about it? Well, not lying, exactly. But she'd covered up the truth with a pink-vanilla mud mask and a cow-print robe. Why?

I dug in the dish towel drawer, looking for ones past their prime. Mom needed to get rid of all of them.

Maybe Deirdre's death had been some kind of tragic accident, and Colleen had panicked. I hated to admit it, even to myself, but it was possible. My sister would never have deserted her friend, though. She would have called 911. Or the Chief. Or both.

Well, plenty of our past talks had gone down over a sink full of bubbles. Extracting a plaid towel with hanging ribbon trim, I turned to toss it to Colleen.

She was gone.

What was *wrong* with her? And with me, for letting her get away again? Wouldn't happen this time.

I peeked behind the green-and-white gingham curtain that blocked off the pantry. Nada. Nearest powder room: also Colleen-negative.

Fury rose inside me like steam in Mom's tea kettle. She'd snuck out the side door while I was talking to Mom. Well, she couldn't have gotten far. I'd cut her off in front of the house. Or in the side driveway, if she tried to take the Mini.

I almost ran smack into an elderly guest with a cane in the hallway. She looked confused. "Oh, excuse me," I said. "I'm so sorry."

The woman placed a frail, liver-spotted hand on my arm. "Could I trouble you for some extra towels?"

I gave her my brightest Colleen smile. "Of course, I'll bring them right up. What is your room number?"

"2A. My husband and I will be turning in shortly. Such a busy day. Is it possible for you to bring them right now?"

"Um, absolutely." I ran upstairs to the main guest linen closet and grabbed two sets of shamrock-embroidered towels. Slightly faded, but they were the nicest I could find. Then I waited outside Room 2A until the guest finally made her way up.

"Thank you, dearie." She fumbled with the room key, so I helped her and made sure she got safely inside.

"Have a lovely night," I said.

No point in trying to chase Colleen around the neighborhood now. I'd heard the distinct start of a car engine as I rummaged through the closet.

Fine. She couldn't avoid me forever. Or even one more night. I marched to our room, hoping I was wrong about the car and she'd miraculously be there, ready to spill.

And . . . no. I took calming breaths, smoothed my hair, and went to say good night to the girls. Maeve would be up for a while, but Bliz was already curled on her side of the bed. Out like a light.

My older daughter seemed more eager to get back to her phone than chat with me, so I headed back to the bedroom. While I waited for Colleen to return, I finally wrote to my boss about my schedule. One item checked off the procrastination list. And while I was in the system, I'd check my email to see what I'd missed at the office, maybe get through some client files.

I'd never fallen asleep working on anyone's taxes—it was my job to stay vigilant on every line and calculation—but I set an alarm for midnight on my phone, just in case. I didn't want Colleen to sneak into bed without waking me up. I considered grabbing one of Mom's little brass bells with the ribbons from the knickknack shelf in the parlor and tying it to the bedroom door, but maybe that was overkill.

I changed into my pajamas and stuck Deirdre's necklace in my robe pocket.

After my evening beauty routine, if you could call it that—I considered myself a "minimalist" because it sounded better than "lazy person"—I settled onto the bed, my laptop on my knees. At first, I kept checking the little clock icon in the corner of the screen, but eventually I focused on the numbers in front of me. Double-checking figures, calculating depreciations, and looking for additional deductions for my clients was almost relaxing for me. Each section completed was like fitting a piece into a jigsaw puzzle. Some of the pieces were easy. Others were more challenging. That's what I enjoyed about my job. Accounting made nice, logical sense, unlike other parts of my life.

At 12:48, the doorknob slowly turned.

Chapter Fifteen

"Oh, hey." Colleen looked surprised to see me sitting up against the headboard, glaring at her. "Didn't want to wake you."

"No worries, you didn't," I said. "I've been waiting up for you. You waltzed out of the house when you knew we needed to talk."

She dropped her designer bag on the shag carpet and crossed the room for the cow-print robe she'd left on a chair. "It was early," she said, her voice muffled as she pulled her turtleneck over her head. "I met a friend. You know, to talk about Deirdre."

"Look, I get you're going through a lot right now. But first of all, that was a dumb move." I slammed my laptop lid. "You're not supposed to talk to anyone outside the family about what happened, remember? And you and I have important things to discuss. You didn't even mention you were going somewhere. You just snuck out. And left me with the dishes, by the way."

"I'm sorry. I should have said something." She belted the robe.

"You've been dodging me ever since I got home," I said. "I dragged myself and the girls all the way out here for some big emergency you don't want to tell me about now. Meanwhile, everything keeps getting worse and worse. I am so done."

"I'm sorry, Katie. I guess I haven't felt like talking." Colleen dropped into the chair. "Everything is such a total mess."

"They'll be worse soon if you don't wake up and take things seriously." I crossed my arms against my flannel pajama top. "You're a freaking person of interest in a murder investigation, Colleen. Do you understand what that means?" My voice rose a decibel or two. "It's one short step to suspect. And one giant leap to jail."

"Stop exaggerating, Kate. You always do that, and it stresses everyone out." Colleen released her shiny blond ponytail from its tortoiseshell claw holder with a snap. "No one suspects me of anything. Well, not for *real*. Especially killing my own best friend. Because they know me. I'm a good person. And Dad is the Chief, for heaven's sake. He knows I didn't hurt Deirdre. That counts for something, doesn't it? It's not like he'd let me be arrested or something."

"Unless you were guilty," I pointed out. "Then he wouldn't have a choice. He'd have to do the right thing, and you know it. Why would you even put him in a position like that by skipping around, acting as if nothing's wrong?"

"Well, I'm not guilty, so it's a moot point." Colleen's eyes filled with tears. "And there is something wrong, because I've lost Deirdre and she's never, ever coming back."

Tragically, true. But still. "Maybe you can explain how you happened to be at Angels Hall with Moira-Freaking-McShane-Kelly on Thursday night, just before Deirdre was killed. And no one saw you leave." I paused. "A witness heard arguing. They told the police."

"I know." Colleen let out a long breath. "Okay. Deirdre texted me that Moira said she was coming to talk to her, and it couldn't wait. Deirdre freaked out because she hates confrontation. She asked me to come and rescue her."

Deirdre didn't like confrontation? Who did?

"Moira and I showed up at the same time," Colleen went on. "So we went in together. I don't know why she thought she had to have a big discussion with Deirdre right then. She was mad because Deirdre didn't want to make her a partner in the Donnelly School. Deirdre said she didn't need one. Moira told her she'd go through with starting her new dance academy, then, whether Deirdre liked it or not."

"I'm sure that went over well."

"Yeah, it was wicked bad," Colleen agreed. "That's when I suggested that Moira go back to New York and stay there. Things sort of escalated from there."

"Did Moira leave?"

Colleen nodded. "She was pretty ticked off. Deirdre and I decided to meet at Farrell's later, because some of our old friends were in town for Paddy's. I went home to get ready, and you and the girls showed up."

"Right," I said. "But when you answered the door you acted as if you'd just gotten out of the shower and put on face goop. Except you were wearing jeans. And you changed into leggings later."

"What?" Colleen looked puzzled. "Oh. I saw you guys from the bathroom window, and I threw on the jeans I'd worn earlier because they were on top of the hamper. I didn't want to run downstairs in nothing but my bathrobe, in case I ran into any guests. You know the family rule."

"But you were acting so weird, as if you were hiding something."

Colleen shifted in her chair. "I ran into a friend on my way back from Angels Hall," she said. "He gave me a ride the rest of the way home. I forgot I was supposed to make a trip to the store for Mom. She would've been really mad if she knew I'd blown it off for a guy."

"Who was this guy?" I asked. "He could give you an alibi for when Deirdre was murdered, for heaven's sake."

"I told the Chief," Colleen said. "But my friend and I only talked for a couple of minutes. Dad said that still didn't cover my whereabouts for the whole time, but he'd mention it to the detectives."

"So who was it?" I threw up my hands.

"I can't tell you," Colleen said. "For all kinds of reasons. But anyway, to answer your other question, I didn't actually take a shower when I got home. My hair was wet from the rain, so I ran upstairs without Mom seeing me and threw on a robe and the face mask."

I stared at my sister. Was my mind processing this crazy story correctly?

"I know," she said. "That was lame."

Colleen's life was one little green lie on top of another. Exhausting. But that story was too crazy for even her to make up. "Why didn't you just say that you and Moira were there with Deirdre before she was killed, especially if you saw a friend right afterward?" I asked. "Why did you lie?"

She shrugged. "I just didn't mention it at first. Before we found Deirdre, it didn't really matter. Some stupid drama with her and Moira. But after we found her, and I told the detectives about it, it did matter. They had Dee's phone with the texts. And Dad and Frank told me not to say one more word unless I had a lawyer present. I don't know what Moira told them. I'm not supposed to speak to her either."

"What? You have a lawyer?"

"Not officially. The Chief's talking to someone."

"Was anyone else there in Angels Hall with you three?"

"I don't think so. The kid who works with Deirdre on music, but he was only around for a while. He went to get takeout. There's no way he would have hurt her. He's a good kid."

I stared at the lava lamp across the room as the blobs split and turned different colors. "I believe you," I said finally.

"*Believe* me?" She catapulted off the chair and stood in front of me with her hands on her hips. "How could you even consider for one second that I'd hurt my very best friend? You're my *sister*. You know me better than anyone."

I shook my head. "That's not it. The cops—"

Her shoulders slumped, and she began to sob.

"Colleen, please," I said, steeling myself against the waterworks.

"I don't want to talk to you!" Now her whole body shook. "Deirdre is dead, and I will never, ever see her again for the rest of my life, and you think I had something to do with it?"

"I never said that."

"What did you mean, then?"

I hesitated. It might make things worse between us, but I had to ask. Slowly, I reached into my robe pocket and brought out the wad of Kleenex with Deirdre's necklace. I carefully unwrapped it and held out my palm.

Colleen stared at the broken heart with the tiny emerald. "Where did you get that?" she said finally.

"I found it on the floor," I said. "I stepped on it, actually. It was in the rug."

"Oh," she said. "Well, I'm glad you found it. It broke, and I was going to have it fixed. I thought I put it somewhere for safekeeping, but I must have dropped it." Her eyes were murky now.

"It's not yours," I said. "It's Deirdre's."

"I have one like it," Colleen said. "I used to, anyway."

"Yours had a ruby," I said. "Your birthstone. July."

"Right." She didn't make a move to take the necklace.

"Colleen, I saw this on Deirdre when we found her. It's an emerald, see?"

Her eyes filled with tears again. "It came off her neck when we were doing CPR. The chain must have gotten caught or something. I . . . I just wanted it to remember her. Us. It's a friendship necklace. We bought them together. I have the other half. Somewhere."

Hopeless. I patted the mattress beside me. "Colleen Queen, come sit."

She obeyed.

"We have to give this to the cops," I said gently, as if she were younger than Bliz. "I know you want to keep it, but you can't. It's evidence. Maybe it broke when Deirdre was attacked. It might be important to solving her murder." *And proving you innocent.*

We sat in silence, side by side, for a minute. "It won't look good that you took this from a crime scene," I said finally. "The investigators will not be happy. At all."

She gave a post-tears hiccup. "I told you, I just wanted to remember her. I was going to wear it. Maybe both of ours together when I find mine."

"There's probably DNA on it," I said. "Maybe even the killer's fingerprints. Unfortunately, when they send this to the crime lab, they'll also find yours."

"And yours."

"True," I said. "But I had neither motive nor opportunity to murder Deirdre. You, on the other hand . . . It's on record that you borrowed money from your friend, and she asked for it back. You couldn't repay her. And then there was the Donnelly School scholarship money that disappeared while in your possession. But even more incriminating, you were on the scene around the time of the crime. Someone heard an argument."

Silence.

I tried another tack. "You want to help Deirdre and Bernie, don't you?"

"Yes." Her voice was slightly muffled by her hair as she hung her head. I felt a little squeeze in my heart.

"I'm sure the cops will give it back to you later, or Bernie will, if you ask," I added. "Shall we give this to the Chief right now? He can explain to them, and—"

Her head jerked up. "No! Not Dad. Please, Katie. I've already told him enough. It would kill him that I was so stupid."

"We could hand it over to Frank, then."

"That's even worse." Colleen's bottom lip trembled again. "Maybe we could give it to the police anonymously. Like, leave it outside the station in an envelope or something."

"Um, no. That'd make things worse. Plus, DNA, remember?"

"Can you turn the necklace in to Sergeant Walker for me?" Colleen looked hopeful.

"That's not such a good idea either," I said. "The cops will have more questions for you anyway. There's no way to avoid talking to them."

"Please, Katie? Sergeant Walker already hates me. She keeps trying to trick me."

"That's her job. To find the truth."

"I know. I just made a mistake." My sister looked penitent.

I sighed. More like, one of her stupidest moves yet, based on a flood of emotion. But did it matter exactly how the evidence was returned, as long as we were honest? And the less talking Colleen did with any cops herself, the better. "Okay," I said. "I'll do it in the morning."

Colleen gave me a huge hug. "You're the best, Katie."

I had no idea what I'd say to Sergeant Walker, but I'd think of something. I reached for the box of tissues on the nightstand and extracted another one to wrap around the necklace.

"Can I take a picture of it first?" Colleen took her phone from her back pocket. "Just to remember it, in case I don't get it back." She swiftly snapped a photo, then flipped the charm and took another.

"Don't put that on social media," I said.

She rolled her eyes. "I won't." Then she looked sad again. "Deirdre never lost her half."

"The girls and I lose jewelry all the time," I said. "Or pieces get broken. Remember the little pearl ring I got for Confirmation? I gave it to Maeve for hers. She left it in the school locker room."

My wedding ring was gone too. I'd sold it in the city, years ago. Not because I needed the money. I just didn't want the reminder.

"Why do bad things always happen to me?" My sister said it so softly, I wasn't sure if she'd meant me to hear.

"Hey, lots of good things happen to you too," I said. "You have tons of friends and a family who loves you. Like the Chief always says, you're young and good-looking, and you have your whole life ahead of you."

I realized my error the second the words left my mouth.

"Deirdre doesn't," my sister said.

She padded off toward the bathroom, carrying her plastic shower caddy full of products. I put away my laptop, crawled under the pink satin comforter, and turned out the nightstand light. The lava lamp was morphing on overdrive.

All those blobby pieces, starting out one way and turning into something else. It was impossible to predict what any one of them might become, or when they would disappear.

By the time Colleen got back to the bedroom, I was almost asleep. "We'll talk again tomorrow, okay?" I mumbled.

"Mm-hmm," she said.

Chapter Sixteen

The next morning, Colleen and I both got up early. She headed to Bernie Donnelly's to go over choreography. I helped Mom bake brown bread and set out the guests' Continental breakfast. Then the two of us sat down at the kitchen table to go over the B and B accounts.

Colleen hadn't told Mom about the "borrowing" yet, it turned out, but at least we could focus on taxes.

An hour or so of numbers later, Mom rubbed her temples again, as if she had another migraine coming on. "How in Mary Nell does that help things at all?" she said after I explained that she and Dad could apply for an extension on filing the taxes, but they'd still need to send the money by the due date.

I placed a hand over hers. It seemed thinner than I remembered. "I know, Mom, it's confusing. Why don't we take a break, and meet again later? I'll ask Colleen to join us, and we'll figure things out together. Then we can come up with a plan for going forward. It's not as complicated as it sounds, I promise."

"I have no idea what happened to all the receipts," Mom said. "I'm sure there must be more. Sometimes I'm so angry with that girl I could spit."

Disgusting image, but I related to the sentiment. "Me too," I said. "But something's been bothering her, I know. I've been trying to get Colleen to talk to me since I got here, but she keeps running away from me."

"Mmm."

"What's that supposed to mean?"

"Well, maybe you need to leave her be for a while. She looks up to you so much, but sometimes not everyone wants your help, Kathleen. You're something of a pit bull, like your father, when you get something in your mind."

Pit bull? Fine, I was done trying to help anyone in this family. For now, anyway.

I got up and rummaged through the pantry. "All yours, Mom." I tossed a bag of Cadbury chocolates onto the table. "Go wild, before Frank gets his paws on them."

Leaving Bliz to work a giant jigsaw puzzle with the Chief in the living room, I headed to the Nest to drag Maeve from her slumbers. "Coffee time!" I announced. "Rise and shine!"

Ordinarily, that enticement would have bounced my older daughter out of bed, but she rolled over and pulled the pillow over her head. "Why are you doing this to me? You can't go with me to PJ's. Sooo embarrassing."

"That's right," I said. "I'm your official chaperone. We can't stay long anyway, because I have actual things to do today. So chip-chop, get yourself ready, and let's go."

Ugh. I sounded exactly like Mom. And I got a drawn-out groan in response, just as I'd always given her.

Last night, I'd laid down the law to Maeve: No going anywhere outside of the Buckley House without prior approval—especially to meet boys or other possible crime suspects. And accompanied, if deemed necessary, by me. She wasn't too thrilled.

The Jig Is Up

As we left the house, I heard Mom telling the Chief that two guests had called to cancel due to an unexpected opening at the Smiling Shamrock. Apparently, the Smiling Shamrock was advertising on social media that they'd installed a brand-new alarm system, to fully ensure the security of their guests.

The Buckley House had old windows, a front lock that easily jammed, and a torn screen at the side door. Plus, a resident murder suspect.

As Maeve and I walked briskly to PJ Scoops, I couldn't help but notice that even more Paddy's Day paraphernalia had sprung up overnight. Irish flags, tricolor wind socks, fat garden leprechauns and mischievous fairies, plastic-stone beer mug fountains—you name it, someone had wasted plenty o' green on it.

Was there some town ordinance that residents were required to go overboard with the decorations? I wouldn't put it past Mayor Flanagan, and I knew exactly what he'd say if anyone objected: "Everyone is Irish on Saint Patrick's Day." The Celtic Emporium needed a T-shirt with that slogan, if there wasn't one already. The back side should say, *Be o' festive. Shamrock loves your cash.*

The coffee and ice-cream shop was much busier than yesterday, with customers streaming in and out the door. The "When Irish Eyes Are Smiling" chime was working overtime.

I trailed Maeve inside after snatching the Moira McShane Kelly Academy of Irish Dance flyer off the door. I didn't want my daughter to think I was petty, or that I believed in any kind of censorship, but really. Deirdre had been dead for no time at all, and her mother was very much alive.

Worse, Moira had taped her ad over one for a candlelight vigil for Deirdre tonight at 7:30. The memorial announcement included a photo of Deirdre in a show costume and another of her surrounded by smiling students from the Donnelly School. Zoe Koo was listed as the organizer, along with her contact info.

I crumpled Moira's nasty flyer as best I could—it refused to die—and tossed it into my purse.

PJ's buzzed with more than caffeine today. The tourist stampede had officially begun. One customer in particular, I noticed, had snagged a prime seat near the window: Detective Garrett McGavin, absorbed in his phone as he sipped from a steaming to-go cup. Off duty, I presumed, judging from his jeans, gray thermal, and brown leather jacket.

Was he playing chaperone too, keeping an eye on his nephew in case Surly Shirley or anyone else showed up to talk to him? Including Maeve and me, I realized, as the two of us got in line.

Or he could be here because Conor gave him free coffee. At least I'd upped the fashion-meter dial today, ditching the sweatshirt look for my lavender tweed jacket I'd found at the bottom of Colleen's closet. Minus the sales tags and one of the little pink-velvet bows that covered the buttons.

The kid waved when he spotted us in line. With all these customers he seemed more animated this morning.

When we reached the counter, he said, "One espresso and a double-shot mocha with extra whipped cream, right? On the house." He looked at Maeve. "I've got a break in a couple of minutes when my cousin gets off hers. I'll bring over your drink then, okay?"

"Thanks." Maeve's eyes slid to mine. "I'll be sitting at a different table from my mom. Oh, and can I also have a mint-frosted chocolate croissant?" she added over her shoulder as I steered her away.

"You got it," Conor said.

She took a table clear on the other side of the shop. Fine. An opportunity to chat with Garrett.

"Hey," he said. "I was hoping you'd show up."

"Can't beat the coffee," I said, pulling out the little wrought-iron chair across from him. Conor delivered my steaming espresso and disappeared before I could thank him. "Recovered from your big night at Lucky's?"

Garrett grinned. "It would have been more interesting if you'd stuck around."

"Right." Was he trying to flirt with me, or just being regular Garrett? The same, really.

He nodded toward Maeve's table, where Conor had joined her. "I'm keeping an eye on my nephew. I promised Siobhan I'd have a talk with him. You know, guy-to-guy. He hasn't been very communicative lately, and she's worried about him. Especially with the whole Donnelly case situation."

"I get it," I said. "I'm dealing with that too. So how is your sister? I haven't seen Siobhan in forever."

"She works a lot," Garrett said. "Paddy's Paws, over on Cork Ave. She's the manager now. The owner lives in Beantown, so it's her show."

"That's great," I said. "I should stop by there. We brought our cat with us from the city, so we need supplies. Who knows how long we'll be here."

"Look at the bright side," he said. "You're here for Paddy's Week."

"Yep, all in on that." I meant to sound enthusiastic.

He took a swig from his cup. "I heard you and Colleen are taking over the dance show for Deirdre's mom. That's really nice of you."

"I don't know what my job is yet," I said. "Colleen's talking with Bernie this morning."

Garrett's cell buzzed, and he checked the screen. "Uh-oh. My presence is requested for a little OT. Between Paddy's Week duty and the Donnelly case, it's all-hands-on-deck at the station."

"You do get time off to sleep, right?" I asked.

"Yeah, but the bad guys never sleep." He grinned. "And I need the brownie points."

It dawned on me that I could get him some extra credit with Sergeant Walker—and help me and Colleen at the same time. At the very least, it would be easier to talk to Garrett than Surly Shirley. Maybe.

I took a quick, extra breath as he rose from the table. "Um, Garrett, could we talk? It's important." My words came out in a whisper. Or possibly not at all.

He cocked his head. "What?"

I cleared my throat and tried again.

"Sure, Katie." He parked himself back in his chair. "What's up?"

"I—I have something I need to give you."

"Okaaay." He drew out the word in a half-wary way, but his expression was encouraging. One lifted brow, a small smile, eyes glinting slightly.

I knew that glint. It wasn't flirty in any way, not that I wanted it to be. It was the same look the Chief got in his eyes when something perked his professional interest.

I reached into the zippered inside pocket of my purse and retrieved Deirdre's necklace, keeping my fist closed around the folded plastic sandwich bag until I placed it carefully between us on the table. The Kleenex had already come undone. "This was at the house. By accident."

"As in, the Buckley House?"

I nodded.

"Is this some kind of jewelry I gave you or something? Hey, that's ancient history. You don't have to—"

"No, you big-headed idiot." I felt less nervous now. "And for the record, you never gave me anything. That's Deirdre's necklace." I nodded with my chin.

"Oh." He almost looked relieved.

"It's a friendship necklace. See the puzzle-edge heart? Colleen has—well, had—the other half."

He pushed gently at the bag. The chain shifted, but I could see there was a knot in it now. "Sorry, not following you here."

Best to rip off the Band-Aid. "Deirdre wore it on the night she was killed," I said. "It may have, um, come off or something when Colleen or Frank was doing CPR. Anyway, Colleen dropped it in her pocket and ended up taking it home with her."

"You're kidding, right?" Garrett hardly paused to answer his own question. "Nope, you're not."

"I wish I were."

He leaned forward, dropping his voice. "You realize this puts Colleen in a bad position, don't you? An even worse one than she's in right now."

"I know," I practically whispered. "She wanted me to give it to you because she was too embarrassed to do it herself."

"Embarrassed?" He sat back again.

"It sounds crazy, I get that," I said. "But Colleen didn't kill Deirdre. I know that for sure. Just like you know your nephew didn't either."

We both glanced toward the kid table. Maeve and Conor looked as if they were having a serious conversation. My daughter was doing all the talking. Between her and Zoe, the guy didn't have a chance.

"You're aware Colleen was seen with Deirdre right before she was murdered?" Garrett said.

"Yes, and so was Moira. Has anyone even considered that she's the killer?"

Garrett tapped his coffee cup. It sounded empty. "We—well, they, since I'm technically off the case—are looking at all the angles, Katie. You know the drill."

I did. Like the Chief, he wouldn't be able to tell me much. "Well, Colleen wanted you to have this," I fibbed. "For evidence. It's probably all messed up with so many fingerprints by now, but maybe there's something on it."

He placed the baggie with the necklace into the inside pocket of his jacket and rose from the table again. "I'll take care of it. Thanks, Katie, but I've got to go."

No smile. No more glint. He was headed straight to the station.

"Is my sister in serious trouble?" I asked, just as he turned away.

"Not gonna lie," Garrett said. "Things don't look good. But I really hope something else turns up, for all your sakes. See you around, okay?"

I barely heard the annoying chime when he walked out the coffee shop door.

Chapter Seventeen

I sipped the last of my PJ's coffee after giving Maeve the "wrap-it-up" signal across the room. I wanted to make sure Garrett was well on his way to the station with Deirdre's necklace so we wouldn't run into him again.

I should have handed it over to Sergeant Walker myself.

"Mom?" Maeve appeared at the table, startling me. I'd been blankly staring at the wall map of Ireland again.

"Ready to go?" I jumped up and adjusted my jacket. "Did you have a nice time with Conor?"

She rolled her eyes. "We were just talking."

"Did he mention anything more about Deirdre, or . . . ?"

"No," she said. "He said he's going to meet Colleen at Angels Hall this afternoon to work out music stuff for the show. But the police still haven't given him his accordion back. And first Colleen has to meet with some parents to talk about safety because of the murder. Oh, and I can go to the vigil tonight, right?"

I hesitated. What was I supposed to do, lock her up? That would make her resentful, and she'd find a way to meet Conor anyway. Besides, being with other kids right now was good for her, even if I was still wary that one of them had been hanging around a crime scene. "We'll all go," I said.

Her expression let me know exactly what she thought of that idea. "I won't hover," I promised. "We'll just walk over together."

"That's almost as bad," she said as we made our way to the door. "But fine."

"Let's head toward Cork Ave," I said. "We need to stop by Paddy's Paws for Banshee supplies." I could say hi to Garrett's sister too. I'd always liked Siobhan, though I didn't know her that well.

The store window held a display of cat climbing towers and dog crates in various sizes, with stuffed animals wearing green T-shirts and headbands with felt shamrocks on antennas.

"Think Banshee would wear one of those?" Maeve said. "He'd look really cute."

"Not a chance," I said.

I found Siobhan stocking shelves near the counter with bags of green dog biscuits. Maeve wandered off to look at the pet community bulletin board on the side wall.

"Hi, Siobhan. Not sure you remember me, but I'm Kate Buckley."

"Katie!" She straightened and gave me a hug, still holding a packet of dog biscuits. "How could I not remember you? My little brother was so in love with you. You broke his heart, I think."

"Hardly." I smiled. "I just saw Garrett, actually. At PJ's. Oh, and Conor too."

She nodded and craned her neck in Maeve's direction. My daughter was petting a senior golden retriever reclining on a plaid dog bed beside the counter. "Gosh, Maeve has grown. Conor mentioned her to me. Can you believe our kids are almost in high school? It seems like we were both just pregnant."

"I know," I said. "You look exactly the same."

True. With her faded-denim overalls, dropped white shoulder tee, black combat boots and short red curls swept up in a Rosie the Riveter–style bandanna, Siobhan hadn't changed a bit. She also didn't strike me as the mom of a killer.

"Ha," she said, patting the stomach of her overalls. "Maybe a few extra l-b's, speaking of just pregnant. I had triplets, so it feels like it. And the girls are seven."

"That is so amazing," I said. "You must be Superwoman. I can only keep up with one seven-year-old."

"Mary Elizabeth, right? I bet she's darling."

"We think so," I said.

Garrett's sister placed the rest of the dog biscuit packets on the shelf, except for one she stuffed in her back pocket. "Did you come in for anything in particular? Hopefully I can find it for you."

I glanced around. The store was stuffed to the studs with merchandise, and there were plenty of cans of gourmet food, but I didn't see the one item we needed. "Cat litter?"

"Oh, that's in the back," she said. "We have another room for all the litter and dry dog and cat food. Brand? Size?"

I had no idea. Usually I bought whatever was on sale. "Medium? Any regular brand."

"Got it. Be right back."

I picked up a plastic shopping basket from the end of an aisle, selected several cans of non-gourmet cat food, and headed toward the counter. Maeve was cross-legged on the floor now, next to the dog, whose head was in her lap. He gazed up at her winningly.

"Isn't he adorable?" Maeve stroked his golden fur, then ruffled his silky ears. "What a good dog."

"He's the sweetest," Siobhan agreed, reappearing with a bag of litter and dumping it on the counter. "His name is Rover—as in,

"The Irish Rover." The song. I sure hope we find him a forever home soon. We're his foster family. His owners left town and dropped him off at the shelter, can you believe it?"

Maeve looked up at me with the same expression the dog had given her.

Nope nope nope. I knew where this was headed. "Gosh, that's terrible," I said to Siobhan. "Wish we could help, but our building back in the city has a pretty strict no-large-breed policy."

"We could hide him," Maeve suggested.

"Honey, no. Some other family will give him the perfect home."

"I hope so," Siobhan said. "We'd adopt him if we could too. I'm already a foster fail. At the moment we have four guinea pigs, a blind Frenchie mix, two feral cats, and a jumbo long-haired rabbit. Oh, and Conor has a very creepy Komodo dragon that lives in his room and freaks me out."

Yup. Superwoman.

"Sorry my son isn't here right now, or I'd have him deliver all this stuff to the Buckley House." Siobhan rang everything up.

"That's okay." Maeve grabbed the bag of litter. "It's not heavy. I can take the cans too."

"Thanks, sweetie. I've got those," I said. But she'd already started toward the door, after a last pat on the head for Irish Rover. He gave her the sad eyes and whimpered a little.

"Hey, how is Colleen holding up?" Siobhan asked as I turned to go. "I can't even imagine how devastated she must be. Especially after she—Oh." She stopped short. "Right, you found Deirdre too. I'm so sorry."

"Thanks," I said. "We're all doing okay. So sad. And such a shock."

146

"Well, if there's anything you need, just ask," Siobhan said. "I know it's been a while since we've seen each other, but I'd love to catch up sometime."

"Me too." I smiled. "And the same goes for you about the asking. It can't be easy for Conor either."

"It isn't." She sighed. "He's been holed up in his room. I'm glad Colleen asked him to keep working on the music for the show. You know, get back on the bike and all." She lowered her voice even though we were alone. "My brother told me Conor's accordion might have been the murder weapon. Can you believe that? They haven't ruled it out yet. Officially, anyway."

It was possible. But striking someone with a bulky instrument took extra motivation. Using an accordion to kill someone had to mean they'd grabbed the nearest potential weapon in sight. A crime of passion. Conor seemed so laid-back. Was that an act? I didn't think kids faked that sort of thing.

It would take a lot of rage and effort to kill his boss with an accordion. The perfectly nice boss who'd just given him a break and asked him to bring her a salad.

Moira, on the other hand . . . Deirdre's frenemy was tall and in great shape. If she'd gotten angry enough, become even more irrational than usual . . . yes, she definitely could have clobbered poor Deirdre with whatever was handy.

But my sister didn't believe Moira was capable of murder, and she knew her a lot better. And to be honest, part of me couldn't help picturing Moira like a cartoon villain, she was so pathetic. A villain who had big, dumb plans, like Wile E. Coyote. Who could take her seriously?

I guessed I should start. I didn't have a lot of better suspect options right now.

"She's a really nice person, your sister," Siobhan was saying. "No one believes any of those ridiculous stories going around about her and Deirdre. And I'm glad she decided not to move to New York."

New York?

Siobhan stopped talking as another customer walked in, behind a highly energetic little boy.

I stepped back against a display of guaranteed, all-natural deodorizers. Colleen had planned to relocate to the city? No, Siobhan was mistaken. Another morsel of misinformation from the Shamrock grapevine.

"Hey, where can I find those green feeler-thingies from the window?" the customer called, her voice booming in the cramped store. She wore patterned leggings that made her legs look extra-skinny, with a long crocheted sweater thrown over a black tank top. Peek-a-boo tattoos. A giant butterfly clip held her ombre hair in a messy bun. "I need one to fit a bullmastiff."

The kid—her grandson?—was already pulling a bunch of studded collars from a pegboard and tossing them on the floor.

"Uh-oh," Siobhan said under her breath. "Theresa Meaney."

The woman looked vaguely familiar. Definitely not a person you kept waiting, unless you wanted to be beaten to a pulp. "Well, I'll be going," I told Siobhan, "but thanks again. Hope I see you around."

"We'll grab a pint." Garrett's sister waggled her fingers goodbye as the energetic kid knocked over a spinner rack of green and orange leashes printed with dog bones and tiny beer mugs. Theresa grabbed him by the arm but left the merchandise on the floor.

Maeve was still waiting outside, the bag of cat litter against her chest. I joined her just as Una and Nuala McShane swept up the sidewalk. Una, a stump next to her sister, was dressed in head-to-toe tweed, with a lace blouse and a fancy gold brooch. She could have stepped straight out of the late 1800s, complete with a dour Victorian-era expression. Nuala wore equally appropriate wicked-witch-wear: long black duster, black stockings, black boots, and a black hat with a hideous pom-pom.

"Isn't this grand, running into the Big City Buckleys again?" Una said.

Nuala said nothing, just stared at us in that unsettling way of hers. Who knew what was going on in her head? Probably planning her next spell.

"Hello," I said. "Would love to chat, but Maeve and I need to get this stuff home. Desperate kitty waiting."

"Ah, of course." Una's eyes flicked to Paddy's Paws behind us. In the display window, Siobhan was trying in vain to extract a pair of green feelers from the head of the largest stuffed dog. I tuned back in to Una's voice, then wished I hadn't.

"We have our Francine's items auto-delivered weekly from the Pampered Pup. They have her favorite gourmet food, *Ciao! Ciao! Ciao!*, which must be kept refrigerated. Standard poodles are very discriminating, you know. Her breeder insists."

"Right," I said.

"And thank goodness for home delivery"—Una nodded toward Maeve's Kitty-O cat litter bag—"because it's a madhouse at the Shamrock right now." She placed a blue-veined hand on my arm. "You've heard Aidan O'Hearne is staying with us? Moira checked him in on Thursday evening. The two of them are very friendly from Irish Steps, of course." She took the latest-model smartphone out of her pocket and flashed a selfie of Moira and Aidan smiling at the Smiling Shamrock's front desk.

"Never heard of him." Maeve shifted the bag onto her hip.

She knew full well who Aidan was. Everyone did. And I wished she'd kept her mouth shut, because Nuala was silently staring daggers at her now. Maeve glared back at her with equal energy.

Una kept right on talking. "Moira tells us Colleen is taking over the Saint Patrick's Day show." Her voice dropped, taking on a conspiratorial tone. "Between you, me, and the kettle, I worry about your sister. A lovely girl, always the rose of the hour. Tell me, might it all be a bit much for her? The children's parents are concerned, and who can blame them? All their little dancers, and with the police investigation . . ." Her words trailed away with a hint of phlegmy cackle.

"No worries, ladies, the show is in very capable hands," I said. "And Colleen has plenty of support."

I brushed past the braggy biddy and her stony sister, and continued briskly down the sidewalk. Maeve kept pace with the bag of Kitty-O, which was starting to rip already. That's what you got with cheap litter.

Maeve glanced behind us, muttering under her breath. "Be kind," I said, even though I agreed with whatever she'd said. "Karma, remember?"

I was pretty sure she mumbled something else. "Are you hungry?" I said. "You can go on ahead and take the litter home, and I'll grab us something for lunch. How does an Italian sub sound?"

Her eyes narrowed slightly. "You're going by Hogan's Hoagies, aren't you? To check up on Conor's story."

"Well, yes," I admitted. "Look, honey, the boy seems very nice, like I said. I know his mom, and he's Garrett's nephew. I doubt he did anything wrong, other than not helping Deirdre."

"But like you also said, it was a good thing he didn't go in there, or he might have gotten hurt too," Maeve pointed out.

I ignored that. "Anyway, where Conor was, and when, is a loose thread that needs to be tied up. If he had a confirmed alibi, he'd be in the clear. Or close to it."

"Don't you think the police checked Hogan's already?"

"I'm sure they did," I said. "I just want to confirm things for myself." *And Colleen.*

Maeve rearranged the Kitty-O bag so her forearm covered the rip in the bag. "I'm coming with you."

* * *

Hogan's Hoagies had to be new, judging by the temporary banner, sparse furnishings, and fresh paint smell. The tourists must not have found the place yet.

I didn't see anyone behind the counter either. I walked up and pushed the leprechaun hat bell. "Hello?"

No answer. Conor had said he'd waited awhile for his order, and the guy kept screwing up, so maybe it was the same employee working. Or not working.

I didn't want to ring the bell again too soon, so I took a menu from the wire basket next to it and handed another to Maeve.

"I'll take a turkey sub," she said. "With provolone and chips. No tomatoes, you always forget that. I'll split with Bliz."

"No provolone, no cheddar," I said, still scanning the menu. "American cheese."

Maeve sighed. "Okay." She needed to learn that every town was not New York.

Colleen might be stuck at Angels Hall all afternoon, between the parent meeting and working with Conor. I'd get something to bring over to her.

I could see now, though, why Deirdre had ordered a salad that night. Hogan's was running some dodgy specials for Paddy's Week.

Ham salad and coleslaw on Irish soda bread? With green peppers. Not even remotely Irish. Just gross.

I hit the bell again. Still no response. Then I noticed the receipts stuck on a long pin next to the cash register. I leaned across the counter and flipped through them. The place hadn't had many customers lately, judging by the paltry number of receipts and zero people in the store right now. Maybe some of the slips toward the bottom were from Thursday evening.

"Mom, what are you doing?" Maeve said.

"Welcome to Hogan's, home of the original Irish hoagie," a flat voice said. I edged gracefully away from the receipts.

The bored-looking young woman stepped out from the back room, texting on her phone. Her employee name tag said "Michi," and she wore the same shamrock antennas we'd seen in the window at Paddy's Paws. Paired with her green apron, they made her look like a strange green bug.

"Can I take your order?"

"Two turkey and cheese subs with mustard, please," I said. "Regular bread. And three packs of chips."

"You mean, Hogan crisps," Michi said. "Drinks are over there." She jerked her chin toward a refrigerator against the side wall.

"I'll get them." Maeve put the bag of litter carefully down on the floor so the clumping sand wouldn't fall through the rip.

I skimmed the menu again as Michi turned away to make our sandwiches. What should I get Colleen? She wasn't big on salads.

"What's in the Mayo Surprise? A lot of . . . mayonnaise?"

Michi looked back at me as if I were the one wearing the bobbing feelers. "No. Mayo as in, County Mayo. In Ireland. It's a different surprise every day." She shrugged. "If you want me to tell you, it's lobster salad with chips today. Irish chips, as in, french fries. That's why it's more expensive. You get extra mayo on the side."

"Ah," I said. "Let's do three turkey subs, then."

"Hoagies, not subs," Michi corrected. "They go in the microwave, so they're hot. Technically, that makes them hoagies. I have to tell people that all the time."

I bet you do. "No need to heat anything up, thanks. We'll take everything to go. By the way," I added as Maeve returned to the counter with two bottles of Club Orange and a lime seltzer, "is there a guy here working with you today? I don't know his name, but he waited on my daughter's friend Thursday night."

"The only guy who works here nights is Nate. He's off on weekends."

"My friend was supposed to get a receipt, but he forgot," Maeve spoke up. "And he really, really needs to get reimbursed by his boss. Could you please check those for us"—she pointed to the paper slips—"and make a copy for him if you find it? Or I could take a picture on my phone. Thursday night, around seven or eight. A salad, maybe a Coke and a bottle of water, and a sub. I mean, hoagie. I don't know what kind."

There was one Buckley woman who had no problem being direct.

A new text came in on Michi's phone, and she pushed the whole stack of receipts toward Maeve. "You can look through them if you want. Nate was supposed to put these in the cash drawer, but he didn't. You can keep the original. I'll make a note for the register."

Well, that was one way to do accounting. I suppressed a shudder. But what a stroke of luck. Michi and Nate could duke it out for Employee of the Month.

The date and time of service were printed at the top of each slip. Maeve quickly pulled out the only Thursday evening receipt for two drinks, a Ham O'Hogan, and a Sligo Salad. 7:38. She stuffed it in her jacket pocket, and I handed over a generous tip.

"Thank you for visiting Hogan's Hoagies, home of the original Irish hoagie," Michi droned as we started toward the door.

"'Bye, thanks so much," Maeve called, but the girl in the bobbing bug feelers didn't look up from her phone.

Chapter Eighteen

As soon as the girls and I finished our subs—Mom declined half of mine when she heard they were from Hogan's—I set off for Angels Hall with an insulated lunch bag for Colleen. Hopefully she wouldn't mind if I sat in on the parent meeting for the show. I was supposed to be helping anyway.

At least she'd appreciate the lunch, as well as the support. There had to be plenty of negativity floating around, and more than a little fear. Who could blame anyone for that? These were their kids.

If I took a seat in the back, maybe no one would notice me. If things got out of hand, I'd speak up. Would people be okay with my sister taking over the show? Express reservations? Sit in stony silence?

I couldn't help wondering whether the killer might be there in the crowd too. Listening. Planning their next move. I shuddered and quickened my pace.

The Chief always said that suspects often turned up at the crime scene. Curiosity? Fascination? Huge egos? Or just some sick little game of cat and mouse?

I reached the parish hall ten minutes past the time Mom said the meeting was supposed to begin. No one was outside, so I took the opportunity for a quick snoop around. The meeting would start on Irish time anyway.

The CSI team had long finished, but maybe they'd missed some tiny clue or piece of evidence. Even though the hall was officially open, there were still remnants of yellow crime tape across the side door, where Maeve and I had seen Conor in the bushes.

I peered in the window to the left of the door. The small section of the downstairs backstage area I glimpsed was dark and dingy. Rubbing the filthy window with my glove, I made out what looked like a large black box lying near the door. It was open and empty, revealing a worn, reddish velvet lining. A musical instrument case—and judging by the odd shape outlined in the velvet, designed to hold something large and bulky. Conor's accordion. The case was clearly out of place, and it looked as if it had been knocked over. Maybe by Maeve, on our way out of the hall that night. Why hadn't the cops taken it for evidence, along with the accordion?

I looked behind me at the killer's likely escape route. They would have had a choice of turning right or left at the side gate at the edge of the parking lot.

Maeve and I had turned right to meet the Chief out on the road. If we had gone straight, we could have cut through backyards until we reached the safety of the Buckley House.

The person Conor saw must have turned left at the gate, or they would have run into the first responder vehicles and all the flashing lights. The paved part of the alley ended with the Lady of Angels property line, several yards down. After that, it was just dirt and what was left of the gravel the town tried to add each year. The Shamrock rains turned it into a muck trail, so cars rarely ventured any farther. In some sections, the muck became a full-fledged ditch each spring.

The Jig Is Up

A person could navigate the alley on foot, though, if they stuck to the less muddy sections where grass and weeds offered some protection. The neighborhood was mostly residential, with the land sloping downhill, but the alleyway eventually led to a major avenue.

Right now, the alley was littered with Leprechaun Lager cans, green plastic cups and cheap sunglasses, along with cigarette butts and fast-food bags and who knew what else. No wonder it seemed like the cops were having trouble finding clues.

No prayer of decent footprints either. It had rained on Thursday night, plus a bunch of other times since then. By now, the team had probably gone over the perimeter a zillion times. Their footprints—the ones that hadn't been washed away or grossly distorted—would be everywhere too.

I retraced my steps to the parish hall. The parking lot was filled with cars. No hope of finding anything here now.

Maybe I could check out the backstage area somehow. The crime tape remnants at the door wouldn't deter anyone at this point. Angels Hall was open for business.

Nope, the door was locked now. Every building in town had probably upped their security precautions.

I gazed at the parish hall itself. There was a small beat-up section of grass at the back, where we kids used to hang out while our parents socialized inside for some event, or after Mass. I'd even gotten my first kiss there—from Garrett McGavin, no less—in fifth grade. A very romantic setting—behind a reeking dumpster spray-painted in colorful graffiti. I could still smell it in my memory.

The dumpster.

I hurried around to the back of the hall. Yep, there was a dumpster—a much newer, nicer, and cleaner one. Beside it, a bright-green recycling bin said, *Keep Shamrock Green.*

The dumpster was tightly sealed, but the lid on the recycling bin was slightly askew. I placed Colleen's lunch bag on the ground and tried to glimpse inside by jumping.

"What's up, Katie?"

I froze with my knees bent and hands extended behind me, poised for a bigger jump. Trust Garrett McGavin to show up whenever I was in the middle of something embarrassing.

He stood there in a blazer, sweater, and khakis with an expression I could only describe as half amused, half disbelieving. "Dumpster diving?"

"Not exactly." My face flamed as I straightened and adjusted my jacket.

"Wait, I get it," he said. "You're hanging out back here by the dumpsters because you were feeling nostalgic for the best kiss of your life."

He *remembered*? "Oh, please."

"If you do want to take a little trip down memory lane, once I'm off duty I'd be more than happy—"

"Thank you, Garrett, that's so sweet of you," I cut in. "If you must know, I was checking for something I . . . lost."

He raised one brow, and I realized how that might sound to an actual detective. As if someone was admitting they'd left an incriminating item behind after a murder and tossed it into a handy recycling bin.

"Okay, so I'm looking for clues," I said. "In case something got, you know, missed."

"You thought maybe we'd neglected to fully comb a crime scene? Thanks, Veronica Mars, for that strong vote of confidence in the Shamrock PD."

"Well, you guys left Conor's accordion case lying around. Maeve almost tripped over it on our way out that night. It could have been the murder weapon."

"Forensics didn't support that."

Aha. "What did they support, then?" When he shrugged, I added, "Come on, Garrett. This is Conor and Colleen we're talking about. Just tell me. Please?"

He sighed. "The murder weapon, or at least what knocked the victim out, was smaller, metal, rounded on the edge. Not an accordion case. Or an accordion."

"Thank you." I couldn't get my Buckley dimple to flash like my sister's, but I tried. "What are you doing here, anyway? I thought you were off the Donnelly investigation."

"I'm checking things out on patrol. You know, seeing who shows up here. So far, the most interesting thing has been finding you at the dumpster."

"I'm here for the dance show meeting."

"I figured." Garrett motioned for me to follow him, and we walked back around the parish hall. A cold wind blew up, and he stuffed his hands in his pockets. "Your dad said Colleen would be here this afternoon reassuring folks, and then staying to work with my nephew. I'm on duty for the vigil tonight, so I told him I'd show up early."

I hesitated, wondering whether he'd handed over Deirdre's necklace for evidence. "Garrett, did you—?"

He reached across me to pull open the front door of Angels Hall. "Taken care of." He held the door and gestured for me to walk past him. "Have a good time."

"You're not coming in?"

"Nope," he said. "I'll be in the parking lot if anyone needs me. In my car. Let me know if you learn anything new, or if things go south in there. Good luck."

Chapter Nineteen

The inside of Angels Hall looked smaller today, and even though the meeting had started, it was a lot noisier. Bleachers were pulled out on the left side of the room, where dozens of parents sat in various groups. Kids under school age zoomed around under the bleachers, or got stuck and cried. Plenty of green everywhere, thanks to all the sweatshirts and ball caps dotting the crowd: navy, green, and gold of Our Lady of Angels; forest green and white of Holy Innocents Academy; Kelly green and gold of Shamrock High; dark green, gold, and black of the Donnelly School of Irish Dance; and plenty of pugilistic leprechaun logos representing the University of Notre Dame. Rah. Oh, and the usual sea of regional sports attire: Go Sox. Pats. Celts. Bruins.

Every head swiveled toward me as I took a seat on the emptiest bleacher, closest to the door. Whispers swirled around me, the kind you heard when you were late for Mass. Irish Time did not apply to church or public meetings with opportunities for important news or gossip. Last one in was a los-ah.

Colleen stood in front of the bleachers, dressed in a short dark-green skirt, a Donnelly School sweater, and Mary Janes that doubled as dance shoes. Her long ponytail was tied with a gold bow.

The Jig Is Up

Beside her, wearing a teal velvet tracksuit this time, Bernie Donnelly sat on a folding metal chair, one thin leg crossed over the other. Deirdre's mom looked like a wreck, understandably, but she had an air of determination about her. Her face may have gained a few extra wrinkles overnight, and her blue eye shadow and dark eyebrow pencil seemed extra-stark under the fluorescent lights, but the way she continuously jiggled one black clog told me she was taking no prisoners. One wrong comment or accusation from a parent, and they were pumpernickel toast.

Colleen waved to me, with a Doublemint smile. "My big sis is back in Shamrock, everybody! Kate and the girls, Maeve and Bliz, will be involved with the show too, so be sure to give them a big Donnelly School welcome."

People clapped politely, and some threw me not-unfriendly looks. I waggled my fingers and smiled, wishing the bleachers would fold up back into the wall with me inside. Colleen loved being the center of attention, but I hated it.

As she talked about Deirdre, and how much they'd all miss her, that dread I'd felt in Angels Hall on the night of the murder crept back. I felt like I was watching a movie in slow motion, without the sound, waiting for some dark evil to make its presence known. My sister, Bernie, and the crowd around me became a strange blur.

I could have sworn that relentless jig was playing again. The blood trail leading behind the curtain reappeared in my mind. I focused on a 2008 Girls Softball pennant on the opposite wall, trying to erase the image.

Now my sister was saying nice things about Bernie, and everyone applauded again. Some rose to their feet, which was good because no one noticed when I suddenly sat up straighter on the uncomfortable metal bleacher.

The blood trail had started on this side of the curtain. Deirdre was attacked out here, then dragged backstage through the curtain. The killer must have pushed her cruelly down the backstage stairs, where Colleen and I found her crumpled at the bottom.

Had Deirdre's attacker snuck up behind her, murder weapon in hand? Or had the two of them been in a heated conversation where the killer grabbed some random weapon nearby, and hit her over the head?

The first scenario was more deliberate. Calculating. The second possibility seemed more a crime of passion. Rage, followed by an impulse that led to tragedy.

In the second scenario, the killer might be remorseful now. Maybe they would even step forward to confess.

Or maybe not. Almost two days had passed. I felt certain Deirdre's murder wasn't some random crime committed by a random person.

So far the police had zeroed in on the people last seen with Deirdre: Conor, Moira, and my sister. They seemed to have eliminated Conor, and I literally had receipts for his whereabouts at the time of the murder. But why was Moira skipping around town, posting her ridiculous flyers?

Probably for the same reason Colleen was here in Angels Hall. My sister had to go on with her normal—well, new-normal—life. Without her best friend. She was taking questions from the crowd now, listening and nodding and periodically flashing her dimple. A lot of people were nodding back. Even smiling.

Except Theresa Meaney, the loud woman who'd come into the pet store earlier. Her grandson was underneath the bleachers, poking at the seats with a janitor's broom. When he headed to my section, I leaned down so he could see me and shook my head at him through the slats. He grinned, dropped the broom, and ducked out to wave at Theresa. She was focused on Colleen, her face a dull red. Too much day drinking, maybe. If I had a grandkid like that, I'd probably join her.

I knew from living with the Chief that detectives never made their moves right away. Questions, yes. Arrests came later, when they were confident they had an airtight case for the DA, and ultimately a jury. No mistakes, no quick moves, unless someone claimed responsibility for the crime. And even then, the cops had to be sure.

As far as I knew right now, the cops had a bunch of highly circumstantial evidence. Moira and Colleen both had motives, and were the last persons known to have seen Deirdre alive. Moira wanted to start up a competing dance school, and she'd always been jealous of Deirdre. Maybe she'd come back to confront her that night, gotten super frustrated, and things turned deadly.

My sister had taken a loan from her friend, and Deirdre told her she wanted it back. But Colleen didn't have the money anymore. They'd had a fight, and then there was the issue of the missing scholarship funds.

Colleen had also interfered with a crime scene. Probably just a dumb move on her part, but still . . .

At least there was that friend Colleen had run into on her way home from seeing Deirdre. He had to have vouched for her to the cops, right? I hoped so. But why, then, wasn't she in the clear with Sergeant Walker?

The woman closest to me in the bleachers stood up. "I love your idea of moving rehearsals to Great Shamrock Hall, Colleen," she said. "It's right by the police station, so there will be even more security."

"And it's on the Square, so it's easy to get to," someone else said.

"Yes!" Colleen lit up the room like a cheerleader at a pep rally. "And it's where we're having the actual show, so the kids can get used to the larger space. Plus, parents and guardians are welcome to stay for rehearsals. We want everyone to feel as comfortable as possible."

I saw Bernie Donnelly wince. She reached down beside her chair and took a swift sip from a thermos. "If you plan to stay, people, there'll be no interference from the peanut gallery about the dancing," she called. "The program numbers are set, and the featured dancers know who they are. No changes, no exceptions. Colleen is in charge."

Bernie was, as she always said with pride, a tough old bird. No one batted an eye, except Theresa, who muttered something. People turned to look at her and frowned.

Someone brought Colleen a chair like Bernie's from out in the hall. She thanked them as she plopped down onto it, her short skirt miraculously staying put. "So what do you think, everybody? Have we answered all your questions about how we plan to keep the kids safe?"

Not a murmur from the peanut gallery.

From the way Bernie's right hand kept twitching, I could tell she was jonesing for a cig. It had to be hard facing all these people so soon after the untimely death of her only daughter. "We don't want anyone feeling awkward," she said, rising to her feet. "We've already heard from a few families privately that they've chosen not to participate in the show this year. I hope Colleen and I have assured the rest of you that your kids and their safety are the top priority for us." She cleared her throat, and her voice wavered very slightly. "Lord knows I understand how important your young angels are to you."

Colleen jumped up to give Bernie a hug. "We're doing this for Deirdre," she told the crowd. "Because Bernie believes—and I totally agree—that Deirdre would've wanted the show to go on."

Another buzz ran through the crowd, but this time it wasn't of the old-dears-clucking variety. More than one person wiped a tear or ducked their heads.

"So okay, last concerns?" Colleen asked. "This is the time, folks. We all have lots to do, we're pumped, and we really appreciate you coming out this afternoon."

"I have somethin'. If no one else is gonna say it, I will." Theresa got to her feet.

"Sorry again for your loss, Bernie," she said. "My granddaughter Darcy says she wants to stay in the show, even if she didn't get a solo like she should have. But ya know, some of us have been hearin' things that aren't good." She jerked her thumb toward Colleen. "About yer one, there."

People gasped. "Sit down, Theresa," someone called.

"Lies," another person said loudly. "All of them."

"Pathetic," a parent near me said to the woman beside her. "No one needs to hear that *(mumble)*. Colleen's a flippin' sweetheart."

Bernie raised one bony hand for quiet. "That's enough, Theresa Meaney," she said. "I've heard those fairy stories, and we're not going there. Shame on you. Colleen and my daughter were the best of friends since Babies class. And Darcy is dancing the slip-jig with three other girls, because that's what Deirdre decided. Plenty of stage time. Anyone else with a word about Colleen here, and—"

"It's okay, Bernie." Colleen gave the woman's wiry shoulders a squeeze, then turned back to the crowd.

Should I jump in to defend her, head things off?

No. My sister was the one looking determined now. This was up to her.

"Okay, everybody," she said. "Yeah, there are crazy rumors going around town, but I promise you, they're not true. You all know me." She looked at Theresa. "Well, most of you."

People nodded in practically every row of the bleachers. "You go, Colleen!" someone called. "Don't listen to that blarney."

The person didn't say "blarney," but that was the general idea. The old Shamrock spirit.

"I get that some of you are worried," Colleen said. "And scared. I am too. I used to dance, but I've never run a show before. Or anything, really, other than Pep Club and prom committee and stuff. But keeping your kids safe is the most important thing in the world to me. More than the show or anything else. Like I said, we're doing this for Deirdre. And the kids too, because they want to dance. Bernie and I both think Deirdre would've wanted the show to go on. Let's make this year's show a tribute to her and prove that evil can't win."

Murmurs started up again, but the tone was softer this time. Theresa sat down and stared straight ahead with a stony expression.

"The real truth about what happened to Deirdre will come out," Colleen said. "Hopefully soon, so everyone can feel safe. As you know, we have a pretty amazing police force in this town. Maybe I'm a little biased, because"—dimple flash—"I happen to be very closely related to a member or two of the Shamrock PD. They'll find out who took Deirdre from us so that the person can be brought to justice ASAP. That's a promise, folks, or I'm not a Buckley." She looked up toward the ceiling and smiled. "We won't let you down, Dee."

The clapping through the auditorium was louder now, accompanied by the shifting weight of people rising from the bleachers, boots pounding metal, and even an earsplitting whistle or two.

Colleen had won them over, at least for now. And she sure hadn't needed my help. As people started leaving, I ran down to the polished floor to give my sister a hug.

"Nice speech, Colleen Queen," I said.

"Thanks, Katie. I'm so glad you came. We're going to kick this show."

Parents stopped to speak to Bernie and offer their condolences. Others, like Theresa, ducked out the door, kids in tow. But several parents wanted to talk to Colleen. Some to say how sorry they were for her loss too, and others to thank her for taking on the show. Despite Bernie's warning, one or two wanted to see if Colleen could work their little darlings into a different show number.

I hung back at first, then went over to sit on the stage. Finally Colleen, Bernie, and I were the only ones left in the hall, and I rejoined them. "Guess this meeting was a success," I said.

"'Twas," Bernie said. "It took guts to face that group, Colleen. Not that the parents shouldn't have been worried, of course. That goes without saying. But the crazy talk about you and my poor Deirdre, God rest her soul . . ."

"Thanks, Bernie, but it's okay," Colleen said. "I feel good about the way things went. Now I can get down to working on the show, and Bernie, you can rest and focus on other things."

"Not sure I want to do that." Bernie sighed.

"How did you get Mayor Flanagan to let you use Shamrock Hall for rehearsals?" I asked. "That was quite a coup." His Dishonor loved nothing more than endless red tape—or in this town, green.

"That was nothing." Bernie waved. "I know how to handle that tub of Kerrygold."

I hid a smile as I imagined Mayor Flanagan as a thick blob of extra-fat Irish butter, and how that convo might have gone down. Colleen was less successful in containing her glee. "You're the Windbag Whisperer," she told Bernie.

"I am." Bernie's lips twitched as she reached into her jacket. "I'm stepping out for a smoke, girls. Colleen, did you talk to Kate here about the piano playing?"

"Piano?" I suddenly remembered the person who was supposed to accompany Conor on his accordion for the show. And on the night of the murder.

"I was just about to ask her," Colleen said.

"Good, I'll leave you ladies to it, then. Cheers." Deirdre's mother hightailed it toward the door for her nic fix. That frail appearance was deceiving.

"Brought you lunch," I said to Colleen, holding out the lunch bag. "Turkey."

"Ooh, thanks."

I held the bag a little higher, just beyond her grasp. "What's this about the piano?"

She snatched the bag and grinned. "I was hoping my musical-genius sister could accompany Conor on his accordion for a few numbers in the show, like Deirdre wanted."

"I'd love to," I said, "but I haven't played for years. Rusty doesn't begin—"

"Seriously?" Colleen rolled her eyes. "Kate, you're a professional musician. Well, you *were*," she corrected. "For a while. Your rusty is, like, a gazillion times better than most people's best."

"Way to butter your big sister up," I said. "Okay, fine, but don't say I didn't warn you. Do you have the music?"

"In my bag." Colleen nodded in the direction of the stage, her mouth already half full of sandwich. "You can take it out if you want. My hands are covered in mustard."

"Want me to stay and work with you and Conor this afternoon?" I eyed the ancient black workhorse of a piano in the corner. So much for any more sleuthing plans today, but a deal was a deal.

"That's okay, thanks," Colleen said. "We decided to check things out at Great Shamrock Hall today instead of rehearsing. He can see what they've got for the sound system, and we'll talk to the lighting guy. That way, we can tell Mayor Flanagan right away if there's anything we need on the tech front." She grinned. "Well, Bernie will tell him."

"Speaking of Bernie, did you ever ask her who was supposed to play the piano for the show?"

"She had no idea," Colleen said. "The detectives asked her too."

Huh. So the mystery person had volunteered their help, then never shown up. Or *had* shown up, and murdered Deirdre.

Colleen extracted a long piece of dark hair from her turkey sub. "Ew. Where'd you get this sandwich again?"

"Don't ask. See you at the vigil tonight, okay?" I started toward the double doors.

"Don't forget to take the music with you," my sister called.

Chapter Twenty

At 6:30, I pulled on another cute pair of boots from Colleen's bottomless closet and stopped by the kitchen to grab some leftover pizza for the road. Not one measly slice left, thanks to Frank. I took a swig of diet root beer, spread a dab of marmalade on a thick slice of brown bread, and grabbed my sister's black leather jacket from the hook. I shrugged into it as I held the bread in my teeth, an easy feat because the bread was stale.

I'd wanted to get back to Angels Hall early for a bit more recon before Deirdre's vigil, but I was running late. Mom had offered to feed the girls and bring them with her.

When I stepped into the hallway, she and four worried-looking guests were grouped at the front entrance, the guests' suitcases lined up near the door. Uh-oh. Not again.

I stepped back into the kitchen. I'd use the side door.

"I do wish you ladies would change your minds," I heard Mom say. "This is a safe neighborhood, I assure you. In fact, my husband—"

"We've very sorry, Ms. Buckley," one of the women broke in. "Your B and B is lovely, but we'd feel more secure over at the Smiling Shamrock."

"To think there was a murder down the block." Another guest clucked her tongue. "We had no idea there would be such a high crime rate here. There's even a gentleman in the living room listening to some kind of crime radio. It's very loud, I might add."

Poor Mom. I hoped the other Buckley House guests—if there were any left by now—wouldn't end up leaving too. How could the Smiling Shamrock keep packing in so many people, with Una and that stupid sign out front broadcasting no vacancies for Paddy's Week? Maybe some of the Smiling Shamrock's guests were being scared away by the bad publicity too. They might feel safer with the off-season witches and ghosts over in Salem.

I pushed through the screen door and walked swiftly toward Angels Hall. The sky was growing darker, which would be nice for the candles. At least it wasn't raining. Turning into the parking lot for the second time today, I spotted two uniforms posted at the front and two at the side of the building. A little damper on my recon plans.

"Ms. B?"

Conor came up behind me, accompanied by Zoe, who carried a plastic grocery bag. I almost didn't recognize her with her hair down. It fell to her shoulders like Maeve's, but she had drawn it tightly back with a thin plaid headband.

"Hi, kids," I said. "You're here early." Over their shoulders, though, I spotted people already coming down the block. Definitely too late for any recon now.

"I just picked up my accordion from the station and dropped it home on the way here," Conor said. "Zoe went with me."

"All he had to do was sign a paper," Zoe said. "They said it wasn't the murder weapon, so he could have it back for the show."

Nice. Some cop casually gave that info to a couple of kids, but I practically had to beg Garrett. My dad and Frank hadn't shared it with me either. "Did they say what the weapon was?"

"Nope," Conor said. "I only got my accordion back early because your dad pulled some strings. The cops didn't have the instrument case, though, so I had to borrow one from a guy at Pauly's Pawn Shop."

"Check the parish hall," I said. Why didn't the Chief just officially go back to work at the PD? I knew the answer: Mom would put her foot down. But he did enjoy consulting with his buddy Chief Ryan and directing things from home in his bathrobe.

A lot more people had gathered for the memorial now, carrying balloons, signs, and teddy bears.

"We'd better get going. I have something for Maeve." Zoe held out her bag, which said "Keep Shamrock Green." Just like the ones I'd seen blown across people's lawns on my way to PJ's earlier. Nice slogan, though I wasn't sure exactly how plastic bags helped the town in an environmental sense. At least she was reusing it.

I pulled out a Donnelly School T-shirt. "Thanks. She'll love this." I wasn't entirely sure about that, but it was thoughtful of Zoe.

"I grabbed her a medium," she said. "That's what I wear. Miss Colleen posted on Facebook that Maeve and Bliz were joining the show. We're all out of kids small, but Bliz can wear one of Conor's sisters' shirts for now."

"It's in there too," he said.

"Everyone from the show is wearing matching shirts tonight," Zoe said. "You know, for Deirdre. It'll be good advertising too."

The Jig Is Up

"Thanks for saying you'd play piano, by the way, Ms. B," Conor said. "The one at Shamrock Hall is all tuned and everything."

I smiled. "Looking forward to it." Another little green lie.

Zoe texted furiously on her phone. "We gotta go help out at the candle table," she told Conor. "They need people to make more drip guards."

Good Lord, that girl is organized, I thought as they rushed off. The mayor should appoint her to head one of his currently useless committees.

It wasn't entirely dark yet, but the parking lot was illuminated by strategically placed spotlights. The yellow crime tape was gone now, and the place swarmed with cops. A furry tail brushed my leg as a K-9 patrol passed me. Shamrock PD wasn't taking any chances with security.

Irish music—quiet, moody ballads—played through speakers as a camera crew set up near the WSCK news van. A petite woman in a green, orange, and white color-blocked dress beneath her open trench coat got her makeup retouched as she did a sound check. I recognized her as a reporter from the evening local news team: Mitzi Dolan-Yung.

And there was Zoe again near the entrance, handing out white candles with paper drip guards as more people streamed in from the sidewalk. Beside her, a whole army of kids passed out little green-and-white ribbons. My daughters were with them.

An old man in a tweed cap handed Bliz a couple of crumpled bills. Bliz flashed her dimple and stuffed the money in the large plastic container Maeve held tightly to her chest, marked "Deirdre Donnelly Memorial Scholarship Fund."

A teen wearing a Donnelly T-shirt over her black Henley approached me. She had a knapsack slung over her shoulder, and her gold choker said "Darcy" in script.

"Hi, want a flyer?" She handed me one without waiting for an answer.

I glanced at it as Darcy disappeared into the crowd.

The flyer featured a photo of young Deirdre, smiling in her simple Irish dance dress, and next to it a glamorous headshot from her Irish Steps days. The larger picture on the back showed Deirdre holding an enormous bouquet of colorful flowers, surrounded by her students. Beneath the photo, three stacked lines read:

Love You 4-Ever, Miss Deirdre!!!

Xoxox RIP.

Dance is Joy.

At the bottom of the flyer were a hand-drawn Celtic cross and an announcement dedicating this year's Saint Patrick's Day show to the memory of Deirdre Ann Donnelly.

And below that: *Approved by the Honorable Raymond F. Flanagan, Mayor of Shamrock.*

As I tucked the flyer into my purse, a tall figure, dressed entirely in retro black velvet—complete with dotted demi-veiled hat—sidled up beside me.

"Hello there! I'm Moira McShane Kelly. I was a good friend and Irish Steps colleague of—"

"We've met," I said flatly.

Moira seemed delighted. "Oh, you're a parent of one of my students-to-be, then. Would you be a doll and pass these around for me?" She held out a thick stack of flyers, more slickly designed than the one in my purse.

I didn't need to glance at them for more than a second. Same flyers she was posting all over town for the Moira McShane Kelly Academy of Irish Dance.

"I'd love to," I said, pasting a smile to match my Colleen-style cheerleader voice. "Please give me as many as you can."

"Fabulous!" Moira pushed half the stack in my hands and hurried away in search of more victims.

I rushed off in the opposite direction, to the nearest recycling bin.

* * *

I tried not to notice the huge, fat raindrops beginning to hit the top of my head as I made my way through the vigil crowd to the platform at the far end of the parking lot.

People were putting up umbrellas now, balancing them with their unlit candles.

It couldn't rain on Deirdre's memorial. That would be so unfair. Nothing had been fair for Colleen's friend, it seemed—in life, or in death.

Under a canopy tent, Conor fiddled with an uncooperative projector. A presentation displaying photos of Deirdre flashed onto the big screen set up on the side of Angels Hall.

The crowd quieted as Mayor Flanagan stepped onto the metal platform. Behind him stood Father Declan, the pastor of Our Lady of Angels, plus a local minister, imam, and rabbi. The multifaith representatives were quickly joined by a very fit and familiar-looking blond guy who took the platform steps in one light bound.

Even for such a somber occasion, he played the fashionista, dressed in a navy fisherman's knit sweater, a jaunty cap, coordinating scarf, and extremely tight slacks. Aidan O'Hearne, Deirdre's dance partner, had arrived. *Former* dance partner, I reminded myself. Deirdre had broken up their hugely successful team.

An excited buzz ran through the crowd as Aidan waved to his adoring fans. He was here in Shamrock in a professional capacity as well as a personal one. According to the front page of the Chief's morning *Shamrock Sentinel*, he'd been named Honorary Grand Marshal of this year's Paddy's Day Parade.

Mayor Flanagan grabbed the microphone. "Welcome, residents and visitors, to our peaceful Celtic haven of Shamrock as we join to celebrate the life of a talented, dedicated hometown girl, the victim of a tragic accident—"

Peaceful? Accident? Everyone knew by now that Deirdre was murdered.

The mayor kept talking, his voice echoing through the parking lot. "On this bittersweet occasion, as we fondly remember one who passed too soon, we look forward to brighter days, thankful for our close-knit community and thriving small businesses . . ."

Seriously? Who said stuff like that under such tragic circumstances? I glanced around the crowd. Here and there, people frowned, and others seemed confused, but most just looked sad. Some tried to light their candles in the rain, even though it wasn't time yet.

The mayor droned on with his infomercial, hardly mentioning poor Deirdre. The rain was picking up now.

"Hey." Colleen came up beside me, carrying a Buckley House guest umbrella.

"Hi," I said. "Where's the friend you were supposed to meet?"

"Up there." She nodded toward the stage and snapped open her umbrella, holding it over both of us. "He got waylaid at the Smiling Shamrock."

I was pretty sure she wasn't referring to Father Declan or any of the other clerics. "I thought you and Aidan weren't speaking anymore."

"I never said that." Colleen pulled her Donnelly School jacket closer. "Deirdre" was stitched over the left front pocket. Bernie must have given it to her. "He's a sweetheart, most of the time. I just didn't like the way he made Deirdre feel like she had to choose between dancing and her mom, that's all. He didn't want her to come back to Shamrock, obviously."

"Did he have a say in that?" I asked. The mayor was on a roll now, but I'd stopped listening.

My sister shrugged. "He kept bugging her to hold off retiring for one more year. Just so he could stay in the spotlight 'til he got his new show into production. He didn't want to start all over again with another Irish Steps partner, you know?" She dropped her voice. "Especially Moira, but we know how that ended." She drew a manicured finger sharply across her throat.

I drew back. "He *hurt* her?"

Colleen rolled her eyes. "Jeez, Katie. There you go again, being so literal. No. He got her fired from Irish Steps because she bugged him so much about it."

The microphone shrieked, temporarily silencing Mayor Flanagan.

"Couldn't Bernie have hired someone else to take over the school?" I asked, when it was safe for us to uncover our ears. "Moira—"

Colleen shook her head. "Nope. Bernie can't stand any of the McShanes. It's never been hearts and shamrocks between them. Besides, she wanted to keep the business in the family. Kind of like Mom and the Chief with the Buckley House."

"Mmm." Probably a lost cause.

"That school meant everything to the Donnellys," Colleen went on. "I mean, they were all champion Irish dancers, going back generations. Mr. Donnelly's parents started it here in Shamrock when they came over the pond."

I glanced at the platform, where Sergeant Walker and Garrett had taken positions at either side. Garrett's head was bowed slightly against the rain—the awning didn't cover the whole platform—but I could tell he was keeping an eye on everything.

Shirley wore black pants and a black coat over her black turtle-neck, every inch the sentinel as her sharp eyes scanned the crowd. Garrett's dark suit was starting to cling to his body in the rain. If those two were freezing, they hid it well.

Colleen turned to say something else to me just as a massive bright light shined squarely in our faces. We both shielded our eyes.

"Colleen! Mitzi Dolan-Yung, WSCK-TV." The reporter thrust a microphone in my sister's face. "You were Deirdre Donnelly's best friend. Tell us what happened here at Angels Hall on Thursday night. Was her death an accident, like the mayor just said?"

Colleen froze. "I—"

Out of nowhere, Frank stepped in and took Colleen's arm. "No comment," he told Mitzi. "Let's go," he added to my sister and me, under his breath. "Start walking."

"I'm not going to tell them anything," Colleen insisted as we hurried through the crowd, which parted to let us through in the glare of lights. "Do you think I'm that stupid?"

"No comment." Frank turned back to Mitzi and the camerap-erson, who were still eagerly following us. "We're done here."

We finally gave the news crew the slip after several people stepped in to block their progress. "You girls should head home," Frank said. "They'll just keep bugging you."

Go home? This was like a déjà-vu from Thursday night. "Thanks, Frank, but we're perfectly capable of taking care of our-selves," I said.

"Yeah, you two have been doing a good job on that so far," he said.

"And FYI, we are not girls," Colleen said. "Check your Big Bro handbook."

Frank's reply was lost in a sonic boom of thunder that shook the parking lot. People screamed as lightning streaked behind the church steeple.

Two uniforms jumped up onto the bleachers to hustle the mayor and everyone else down from the platform. One of the officers had to remove the microphone from Mayor Flanagan's grasp. "Just a little spring burst, everyone!" the mayor shouted.

"Proceed quickly and in an orderly fashion to the nearest exit," the officer announced as the mic screeched again. "Do not run. No need to panic. I repeat, do not run."

Mayor Flanagan grabbed the mic back. "The memorial will be rescheduled," he said. "All is well."

Another bolt of lightning exploded in the sky, and I frantically searched the crowd for the rest of my family. I didn't spot them, but I did see the McShane witches standing serenely on the covered church steps. Was Nuala actually *smiling*?

There was Mom, herding Bernie, Maeve, and Bliz straight toward the same church steps the McShanes were hogging. She marched them all up past the evil ones and pushed on the double side doors, which opened like some kind of miracle. Eileen Buckley was on excellent terms with Saint Jude.

Frank kept checking over his shoulder as he escorted Colleen and me to the gate, making sure Mitzi didn't catch up with us. Fortunately, the cameraperson had turned off his light, and the pair had disappeared.

I checked my phone and saw a text from Maeve. She and Bliz were going home with Mom after they lit some votive candles for Deirdre.

A nun with an umbrella was inviting other people to take shelter in the rectory now. A shame they couldn't move the whole memorial to the church, but everything was a mess right now.

People scattered in all directions as the rumbles of thunder and occasional streaks of lightning continued.

"See you ladies later," Frank said. "I'm going back to make sure everyone else evacuates the vicinity safely. Remember, no talking to the press or anyone else about the case. Got it?"

"Got it," I said quickly.

"Thanks, Frankie," Colleen called as he headed into the fray. "Come on, Kate, we're going to Farrell's."

"We are?" At this point, half the people had run into the church or the rectory, with the other half scurrying toward the pub at the corner. "We'll never get a table."

"A little positivity, please." Colleen texted as she walked. "I've got connections. Mr. Honorary Grand Marshal is meeting us there."

I felt the next rumble of thunder in the middle of my chest before I heard it, and another crack of lightning branched through the sky. "Okay," I agreed, and not just because we were about to be fried. This would be a perfect opportunity to find out more about Aidan O'Hearne.

Had Deirdre's former partner, angry over her desertion of both him and Irish Steps, been involved somehow in her death? Did a killer lurk behind that polished, charming exterior? Maybe Colleen was fooled by the guy, but I sure wasn't.

I glanced back one last time at the nearly empty parking lot, feeling a wave of sadness. Deirdre's memorial was ruined. That was how things seemed to go in Shamrock.

From bad to worse.

Chapter
Twenty-One

I inhaled the familiar stale-beer-sawdust-and-fry-oil smell as I followed my sister into the comforting warmth and bustle of Farrell's. Colleen was right. We had no problem getting in, even though Aidan hadn't arrived yet. She breezed us both past the people waiting outside in the rain and the burly-looking bouncer with a waggle of her royal fingers.

The crowd good-naturedly parted for us, just as they had at the memorial in the Angels parking lot. I felt the way Maeve must have when she was Little Miss Shamrock following Colleen around town. Women gave my sister hugs, men offered to buy her drinks, and a fiddler from the band warming up in the corner tipped his cap. Colleen waved to all and pulled me toward a prime booth in the pub section, which two guys insisted on vacating for barstools.

Who'd ever imagine she was a murder suspect?

I avoided the blob of ketchup on the seat as I slid in across from my sister. Foam stuffing spilled from a gash in the green leather. Farrell's needed an update, like many places in town, but the locals preferred it shabby.

"Hey, Colleen. Really sorry about Deirdre. You guys don't need menus, right?" A waitress with thick, dark eyebrows dumped down two glasses of ice water.

"Thanks, and no," Colleen said. "How's it going, Carmel?"

The waitress shrugged. "The same. Vodka cranberry, onion rings to start, and . . . ?" She looked at me.

"A Harp," I said. "Just a half-pint, please."

"We don't do half-pints." The eyebrows drew together. "And nobody drinks Harp here. Want a Guinness? We have those freakin' sour beers and seltzers too."

"Guinness," I said quickly, and she took off. I leaned across the table toward my sister. "Before Aidan gets here, I have to ask you something."

Colleen visibly froze. "Sure, what?"

"I know Deirdre and Aidan were dance partners, obviously, but were they ever a couple?"

My sister's expression immediately clouded. "*No.* Are you kidding? They had this amazing chemistry onstage, but off it they were like brother and sister. They fought a lot, but Aidan always won."

"Until Deirdre quit and left him high and dry without his better half."

"He's a really good dancer," Colleen said. "They were equally good."

"Not what I meant."

"Oh," Colleen said. "Yeah, he kinda went a little crazy when she left Irish Steps. He told her she could run the dance school later. But he just didn't get it about Bernie. Deirdre felt like she owed her mom a lot. Bernie made tons of sacrifices over the years for her dance career—the dresses alone were super expensive—and when Mr. Donnelly died, it was just the two of them."

"They had friends in town," I said.

Colleen gazed up at the "My goodness, my Guinness" poster over our booth. "Yeah, well . . . that's not the same as having family around."

I nodded as a different waitress dropped off two menus at our table without looking, on her way to wipe up a full-pitcher spill across the bar. I had to admit, I felt lonely myself in the city sometimes without my crazy family, even though the girls and I had plenty of friends and acquaintances. But I knew full well the grass wasn't any greener in Shamrock, despite the annual rainfall percentage.

Colleen pushed the greasy menus to the side. Farrell's fare hadn't changed much in either of our lifetimes: corned beef and cabbage, mutton stew, shepherd's pie, Irish nachos, burgers, and every imaginable dish that was fried and/or contained potato. The place wasn't overly concerned about online reviews that criticized their old-school Irish American pub fare. That was Farrell's entire culinary goal.

"Did Deirdre have a boyfriend?" I asked. "Anyone at all?"

My sister shook her head. "Don't think so. Deirdre was really private about that kind of stuff. I'm sure she would have told me, though. Especially if it was Aidan."

"Yeah, I guess those two would have made a strange couple," I said. "Deirdre was so shy when she wasn't onstage, and Aidan seems in love with himself."

"He's not that bad, Katie. You don't know him." Colleen swirled her ice. "The Irish Steps producers loved all the publicity and rumors. You know, the whole dancing sweethearts deal. Totally fake."

We both turned toward a sudden flurry of activity at the door. The King of the Dance had arrived.

"He sure is popular here," I said. Understatement of the year.

"He's popular everywhere." Colleen shrugged.

"You think Aidan would have become such a big star without Deirdre?" I asked. "Could he have gotten so angry with her for deserting him that he killed her during some big argument?"

Colleen reached for the breadbasket and extracted every last package of oyster crackers. "Seriously?" she scoffed, tossing one across the table to me. "I know I said Aidan went ballistic on Deirdre, but I was exaggerating. He doesn't ever get ticked off about anything, really. He turns on the charm to get his way."

I swallowed a smile. *Pot and kettle.*

"His blarney didn't work on Deirdre because she knew him too well. They had some pretty intense discussions, but that was it."

I'd keep Aidan on my mental suspect list with an asterisk anyway. Right under Moira. Conor said he'd heard women's voices arguing in the parish hall that night, but he could have been wrong. Or Aidan could have been a bystander at first. Maybe he'd gone to Angels Hall to try one more time to persuade Deirdre to come back to Irish Steps, and things went south.

But he had his own show now. Or would, very soon.

The commotion moved closer to the bar area. I couldn't see the man of the hour in the swarm of fans, but Colleen jumped up, waving. "Aidan, over here!"

I finally spotted the blond guy in the tweed cap heading confidently toward our booth, smiling at fans along the way. He pulled out a gold pen from the breast pocket of the blazer he'd thrown on over the Irish sweater and signed a napkin for an elderly tourist, as well as the arm of a teenaged girl.

Finally, he dropped into the booth beside Colleen in a cloud of pricey men's cologne. "Hello, again, gorgeous," he said, giving her a kiss on the cheek. A group of guys whistled and called joking encouragements from across the room.

"Save the charm for your big admirers," Colleen told him. "You remember Kate, right?"

He turned his infectious smile to me, his blue eyes crinkling at the corners. Closer up, I saw that his face was scattered with light freckles. "Ah, the very serious big sister," he said, with a touch of studied brogue. "Every inch the Buckley too."

Please. Where was our waitress with our drinks?

Our server rushed right up. No hairy frown this time. "So nice to meet you, Mr. O'Hearne," she gushed. "Huge fan here. What'll you have? On the house, of course."

"You're very kind," Aidan said. "How about your finest Cabernet Sauvignon? Napa Valley, say, 1992?"

The waitress's face dropped. "Oh. Um . . ."

"Just pulling your leg." Aidan gave her a twinkly look and patted his perfectly flat abs. "Your lightest lager for me. I'll take a Harp."

"Nobody drinks Harp here," I informed him. I smiled at the waitress. "A burger with fries, please. And our drinks."

"Me too," Colleen added. "And don't forget the onion rings."

"Afraid I can't stay long," Aidan said to Colleen, after Eyebrows left. "I promised Bernie Donnelly I'd stop by to see her tonight."

"Where are you staying?" I asked, knowing the answer.

"He's at the Smiling Shamrock." Colleen rolled her eyes.

Aidan shrugged. "Couldn't turn down the free accommodations."

No wonder he'd ended up at the McShanes' B and B. On the other hand, who hadn't?

"Your loss," Colleen told him. "The Buckley House is tons nicer."

"It is," Aidan said. "I wasn't sure that would be a good idea, though, under the circumstances."

What was that supposed to mean? Was he talking about Deirdre's murder or Colleen being a suspect or . . . ? My sister twirled her straw in her ice water again.

"So how are things going with the new show?" she asked. "You started to tell me, but—"

"It's brilliant," Aidan said as our drinks arrived. I immediately slurped the creamy foam—the best part—off the top of my Guinness. "We have interest from major investors, and I've worked out some fine choreography, if I do say so myself. I was holding auditions in Chicago earlier this week."

"What time did you get here Thursday night, exactly?" I asked.

The faintest of lines appeared on his forehead. "Around eight or half past eight, I suppose. Why do you ask?"

"Just wondering," I said. "Must have been a stormy trip into Hartford."

"Boston," he corrected. "The Uber trip was worse."

His itinerary would be easy enough for the detectives to confirm. I'd talk to Garrett. "Guess Moira checked you in, then. She must have been excited to see you."

"Ah yes. Over the moon." He rolled his eyes slightly. "Better her than those two old dears." He shook his head. "I still can't believe you girls found Deirdre that same night."

His tone sounded weirdly flat. Was he heartbroken? Still in shock?"

"It was worse than awful." Colleen crumpled up the now empty oyster cracker bags and tossed them back in the breadbasket. "I can't even talk about it."

"It's good to get things out," Aidan said.

Colleen's eyes filled. "No. Like, literally, I can't. I've been advised not to say anything, anyway."

"Ah. You have a lawyer, then?" Aidan asked. "Do you need money for legal fees? Just say the word."

"Thanks. I'm okay on that," Colleen said. "A friend of the Chief's is taking me pro bono. Well, pro bono-*ish*. If I need him. Hopefully I won't."

"So did Colleen tell you she's directing the Paddy's Day show for Bernie?" I asked Aidan.

"She did." He leaned in closer to my sister. "Remember when you came to the final auditions for Irish Steps, years ago? With Deirdre, and maybe Moira, I can't remember. You had it all: talent, looks, personality. You knocked the audition panel out of their chairs. It should have been you up on that stage with me every night."

What? The Guinness swirled bitterly in my gut. Was he hitting on my sister? Completely inappropriate—no, downright sleazy.

Colleen gave a funny little laugh. "I don't know what I was thinking, even showing up. All those rehearsals, the travel . . . No thanks. Deirdre was better than me, anyway."

That's what my sister always told herself. It made me sad when she talked like that. But right now I was thinking about Aidan's whereabouts at the time of his former partner's murder.

He and Moira had both been at the Smiling Shamrock that night. Moira had definitely checked Aidan in, because outside Paddy's Paws today, Una McShane had bragged about that selfie Moira had taken with him. It had to be time-stamped.

Moira and Colleen had walked into Angels Hall around seven, according to Conor, to see Deirdre. Aidan could have shown up there later. What if he and Moira had even worked together after Colleen left, ganging up on Deirdre for different reasons?

At least I could rule out the Witch Sisters, who had zero motive, other than their ongoing game of Family Feud with the

Donnellys. The girls and I had encountered Una in the driveway of the Smiling Shamrock around the time of the murder, out in the pouring rain. Nuala had spied on us from the upstairs window.

My nose twitched, then burned, as I inhaled another wave of strong perfume, more flowery than Aidan's.

Like a determined racehorse, Moira McShane Kelly pushed her way past a group of elderly men toasting each other with Farrell's homemade root beer, nearly knocking them off their stools. She was headed straight for our table.

Trapped.

"Aidan!" Moira squealed, sliding into the booth beside me without an invite. Straight on the ketchup stain. "I figured I'd find you here."

He smiled, but his eyes didn't crinkle quite as charmingly at the corners. "Moira, lovely of you to join us."

She beamed, then seemed to notice my sister and me. "Oh, hey, Colleen," she said. "Heard your show meeting with the parents went well. Best of luck and everything."

Colleen sipped her vodka cranberry. "Thanks, Moira. That means a lot. You remember my sister, Kate, from New York, right?"

Moira gave me a less-than-dazzling smile. "Sure."

Hopefully she hadn't seen me trash all those flyers I'd offered to distribute.

"Tell me more about what you've been up to, Moira, since you left Irish Steps," Aidan said. "We didn't have much chance to chat the other night. You started a dance school in the city, your auntie said?"

"Oh, that." She waved as if the Moira McShane Kelly Academy of Irish Dance was no big deal. "I'd much rather hear about your exciting new show. Crossroad Dreams, right? Because in the old days, Irish people met at the village crossroads to dance."

"Crossroad Dreams with Aidan O'Hearne," he corrected modestly.

"Even better." Moira actually batted her fake eyelashes. "Started casting yet?"

"We have," Aidan said as the bar became oddly bright. Mitzi Dolan-Yung and her cameraperson had arrived, along with a stylist and a young woman lugging a heavy-looking bag. The intern.

Mitzi stopped to interview the old men with the root beer, but the intern kept glancing toward our booth. Only a matter of time before they headed over. Of course they'd want to talk to Aidan O'Hearne for the late news. But murder suspect Colleen Buckley would be a bonus.

"Mitzi alert," I said to my sister in a low voice.

Colleen was already on her feet. "Sorry, guys, gotta go," she announced. "Kate has to tuck the kids into bed. Stop by rehearsal if you can tomorrow, Aidan. The students would be thrilled. Seven o'clock, Great Shamrock Hall. See you around, Moira."

Aidan looked puzzled. "What about your meals?"

"You two can have them," Colleen said. "The burgers are wicked awesome here." She glanced toward the other end of the bar, where Mitzi and her entourage were making steady forward progress.

"This should cover it," I added quickly, tossing two twenties and a ten on the table. I felt Moira's lizard eyes boring into us as she moved aside to let me out of the booth. "'Bye."

I caught up with Colleen at the emergency exit, just past the ladies' room. "Doesn't this door have an alarm?"

"Maybe, but at least we'll be out of here." Colleen pushed on the bar.

Fortunately, no alarm sounded as we stepped into the pouring rain. Another streak of lightning zigzagged through the sky.

"Better than Mitzi," Colleen said. "Race you home."

* * *

Miraculously, my sister and I made it back to the Buckley House without being charbroiled. Mom and the girls had gone to bed, so the Chief and I ate bowls of cold cereal in the kitchen as Colleen dug into the freezer for ice cream.

I hoped Moira and Aidan enjoyed our food.

"Be a good girl and put on the news, would you, Kathleen?" Dad asked, crunching away.

"There's probably something about Deirdre's memorial getting rained out," Colleen said. "And Aidan. And . . . me." She bit her lip, which had given a sudden little quiver.

"Not on my watch, pet," the Chief said.

I felt around the counter for Mom's TV remote. Yup, Mitzi Dolan-Yung was on the story, huddled under a WSCK umbrella in an empty Angels Hall parking lot. She looked cold. Good.

"Shamrock residents, visitors, and Broadway royalty alike came together tonight to pay their respects to Deirdre Donnelly, the former world Irish dance champion and Irish Steps star, found dead Thursday night in Our Lady of Angels Hall. Sadly, Donnelly's death fell in the middle of the town's annual Saint Patrick's Week celebration."

Even Dad stopped chewing. Now Deirdre's murder was a bummer for the Paddy's celebrations?

With a sweep of her arm, Mitzi showed viewers the darkened parking lot. "Hours ago—"

"We don't need to see this." Colleen still sounded nervous. "Find something else, Katie."

"Hold on, now," the Chief said. "Let's see how the media spins things."

I threw up my hands, and Mitzi's report continued by default.

We heard the story of how Deirdre returned to her hometown to teach Irish dance and how her devoted students planned a moving candlelit vigil under the direction of the town's very popular mayor, Ray Flanagan.

Next up: an edited clip of the mayor giving his infomercial on the stage, featuring the part where he'd extolled Shamrock's near-zero crime rate.

The Chief choked a little on his cereal.

"Guess the police are doing an awesome job of deterrence, Daddy," Colleen said.

"How did that guy get elected, anyway?" I asked.

"Greed and money," the Chief said. "This town is full of both."

"The vigil ended early due to tonight's severe thunderstorms," Mitzi continued. "Be sure to check the WSCK website for the rescheduled memorial date."

Behind her, an SPD cruiser turned on its lights and started to pull out of the parking lot. Mitzi ran toward it with her umbrella. She hurried around to the passenger side, where Detective Sergeant Shirley Walker frowned and gave her a brush-off wave before the vehicle zoomed off. Ouch.

Mitzi recovered quickly. "To end our broadcast on a more festive note, here is a live shot from inside Farrell's Pub, where Ms. Donnelly's Irish Steps costar, the legendary Aidan O'Hearne, was spotted by our news crew." She paused. "Aidan, can you hear me? Christina, can you get his attention?"

The intern, holding a microphone as she was jostled by enthusiastic revelers, helplessly shook her head.

Aidan toasted the crowd, and people cheered. Moira was right behind him, waving to the camera.

The live feed returned to Mitzi in the Angels Hall parking lot—flanked by two eager interviewees.

"Meet Shamrock's own Una and Nuala McShane," she said brightly. "Co-owners of the Smiling Shamrock, a charming bed-and-breakfast awarded four full shamrocks from the Chamber of Commerce, they also happen to be twin sisters, originally from the Emerald Isle."

The Chief very noisily shook more cereal into his bowl. I had lost my appetite by now.

"Such a shame, this terrible tragedy," Una said.

Beside her, Nuala looked her usual bloodless self, but she managed to add, "May that poor girl's soul rest in peace."

"As a highlight of Saint Patrick's Week, we'll hold a Blarney Breakfast in Deirdre's honor at the Smiling Shamrock on Monday morning, from half past eight until midday," Una said. "It's open to all—first come, first served—after our VIP guests, of course. And we'll offer a ten percent discount to anyone who books a future reservation at the Smiling Shamrock."

"Blarney Breakfast?" Colleen hooted. "That's a big honor, all right. Deirdre would have absolutely loved that."

"You can turn off the TV now, Katie," the Chief said. "I think we've heard enough."

I silenced Una McShane with the push of a button.

Chapter
Twenty-Two

At nine o'clock sharp the next morning, I answered the front door to find Zoe on the porch.

"Hi, Ms. B. I'm here to see Maeve."

"Hi, Zoe. I don't think she's up yet." At home, my daughter rarely dragged herself out of bed before ten on non-school days. "Come on in."

"Thanks." Zoe stepped past me, wearing black leggings and a sports bra with a wrap-style ballet sweater over it, knotted above her tiny waist. Her dance bag was slung over her shoulder.

A fully dressed Maeve materialized in the hallway outside the kitchen. Shocker.

"Morning, Maeve," Zoe chirped. "Brought you a bagel and some dance shoes that might fit. Your first practice tonight, remember?"

Practice? Another surprise. "Is the bagel green?" Maeve asked.

"Sorry to disappoint, but no." Zoe pulled a small brown-paper-wrapped package from her bag and held it out. "Gluten-free."

"Thanks." Maeve unwrapped the paper and took a bite.

"I figured you'd like it, since you're from New York. My mom won't let Mikey and me have bagels. She owns a yoga studio, and she's always campaigning for healthy food in Shamrock."

Ms. Koo had her work cut out for her. The town had never been known for either healthy food or yoga fans, but that was changing. "Shall I bring out some juice for you girls?" I asked.

"Yes, please," Zoe said.

"Can I have coffee instead?"

Maeve did look a little bleary. I still couldn't believe she was going to a dance practice. Hadn't she told us she didn't want to be in the show?

When I returned with a pitcher of orange juice, my daughter was sprawled at one end of the couch in the living room. Zoe was curled at the other, intent on her phone. She'd changed into a pair of soft leather dance shoes.

"Okay, here you go." Zoe put down her phone and tossed Maeve the dance bag. "The shoes are called ghillies, by the way. I brought a pair of eights and a nine."

"I wear a nine and a half," Maeve said.

"Oops," Zoe said. "Well, they lace up, so you can adjust them. I'll get a bigger size for you tonight. There are socks in there too. We all wear the same kind so they match when we do the steps."

She turned to me. "I brought shoes for Bliz too. The little girls start with regular ballet shoes. They get really excited about earning their first pair of lace-ups. Did the T-shirt fit?"

"It did," I said. "She's thrilled, thanks. She wore it to breakfast this morning."

"Did you hear Mayor Flanagan wants to reschedule Deirdre's vigil for after Paddy's Week?" Maeve said. "Like, after the funeral."

Zoe sipped her juice. "He's worried any more publicity about the murder will scare the tourists away. Plus, he's making me dance at some stupid Blarney Breakfast tomorrow morning. At the Smiling Shamrock. I hate that place."

Me too, I wanted to add. But as a mature adult, I didn't.

Zoe rotated each of her ankles in a circle, then bounced off the couch. "Okay, let's get started. We've got a lot of work to do before tonight."

I handed Maeve a steaming mug of coffee and dropped into a nearby wing chair with mine. "Mind if I watch for a while? I could use a refresher on the dances myself for the music."

"If you want." Maeve took a big swig of coffee. "It may not be pretty."

"You'll do great." Zoe demonstrated some basic steps for Maeve, then stopped and cocked her head. "You're not following this, are you?"

"Not exactly," Maeve admitted. "I'm trying, I swear. It looks so easy when you do it."

I was hardly an Irish dance expert, but I could tell Zoe was a pro. Even doing baby steps, she was a perfect package of precision and grace. And patience.

"We'll start over," she said. "Just listen first, and then watch me again, okay?" She pointed for Maeve to sit back down on the couch.

I went over to sit beside my daughter and put an arm around her shoulders. "You're doing an awesome job," I whispered.

Maeve sighed. "I hate it when you say that and I'm not. This is hopeless."

"You don't need to dance in the show, honey," I said. "We talked about that."

"I told Zoe I'd try. I was delusional."

"There are a few things to remember," Zoe said. "They'll help make you look like a really good Irish dancer, even if you're not."

Maeve nodded.

"First, keep your feet turned out, all the time. Like this." Zoe placed one foot in front of the other. "See how my toes point at ten o'clock and one o'clock? It's fifth position in ballet, but first posi-tion in Irish dance."

I hid a smile. Maeve had taken ballet lessons in New York years ago, with all her friends. She'd lasted two weeks.

"Next thing, you have to stay up on your toes."

Maeve groaned and flopped dramatically back against the cushions.

"You also need to keep your legs crossed the whole time, so you can't even see one of your knees behind the other. And then you just listen to the music and remember your steps."

Maeve covered her face with her hands. "I can't do this."

"Oh, and it's super important to keep your arms at your sides. With your hands in fists. All. The. Time." Zoe gave a brilliant smile. "Got it?"

"Yup." My daughter rose from the couch.

"Let's try it again. Step, hop, one-two-three-four. Step, hop, two-two-three-four . . ."

Maeve tried her best. "You've got this, sweetie," I encouraged her.

"Okay, stop," Zoe said finally. "You're flopping around like Big Bird trying to fly. Arms down, remember? Make those fists. See, like this."

"I am keeping my arms down." Maeve step-hopped uncon-vincingly around the living room.

"Wait, I have an idea," Zoe said. "I brought something else for you, just in case." She ran to her dance bag.

Maeve stopped hopping. "What is it?" she asked warily.

"Close your eyes," Zoe directed, "and put your arms at your sides, nice and tight."

I watched, half fascinated and half horrified, as she quickly wrapped Maeve's arms to her body with a roll of shamrock-printed tape. The kind people used to keep their suitcases closed.

Maeve's eyes flew open. "Are you serious? I can't even move now. Look." She jumped up and down like the spare key in Mom's baby food jar, almost falling sideways once or twice.

Zoe grinned. "Much better."

"Mom, you're making me nervous," Maeve said. "Can you please leave?"

Not exactly a question. I didn't want to be "that mom" who hung out with her daughter's friends anyway. I'd done enough of that already. "Sure, have fun."

I retreated to the kitchen, where I soon found myself elbow-deep in liquid soap bubbles, after offering to help Colleen with the dishes from the guests' Continental breakfast.

"You missed a spot." My sister pointed to a stubborn streak of dried jam. "Wash it again, please." She handed back the plate.

"Nope. What the washer misses the drier wipes off, remember?"

"Fine." Colleen snapped me lightly with the dish towel. "I'll wash, then, and you can dry."

"We're almost done."

"I know." My sister smiled and flipped the towel onto her shoulder. "So what's the deal with you and Garrett?" she asked, leaning casually against the counter. "You two rekindling your big romance?"

"No." I hit the faucet harder than I'd intended, and the soap bubbles rose precariously high in the sink. "What gave you that crazy idea?"

She shrugged innocently. "I can just tell."

"We hardly know each other anymore. Besides, he's a cop."

"Is that a problem?" Colleen flicked the jam off the plate with one fingernail.

"Careful," I said. "You'll scratch the gold edge."

She dropped the plate back in the water. "What do you have against guys on the force? He came by the house this morning, you know. To talk to the Chief, but I bet he was disappointed he didn't run into you."

"Mm-hmm." I hit Spray, and foam flew in every direction. "Look, Garrett's a great guy, but I have no interest in dating him or anyone else right now. I have my hands full enough with the girls and trying to make ends meet."

And you, I almost added. How could she be thinking about my love life when she was a suspect in a murder investigation?

"Quit it, you're getting my top wet," Colleen complained, brushing droplets from her cropped pink sweatshirt. "But you still think Garrett's cute, right?"

"Even if I did, it's not like the girls and I live here," I said. "And for all I know, he could have a girlfriend." I removed a long tail of foam from the edge of the sink.

"Nope," Colleen said. "He's still probably crushing on you after all these years. You two are getting up there, you know." She tried to balance a platter on top of a precarious pile of clean dishes, before giving up and setting it on the table. "He was seeing Megan Feeley for a while, but I don't know how serious they were. She wanted to get engaged, I think."

I truly wasn't interested in another relationship right now—maybe ever. One failed marriage was enough.

"Megan's nice," my sister said. "But not as hot as you, if you'd put in a teensy bit of effort."

"First, Garrett and I aren't *old*," I said. "And I'm a mom. I don't have to be hot. I wouldn't be interested in a guy who was shallow enough to care about that, anyway."

"Moms can be hot." Colleen started on a serving bowl.

"I know," I said. "That just isn't me." My sister had plenty of free time to spend on her appearance and going to parties and bars. She didn't have a ton of responsibilities, other than helping Mom and Dad. But I wouldn't trade places with her for a second. I liked my life, and Colleen was happy with hers. As far as I knew.

"I heard you were thinking of moving to the city," I said casually. "What's up with that?"

"I'm not going anywhere," Colleen said. "I can't leave Mom and Dad. And I can't afford to live in New York like you. Or Boston either." She hunted in a drawer for a fresh dish towel and pulled out one with a sheep embroidered on it. A tiny brass bell hung from its neck. "You know, I was thinking, Katie. What if you and the girls stayed here in Shamrock for a while? I mean, Mom and the Chief would be thrilled. We could always use more help running this place, with Mom getting older and all."

I stared at my sister. Did she mean for a week or two? After Deirdre's murder was solved? Or permanently?

"And the Chief really misses you. You're his favorite, you know."

"That's ridiculous." Our dad loved all three of us kids equally. Maybe not in the same way, though. We had pretty different personalities.

"You could work from here, and Mom and I could help with the girls," Colleen went on. "Maeve's growing up so fast. She'll be in college before you know it. And I'd love to spend more time with Bliz." She threw me a sideways look. "Plus, maybe you and Garrett could see how things go. Added bonus."

I ignored that last part, but I felt a little pang about the rest of what she'd said. Mom and Dad were slowing down. The girls were speeding up. But spend more time in Shamrock, a place I both loved and hated? My childhood home? My life would be moving backward, not forward.

I was saved from answering when Maeve and Zoe burst into the kitchen. Maeve's cheeks were each dotted with one rosy spot, and she looked sweaty. Zoe was completely put together, as usual.

"How'd the rest of the dance lesson go?" I asked.

"She made a ton of progress for her first day. Right, Maeve?"

"Oh, yeah." My daughter rubbed at the sleeves of her long-sleeved T-shirt, where the tape had left some glue. "I'm a real pro now." She looked at me. "Zoe invited me over to her house. We're going to hang out at the Square first. Is that okay? I can walk over with her to practice tonight."

Officially, I'd never handed down the grounding I'd planned after her Lucky's stunt. But it was a good thing for Maeve to have friends her own age here in Shamrock, especially after the murder. And Zoe was a nice girl. "Fine," I said. "Have fun, and we'll see you there. Make good choices," I called after them as they left.

Maeve didn't look back, but I felt the eye roll.

"What's on the dinner menu?" I asked Colleen, who was poking around in the cabinets.

"Not sure yet," Colleen said. "Something easy. Aha. Potato leek soup. I'll throw it into the crockpot now. And then we can have toasted cheese sandwiches with onion and tomato."

"So . . . pizza again, pretty much?"

"Sort of," Colleen said. "I don't have time to go to the store, with rehearsal coming up. And Mom can offer any leftovers to the guests when they get back from the Touch o' the Green sidewalk sale."

The event, put on by local merchants, was held multiple times a year. A chance for retailers to get rid of seasonal touristy junk to make room for more.

"Do we have any guests left?" I asked. "Seems like they've all been leaving."

"Just a few," Colleen said. "I think I've talked Mom out of officially adding guest meals, but soup and sandwiches are easy. You know. The home-cooked touch."

I headed to the fridge. "Okay, I'll chop the leeks."

Colleen waved. "Thanks, but I've got this. You go do something else." She threw me a little smile. "The show music is in my bag. In the hall."

"Right," I said, taking the hint. "I'm on it." If Maeve was making a brave attempt to dance with the Beginner kids in the show, I could plunk out a tune or two on the old Buckley piano.

I extracted the ream of faded sheets from Colleen's jam-packed designer tote—how could she lug around that much *stuff*?—and headed to the corner by the drapes. At least the police scanner was off, for once.

I dropped onto the bench, arranged a few pages in front of me, and stared at the music. The notes and registers looked like some kind of foreign language. I frowned and leaned closer. Maybe I needed glasses. I placed my hands tentatively on the yellowed keys but couldn't bring myself to press down.

What was wrong with me? This was ridiculous. All I kept seeing in my mind was Ian, jamming with his band under the bright spotlights of some steamy stage.

Then my ex and his bandmates disappeared, replaced by three Irish dancers. One in front, two in the back. At first, I thought the main dancer was Deirdre, with Moira and Colleen. But the more I tried to see their faces, the blurrier they got. And then there was the music: that awful jig from Angels Hall on the night of Deirdre's murder.

I covered my face with my hands, willing it all to stop. The stress of the past few days was getting to me. To distract myself, I reached for my phone on top of the piano.

201

I was going to check my email, but instead I started googling info for the case. Deirdre's death seemed to be getting more attention internationally than in the States. The Irish sites all glowingly mentioned Deirdre's mother, the former world Irish dance champion Bernadette McFadden. Sometimes I forgot she'd been a champion too.

I hardly recognized her in the old photos, except for the wry smile. She looked a lot like Deirdre back then. So sad.

I was relieved that none of the articles mentioned Colleen. They didn't name any other persons of interest either. Mayor Flanagan and the Shamrock PD were doing a fine job of squelching information.

Next, I pulled up the Donnelly School of Dance website, which I'd only glanced at earlier. I found outdated class times, links to their Facebook page and Irish Steps, bios of Deirdre and Bernie. A short history of the school. Old photos of dancers and performances.

I even spotted one of Maeve from years ago, sitting cross-legged on the floor and drinking from a water bottle. *Aww.*

I saved the photo to my phone, then skimmed the text on the landing page. No mention of Deirdre's death—not even the vigil info—and it was clear no one had updated anything on the site in a long time. This was where Moira's marketing skills could be useful, I had to admit.

I hated to google her dance academy because I didn't want to up her search rankings. I also didn't need any ads popping up whenever I went online. But I couldn't resist.

A couple of clicks later, I discovered that Moira's school in New York was . . . closed. Permanently. No details.

Huh. So that explained why Moira was so eager to open her business in Shamrock.

I backtracked to the Donnelly School's Facebook page. It was private, like the one for Maeve's soccer team back in the city. Group administrator: Theresa Meaney. I'd need to be approved before I could view any posts. No thanks.

I also checked Deirdre's fan page—she didn't seem to have any personal social media accounts, just a few that the marketing folks at Irish Steps probably handled. I found mostly clips and tributes to their late star—and a banner announcing that tickets were still available for the week's performances. Kerri Coyle would dance the lead with Aidan O'Hearne's understudy, Milo Washington.

I frowned. Irish Steps shows were almost always sold out. Now they were advertising tickets. Could anyone else at Irish Steps besides Aidan have been angry with Deirdre for retiring at the top of her game?

Probably not. Dancers got injured, burned out, or aged out of productions all the time. That was the biz. And the show always went on, just like in Shamrock.

That tradition was supposed to be inspiring, but it was a little sad in Deirdre's case. No matter how big a star she'd been in the Irish dance world, that tiny galaxy was just a part of a much larger universe. Someone had put out Deirdre's star, and I wouldn't let them get away with it. Not just because some thought my sister was the murderer. Because it was the right thing to do.

I placed my phone back on top of the piano, then sat there again, staring at the keys. I didn't feel overcome with stress this time. No weird visions. Just . . . empty.

The Chief had creaked into his usual spot in his wheelchair. He nodded toward the piano. "What do you have there, Katie?"

"Just some music for the show."

"Grand," he said. "Play us a tune."

My eyes filled with tears. "I-I can't."

"Sure you can."

"Dad, I don't know what's wrong. I'm frozen up or something."

The Chief did his fingertip-steeple thing, and I had the distinct feeling he was reading my mind. "You're a talented girl, Kathleen," he said. "Your mother and I never understood why you gave up your music. You used to love it so."

I bit my lip. "I'm . . . worried about things right now. Colleen, the case, my life. I keep thinking—"

"Maybe you think too much," my dad said. "There's a time for thinking, and a time for doing."

I didn't answer, because I really hated to admit he was right. Poor Dad. He had one daughter who thought too much before doing, and another who did too much without thinking.

"You play, and I'll rest my eyes for a bit." He leaned back in his chair. "Go on, now. I'm half deaf anyway."

Totally untrue. The family joke was that the Chief had very selective hearing. He heard what he wanted to hear, and woe to anyone who tried to slide anything past him. I smoothed the page in front of me: "Irish Wedding Dance."

Of course. That was the song the band had played at my and Ian's reception at the local FOP Lodge banquet hall. My dad and I had danced to it together, mere weeks before his accident.

"Sorry, Dad," I whispered. "I can't."

Chapter Twenty-Three

I waited in the kitchen for Bliz and Colleen, finishing off a Flake bar as Mom whipped up a batch of brownies. Six forty-five. At this rate, we'd be late for our first official show practice at Great Shamrock Hall.

Bliz burst into the kitchen, wearing her new Donnelly School T-shirt and her little plaid school skirt. She was followed by the Chief in his wheelchair, his *Shamrock Sentinel* folded on his lap. The front-page headline was only partly visible, but I could make it out: "All Eyes Are Smiling in Shamrock—It's St. Paddy's Week!"

I could think of plenty of eyes that were not smiling at all.

Oh, and there was also a photo of guys in a speedboat turning Emerald Lake electric green for Paddy's Week by adding orange vegetable dye. Who knew how that combo worked. Completely nontoxic, they claimed.

"Guess what, Mommy?" Bliz was ready to pop with excitement. "I know how to Irish dance for real now!"

"That's great, honey."

"She's been dancing all over the house." The Chief smiled indulgently at his younger granddaughter. "A real firecracker, this one. Think it'd be safer for the furniture and all those cockamamie knickknacks of yours, Eileen, if she stayed in here with you."

"Watch me, watch me!" Bliz sang. She danced around the kitchen, her strawberry-blond braids bouncing. "Step, hop, one-two-three-four; step, hop, two-two-three-four . . ."

I stared at her happy little self as she circled the kitchen table. Toes pointed. Balanced hops. Light, quick steps. Chin up. Even Zoe would be impressed. Bliz didn't need any tape to keep her fists firmly at her sides.

"Wow, where did you learn that?" I asked.

"Aunt Colleen," Bliz replied. "She showed me this afternoon. She's a really good dancer."

"Oh." I shook off a tiny pang of jealousy as Colleen appeared in the doorway. "Guess she's a good teacher too."

"Bernie was right, the kid's a natural," my sister said as Bliz danced over to throw her arms around Colleen's waist.

"Mary Elizabeth, you will tire yourself out before the rehearsal," Mom said. "Want a taste of mint frosting from the beaters?"

My daughter abandoned her blossoming Irish dance career faster than Michael Flatley's feet. "Not too much," I called as she zoomed toward the counter.

"We'd better get going," Colleen said. Like Bliz, she wore black leggings, but hers were shiny and clingy. She wore a flippy little black dance skirt over them, with a low-scooped black leotard top and sky-high purple heels.

"Think you'll be able to, um, move in those shoes?" I asked her.

"Sure," Colleen said. "I can dance all night in these things. Flat shoes make my feet hurt. I need the arch support."

I looked down at my sneakers. I couldn't remember the last time I'd danced. Or even worn cute shoes. But I had plenty of arch support.

"We can take my car," Colleen offered.

I stuffed the show music packet back into the tote on her shoulder, and the three of us were soon squeezed into the Mini Cooper. Bliz and I sat in back, because the front seat was packed with more of Colleen's stuff: a plastic file box, a bulging Target bag, and who knew what else. It felt like we were crammed into a clown car. At least I could redo Bliz's braids on the way.

"Take this, will you?" Colleen dumped her giant tote over the seat. I put it on the floor between my sneakers.

It was a short drive to the Square, especially the way my sister drove. "Hold still," I told Bliz. She was wiggling so much in her excitement as I tried to tame her slippery curls that I dropped the plastic barrettes on the floor.

As I reached to retrieve them, I noticed a binder-clipped document behind the stack of sheet music. The clip had caught one of the pages. I pulled the whole pile out and carefully freed the trapped sheet, then froze. The clipped packet looked very legal and official. Strangely familiar too.

"Hold on a sec, honey," I told Bliz, scanning the front page. Colleen was switching her playlist and zooming the Mini toward Great Shamrock Hall like a guided missile.

The document was a lease for a studio apartment in Brooklyn, New York, starting March 15. No wonder it looked familiar—the property management company and the listed address matched the building where the girls and I lived.

So Colleen planned to move to the city after all. Not just to Brooklyn, or our neighborhood, but to our exact building. What was all that she'd told me about not having the money, then? And suggesting we could all stay here in Shamrock and help Mom and Dad?

March 15 was tomorrow, for heaven's sake. Was my sister not so broke after all? The down payment alone of first and last months' rent, plus security deposit and broker's fee, was an astronomical amount. But why was she pushing us to uproot our lives and move to Shamrock, while she planned to live the high life—without a job, as far as I knew—in the Big Apple?

Or ended up in jail. Either way, so much for all being together as a family.

"Mommy, hurry up," Bliz said. "We're here already."

I snapped the barrettes back into place just as Colleen swerved expertly into a parking spot across from the municipal building. "There you go. You're gorgeous."

As we started up the wide marble steps to Shamrock Hall, I had a pretty good idea of how criminals felt on the way to face the judge at the courthouse next door.

Confused. Nervous. Angry. Hopeless.

"Ow!" Ahead of me and Bliz, Colleen grabbed her foot and leaned against a scrolled white pillar at the top step. "I think I twisted something."

At that very moment, Maeve arrived with Zoe and two other girls. "Hi, honey," I called to Maeve. "Can you take Bliz and go on ahead? We'll catch up."

"Through the double doors, downstairs, and to the right," Colleen added, wincing in pain. Maeve already had her little sister by the hand.

They looked worried, but I waved them on. "She's just resting her foot for a minute."

"I'm fine." Colleen straightened and hobbled after the girls as they disappeared into the building. "I'll walk it off a little."

I took her by the arm. "Well, take off those heels, or your foot will swell."

With a deep sigh of frustration, she took my suggestion for once and wedged them in her bag.

"So, you're moving to New York after all?" I asked.

She took a wobbly step back. "What?"

"The lease in your bag. It was with the music. I wasn't snooping."

"I told you, I was planning to move," Colleen said. "But things didn't work out. I didn't sign that lease because I didn't have the money." She sighed. "Well, I did. For a while."

"You mean, you spent the money Deirdre lent you on something else?" I said, incredulous.

My sister's eyes flashed. "You can lose the attitude, Kate. You don't understand my life at all, or how much stuff costs."

"Oh, please." I threw up my hands. "I live in the city with two kids, and I have plenty of life stuff of my own going on, thanks very much. Things cost way more in New York than they do here in Shamrock."

"It's none of your business anyway."

"It is when it affects my life." My pulse pounded in my temples. "And the kids'. Did you really think you could just move to the big city for kicks, and we'd switch places so I'd help run the Buckley House? Have you lost your freaking mind?" I was so mad I felt dizzy.

"Stop yelling. It's nothing like that at all. And can we talk about this later? We'll miss the whole practice."

Theresa Meaney was heading up the steps now, with her overactive grandson and Darcy. Colleen was right. We couldn't have this discussion here in public. Her new students were waiting for her. But we would hash this out ASAP.

"Just tell me one thing," I said. "Why did you want the girls and me to come out here to Shamrock, and why do we have to stay?"

"You don't," Colleen said, almost in a whisper. Her face had paled under her rosy makeup. She looked . . . crumpled.

Something was definitely off, but there was no point in pushing it. She needed to be upbeat and focused right now. I sighed. "Come on, let's go. The kids are counting on you."

"Us," Colleen corrected.

"Right." I held one of the doors open, and my sister limped through it. *Why couldn't she be straight with me for once?* I wondered as we headed along the swirly green carpet and down the stairs to the auditorium. She could have told me she wanted to move to the city. Maybe we could still work something out. Our apartment was miniscule, but she could surf on the foldout couch. Temporarily.

But that left Mom and Dad and the Buckley House high and dry.

I heard the tapping and pounding of hard shoes even before we entered the giant hall. Plenty of dancers had already arrived, their family members and guardians settled into velvet folding seats.

I gazed in awe at the polished mahogany balconies, glittering chandeliers, and paneled murals. A huge, dark-green dome arched overhead, dotted with pinpoint lights like Shamrock's version of the constellation ceiling in Grand Central Station's main concourse.

None of the kids noticed us at first. Most were too busy dancing around the stage in all different directions—jumping, kicking, stomping, twirling. Even the beginners were intent on their steps, except for one who sat on the edge of the stage, munching a bag of pretzels and swinging her legs. Maeve.

Bliz spotted us and ran up to take my hand. Guess she wasn't ready quite yet to join the other dancers after all. She looked up at me, and I gave her hand a little squeeze.

"We can wait on the piano, Kate," Colleen said. "We'll just be organizing and working on steps to start, I think. Conor's talking to the sound guy again. Some kind of tech stuff for the Irish Steps numbers. Aidan pulled some strings and got permission for Zoe to use Deirdre's old music."

"Okay, I'll just watch for a bit, then," I said, but my sister was already marching down the aisle with her giant bag. She'd slipped on her old dance shoes, and the limp had disappeared. Colleen was tougher than she appeared sometimes.

Bliz and I watched as Zoe zipped diagonally across the stage like lightning, whirling her way through the other dancers without missing a step. She leaped into the air with one foot tucked under her butt and the other pointed straight out, landing about two inches from another dancer, who executed a fast kick of her own above her head.

Yikes. Kids could get hurt out there.

"I want to dance like Zoe," Bliz said. "Maybe Aunt Colleen can show me how to jump like that."

"Someday, sweetie," I said. "Why don't you go have fun? I'll walk down with you."

My daughter nodded, and we headed down the aisle. At the stage steps near the piano, Bliz suddenly stopped short, squeezing my hand a little tighter. "Want to stay with me and watch for a while?" I looked for Maeve but didn't see her. Colleen was busy trying to call for attention.

Bliz followed me over to the shining grand piano. I carefully lifted the lid over the ivory keys, then slammed a loud chord. At the same time, Colleen gave an earsplitting whistle.

The tapping and thudding ceased on a dime.

"Okay, dancers!" Colleen called. "Time to start our first official practice in Great Shamrock Hall. Are you all excited for the show?"

Cheers and clapping sounded through the auditorium. The acoustics seemed pretty good to me.

"Everybody over here to the front, please," Colleen said.

There had to be at least sixty kids in all, most but not all of them girls, ranging in age from four or so to teen. Maeve stood in the shadows at the other side of the gigantic stage. I smiled encouragingly from the piano, but she pretended not to see me.

Colleen introduced herself as a past student and the new show director. Then she told the kids how sorry she was about the loss of her good friend, Miss Deirdre, and how much the Donnelly School and all her students had meant to her.

Most of the dancers stared silently down from the stage. Others looked away. One girl burst into tears, and then another. In seconds, half of the kids were crying. The adults swiped at their eyes or loudly blew their noses.

Oh no. The pomp and grandeur of Great Shamrock Hall and the reality of Deirdre's loss had added another degree of sadness to the situation. My sister looked helplessly over at me.

I rose from the piano and jogged up the stage steps. "It's okay to be sad, everyone," I said over the sobs and sniffles. "I'm Ms. Buckley, Miss Colleen's sister, and I'll be helping with the music. All of this is very, very hard, we know. But just think of how proud you're going to make Miss Deirdre and Miss Bernie. I promise, you're in great hands with Miss Colleen. She's a fantastic teacher, and like she said, she used to dance with Miss Deirdre. She was also her very best friend, so she knows how sad you feel right now."

Was it my imagination, or did Theresa Meaney give a gravelly harrumph? I ignored it.

"Everything's going to be just fine," I said. "So let's get started and do Miss Deirdre and Miss Bernie proud."

A borrowed line from the Chief, but it seemed to work. The tears and sniffs slowed, and the first group of dancers stepped forward and gathered around my sister. Colleen smiled at me and mouthed a thank-you.

I returned to my bench, just as Garrett's sister, Siobhan, pushed through the auditorium doors. Behind her tumbled three little girls, laughing and pushing. Aside from their wildly assorted hair colors, they looked like mini clones. Siobhan waggled her fingers at me as she came down the aisle. She headed straight to the piano, the rambunctious triplets still in her wake. When she stopped they dominoed against her.

"Hey there, Kate," she said. "We made it. Have you seen Conor?"

"Hi," I said. "Not yet, but Colleen said he's here."

"Okay, I'll find him. I brought the rest of the crew." Siobhan pointed out each of her daughters. "Fiona here with the dark hair, Brogan's our blonde, and the carrottop is Ginger."

"And this is Bliz," I said. She peeked out from around me on the bench.

"What kind of name is that?" Fiona wrinkled her nose. Bliz shrank back.

I willed myself not to intervene. Bliz wasn't shy with other kids, exactly, but she could be a little sensitive sometimes.

Her excitement over her first practice must have won out, though, because she jumped off the bench. "It's a nickname," she said. "My real name is Mary Elizabeth."

"I have a funny name too," Ginger said. "It's Sinéad, but everyone calls me Ginger because of my hair."

Brogan, the blonde, ran forward and linked Bliz's arm through hers. "You dance, right? Now we'll have four for the ceili reel. You can be my partner."

The Murphy girls and Bliz took off toward the stage, giggling, and I breathed a sigh of relief.

"Looks like she's all set," Siobhan said with a grin. "Adorable. I've got to pick up some things at the store while my little darlings are occupied. Will you text me if anything . . . goes wrong?"

"Sure," I said. "But no worries, everything's under control here, and the cops are around somewhere too. I'll keep an eye on the girls." We exchanged numbers, and Garrett's sister was off with her thanks and another wave. "Don't forget about that drink," she called over her shoulder. "You have my number now."

I turned my attention back to the stage. The dancers seemed calmer now, listening intently to Colleen as she explained what numbers they'd run through first. Zoe stood behind her, making notes on a clipboard.

"Hi, Ms. B." Conor appeared beside me, now that his mom had left, and set down his pawn-shop accordion case.

Zoe came up within two seconds. "Good, you're back," she said to Conor. "Miss Colleen changed her mind, so we'll need you both for the accompaniment soon."

"No problem," I said, amused to be directed by a fourteen-year-old. My sister was busily arranging dancers in rows.

"Did you remember to bring the music?" Zoe asked Conor.

"Ms. B has it. I think."

I brought out the sheet music from the bag, minus the rental lease. "Got it."

Zoe consulted her clipboard and frowned. "Uh-oh. Miss Colleen signed Maeve up for the Beginner Slip Jig. Not sure she's *totally* ready for that, but . . . hey, check out Bliz up there. She's doing great."

Bliz and Brogan skipped in a circle across from Fiona and Ginger, holding hands over their heads. They seemed to be having fun.

Maeve was nowhere in sight. "Natalie!" Zoe called to the girl with the braids from Lucky's, who was changing into her hard shoes at the corner of the stage. "Can you find Maeve and help her with the slip jig? Take her out in the hall so you'll have more room."

Conor and I chose pieces for each number, then started to play for the first dance on Colleen's cue. Half an hour into the practice, I finally began to relax into the music. As my sister led the dancers through short drills, we played the same short sections over and over, with plenty of breaks between numbers as Colleen worked with kids on steps.

Bliz took to the stage like a baby turtle to the sea, and after her quick private lesson with Natalie, Maeve seemed more comfortable too. She'd been grouped with older beginners, but many were still half her height, so she was assigned to the back row.

Halfway through the practice, Colleen called a twenty-minute recess. Some of the dancers flopped onto the stage, while others practiced steps. Time for me to take a bio break. Plus, my head hurt from all the floor pounding.

Hoping to find a more private powder room, I left the auditorium through the back doors and took a right down the carpeted hall toward a gilt-framed sign that said "Ladies." On the way, I spotted a flash of black-and-white stripes in one of the floor-length mirrors, also framed in gold. Behind me, Moira McShane Kelly was sneaking in one of the side doors to the auditorium.

What was she doing here? I glanced around, but it was just the two of us. When I looked back, Zebra Woman had already disappeared. Had I imagined her?

Retracing my steps, I slipped through the same side door. The back of the auditorium was dark, and taped Irish music played in surround sound. I didn't see Moira anywhere. Maybe—

Someone grabbed me roughly from behind, clapping a leather-gloved hand tightly over my mouth. I couldn't tell if my attacker was male or female, but I sensed the person was tall. Then I felt something hard and metal pressed into my back.

A gun?

The gloved fingers covered both my nose and mouth, and I couldn't breathe. The darkness swallowed me up.

Chapter
Twenty-Four

Next thing I knew, I was gasping for air in a pool of sweat, my cheek lodged against the back of a velvet auditorium chair.

My mysterious attacker with the leather gloves was gone. And so was Moira.

"Kate, are you okay?"

Aidan O'Hearne's handsome face frowned down at me, his blond hair strangely pink in the glow from the fire exit sign.

I nodded and struggled to a full sitting position, feeling disoriented in the dark auditorium. I must have passed out. From what seemed like very far away, I heard scratchy Irish music playing.

The music abruptly stopped. "Okay, that's better," a familiar voice called. Colleen. "But ladies, this number is a group effort. Let's work together more this time. One-two-three, two-two-three . . ."

"She doesn't look so hot," another voice said over Aidan's shoulder. Theresa Mooney. No, Meaney. "You hit your noggin?"

"No," I said, gingerly testing. "I don't think so."

"Okay, then, back on your feet, Princess." Theresa grabbed my hand and practically yanked me out of my sneakers. "You wasted or somethin'?"

Ms. Tea and Sympathy. I felt like kicking her, and my foot unconsciously jerked a little in her direction. Instead it hit something metal, a cylinder, which rolled somewhere under the seats. A flashlight. That must have been what my attacker pushed against the middle of my back, trying to scare me. Not a gun, thank heavens. "No," I said again. "I'm fine. I must have fainted or something. Low blood sugar."

No way would I tell Theresa and Aidan I'd been attacked. Not yet, anyway. It could have been either or both of them. Or Moira. Had she doubled back from wherever she'd disappeared to and scared the living daylights out of me as a warning to mind my own business?

"Do you need an ambulance?" Aidan glanced toward the seats. "We must have some medical professionals here."

"Really not necessary, thanks. I feel super," I lied.

"All right, then, let's get you to a seat, if you're not too wobbly." Aidan didn't seem completely convinced. "I'll tell Colleen." He waved in the direction of the stage, but my sister didn't notice. No one did.

"Please don't bother her," I said. "Or anyone. I don't want to interrupt the rehearsal. I'm supposed to be playing the piano," I added, as Aidan and Theresa escorted me down the aisle.

Theresa's grip on my arm was extra-tight.

"You need a sit-down," Aidan said firmly. "You've had a spell of some sort. They're working on steps right now, so they'll use the tapes. Or that kid on his phone up there can play the accordion."

"Here." Theresa dug in her jacket pocket and pulled out a pack of gum. "Have a piece. There's a lotta sugar in it. Heck, take the whole thing."

"One is great, thanks." I politely extracted a wrapped stick. Hades would freeze over before I put it in my mouth. Probably poisoned.

"I'd be happy to run you back to the Buckley House," Aidan offered. "My Mercedes is parked out front in the mayor's VIP spot."

"Appreciate the offer, but I'm good." I frowned. "Didn't you say you took an Uber from the airport?"

He looked puzzled. "Are you some kind of travel agent, Kate? You have a keen interest in transportation and itineraries. Thought your sister said you were an accountant."

"I am."

"The Uber dropped me at Emerald Prestige Auto Rentals. They opened up just for me."

"How nice." And how convenient that he'd been the one to find me after I'd been attacked. So quickly too. Had Aidan been lurking in the back of the auditorium the whole time?

And where were the cops who were supposed to be working security? My attacker might go after someone else next. Garrett and Frank had to be here somewhere. I'd text them as soon as I got rid of these two.

"Oh, poor Colleen's sister! Are you okay, hon? You look like death." Moira McShane Kelly popped up from a row of seats midway down the aisle. "You and Aidan can sit right here with me if you don't feel well. We'll keep an eye on you."

I bet. Hadn't I been chasing after her just before I'd been attacked? Maybe she'd snuck in and settled into the seats so she could pretend she'd been there the whole time.

Moira had a lot of moxie, as Mom would say. What was she doing at a Donnelly School practice? Scouting? Pilfering students? Stalking Buckleys?

This wasn't Moira's show. Had Colleen spotted her yet?

No, right now my sister was mediating some intense discussion between Darcy and Zoe.

"Gotta go." Theresa glanced toward the stage. "Feel better, kid." She stomped down the aisle.

Moira patted the seat next to her. "Bring Kate right over here, Aidan. We'll take good care of her, won't we? We have so much to talk about."

She and I, or she and Aidan? Moira had shown up because she'd heard my sister invite him last night to stop by the rehearsal. She was dying for him to cast her in his new show. Or get his endorsement for her new dance academy.

Zero concept of reality, but Moira was no quitter. And maybe, somehow, a killer.

Aidan gestured ahead of him into the row with a gallant flourish. I dropped down next to an ecstatic Moira.

Fine. I could keep an eye on both of them and watch the onstage action at the same time. Everything seemed okay up there now. Darcy and Zoe were taking water bottle breaks while Colleen worked with a group of younger girls.

Someone in the audience spotted Aidan, and an excited buzz ran through the auditorium. He waved away the attention with a good-natured smile and pointed toward the kids onstage.

Colleen threw him a quick dimple.

I didn't get it. Babysitting me and having a little chat with Moira McShane Kelly couldn't have been what the great Aidan O'Hearne had in mind for his Sunday afternoon in Shamrock.

Then it finally dawned on me. He wanted my sister. *Duh.* It had been totally obvious last night, but I'd been too busy focusing on him as a murder suspect. They'd known each other for years, through Deirdre.

And if Aidan and Moira had both murdered Deirdre—or one was covering for the other—was this whole thing between them an act? They were seasoned performers. Had that selfie Una had shown me outside Paddy's Paws been edited?

One thing was for sure. My gloved attacker had shown up to play. He or she knew I was snooping around on the case, or at least that I'd been following Moira. They'd succeeded in scaring the bejeezus out of me. But what did they *really* want? And if the person wasn't Aidan or Moira, who were they, and where were they now?

This sucked. Here I was, wedged in a cramped seat between two of my prime suspects and their dueling perfumes.

Wait. Had my nose burned like this as the mystery attacker approached? *No.*

The person had been quick in covering my nose and mouth, but still. I needed to alert Garrett or Frank right this second.

Moira was already talking Aidan's ear off again about his show and the new dance video of herself she was about to post online. He kept his eyes on the stage, and probably my sister.

As I reached down toward my bag for my phone, I noticed that Aidan was not wearing gloves. Had he worn a pair at Deirdre's vigil, or when he'd appeared at Farrell's? No idea. But he might have them in the pockets of his suede jacket right now.

Trying to confirm that might be risky, with me seated this close to him. Not to mention embarrassing. What if he thought Colleen's much-older sister was trying to hit on him? With his big head, he probably would.

Moira was so busy chatting she didn't notice me check out her half-open bag on the floor next to mine. Not as packed as Colleen's, mostly flyers and makeup, but I spotted a pair of black gloves tucked on one side near the top. Velvet. Not leather.

Scanning the floor near the seats reminded me of the flashlight I'd kicked away earlier. The one that had felt like a gun at my back. The person must have dropped it as they fled.

Still keeping my head down, I shot Garrett a quick we-have-a-situation text. I told him to meet me near the main doors to the auditorium ASAP—and if he wasn't in Great Shamrock Hall already, to send Frank or someone else.

Then I added another text asking him to let me know when he got to the doors. I didn't want to leave the auditorium until someone from the force showed up. I needed to keep an eye on the rehearsal—and Aidan and Moira—in the meantime.

"Excuse me," I said to my caretakers, rising to my feet. "I have to use the ladies' room."

"Want me to go with you, hon?" Moira was all heavily-mascaraed sweetness.

"No, thank you," I said. She looked relieved as Aidan jumped up to let me out of the row. "Be careful, Kate," he said. "We don't want another accident."

Was that a semi-veiled threat, or did he just think Colleen's sister was a total klutz?

I kept my phone tightly in hand as I hurried up the aisle. I wasn't dizzy anymore. If anyone came near me, I'd be ready this time—and I'd scream like a banshee before anyone could silence me.

When I reached the spot where I'd been attacked, I dropped to all fours and checked as best I could under the seats with my cell phone flashlight.

My attacker's flashlight was gone, as far as I could tell. Had it rolled all the way down to the stage without anyone noticing? Or had someone come back to retrieve it?

I was taking a final look when Garrett squatted beside me. "Katie?"

No time to waste being mortified, on top of the dumpster diving deal. I snapped to a sitting position. "You were supposed to meet me outside the doors."

"Your brother's there. Thought you might want a heads-up. I told him you needed help, and I was going in."

Great. I'd be in for a Frank lecture later.

I briefly filled Garrett in on what had happened, and his mouth formed a thin line. "You should have texted right away. You or someone else could have been hurt worse. A kid, even. Who knows where the perp is now?"

All true. Whatever reasoning I'd used in my oxygen-deprived daze had been totally stupid. "I know. I'm sorry. I was disoriented."

"Well, glad you're okay," Garrett said. "Sure you don't want to get checked out?"

I shook my head as I pulled myself up. "I'm fine. Where were you guys?"

"I was in the parking lot," he said. "We've got two cars out there, plus unis manning all entrances and exits to the building. Two more backstage. And Frank. He just came on duty."

"No one was at these doors when I came into the lobby. Not that I noticed, anyway."

"Maybe you just didn't see them, and they didn't notice anyone suspicious, so they stayed in place."

Well, that was possible. A lot of people had gone through these doors. Parents, guardians, kids, Moira, Aidan . . . And plenty of them wearing gloves, I was sure.

"I thought the point was to make everyone feel safer."

"Flanagan didn't want the security to be too obvious."

Pathetic. Was the Shamrock PD scared of Mayor Windbag? Did they need funding approved for a new police cruiser or something? The Chief needed to have a serious talk with his old buddy Bob Ryan.

"At least we know one thing," I said. "If the person who attacked me was Deirdre's murderer, it wasn't Colleen. She was up onstage the whole time."

"Or it could have been a completely unrelated situation. And the way a detective might look at it, well . . . you're her sister. You could have . . ." He hesitated.

"Made up the whole story to throw off suspicion? Seriously?"

Garrett shrugged. "I'm just saying, that's a possibility. Technically."

The double doors clicked, and light poured into the back of the auditorium.

Frank. And he didn't look happy.

* * *

By the time I got to bed that night, I was done.

First I'd been grilled by Frank, and then Sergeant Walker, at Great Shamrock Hall. The rehearsal ended early as an "extra security precaution," and Colleen and the girls and I got a special police escort home, courtesy of Frank. Mom and the girls watched TV while Colleen and I were treated to a private debrief with the Chief in his office.

"I can't believe it," my sister kept saying in between tears. "Katie, what if something had happened to you? You should have *told* me."

Now I was the secretive sister. No one else saw the irony.

After much discussion between the Shamrock PD and the Chief and the mayor and the Saint Patrick's Day Committee and Bernie and Colleen and parents and who knew who else, all future show rehearsals were canceled except for the final dress rehearsal.

Of course the media got word there had been a "minor incident" that caused today's rehearsal to end early in "an abundance of caution," but no details were released. People started calling, and Mitzi and her news crew showed up at the front door. Two guests had to push past them to enter the Buckley House. They weren't very pleased.

Incredibly, Colleen went out again. She shot me a text that she was with Aidan, and not to worry, she'd be home late. Then she shut off her phone.

Not worry? What if Aidan was Deirdre's murderer? Or Moira was, and she stalked the two of them and something terrible happened? Or Aidan and Moira were in cahoots and ganged up on my sister?

Worst of all, how could Colleen go on a date, or whatever she wanted to call it, with that jerk Aidan O'Hearne?

The Chief sent Frank to find her, and when my brother had no luck, the Chief left for an impromptu poker game with his buddies. That's what he told Mom, anyway. He was probably driving every street in Shamrock in his van right now.

I stayed home with the girls. I tucked in an exhausted Bliz early and checked on Maeve, who wanted to know what had happened at rehearsal. I gave her an abbreviated account, and her eyes filled with tears. "Mom, you could have ended up like Deirdre."

"No, honey," I lied. "It wasn't like that at all. I'm perfectly fine. But you know you don't have to be in the show if you don't feel safe. No one does. Everyone would understand."

"I'm not quitting," Maeve said. "And I'm going to the Blarney Breakfast at the Smiling Shamrock tomorrow morning to support Zoe. Darcy's dancing too."

"Are you sure you want to do that?" I said. "Bliz is going to stay home with Mom and the Chief, and I'm only going to help Aunt Colleen." The last thing I wanted to do was spend any time at all with the McShanes and the mayor, but there was no way out of this one for me and Colleen. If she ever came home.

"I set my alarm. Good night." Maeve put on her headphones and closed her eyes, giving me a little wave.

Dismissed. Well, I'd tried.

Mom had retired to read with a glass of sherry, so I went to my room and tried to do some work. I had a hard time focusing, especially with Banshee continually walking over my keyboard. Was he nervous too? Finally, I settled into answering client emails and researching new or obscure out-of-state tax rules. Not my favorite part of the job.

I called it quits when both hands of Colleen's loudly ticking bunny clock passed twelve. I lay awake, waiting, for what felt like forever, with Banshee now curled beside me, snoring. The next thing I knew, both the bunny hands were past two, and I was burning up from the heat generated by a combo of laptop and extra-large cat.

Someone had left a light on near the garage, directly below my window. No, I remembered, that light was triggered by a motion detector. Faint but distinct tapping sounded from the blacktop section of the driveway.

Grabbing Colleen's bathrobe, I crept to the open window, careful to stay out of sight.

Cold sweat broke out through my tank top. Was someone trying to break into the Buckley House? Should I wake up the Chief? Make Bliz and Maeve hide in the Nest's wardrobe? Call 911, like I should have done earlier tonight?

More taps. The rhythm was familiar. One-two-three-four. Two-two-three-four. Three-two-three-four . . .

I jumped away from the window and bolted myself against the wall, pulling one of the drapes over me for good measure. That creepy jig played again in my mind, punctuated by the taps. I recognized the rhythm even without the music.

The Jig Is Up

Was Deirdre sending me some kind of message?

No. That was insane. And I was being ridiculous, hiding under a drape. I was a strong, empowered woman, a single mom with two kids, two elderly parents, and one exasperating sister. I needed to be brave for all of us.

I peeked around the drape, gently moving aside the sheer white curtain blowing slightly in the night breeze.

There was no such thing as ghosts. It might have been the filmy curtain, or the way the light hit the blacktop, but other than her earbuds and black leather jacket, the figure dancing in the driveway of the Buckley House almost didn't seem human.

Maybe I was dreaming, or I'd watched too many jigs and horn-pipes and reels today in Great Shamrock Hall. But the determined, high-ponytailed blonde with the flying feet and sky-high kicks wasn't just good. She was breathtaking.

Better than Zoe. Maybe even better than Deirdre. The dancer didn't need to turn around for me to know who she was.

My sister.

Chapter Twenty-Five

"Need anything from Kilpatrick's?" I asked Mom bright and early the next morning, shrugging on my coat. "I'm making a quick run." With luck, I'd be at the market the minute they opened.

"I just used the last of the scone mixes," she said. "Blueberry, please, and a cheese. Oh, and one more jar of jam."

"You got it."

"And Kate?" she called after me. "Don't flash the boxes about, please."

"I'm the queen of discretion," I said. "Family secrets are my specialty."

I lucked out. Colleen's friend Kenya was my checker. She wore a green Kilpatrick's apron with a green polka dot headscarf.

"More raspberry jam?" She grinned. "Must be our last one. Between the Buckley House and the Smiling Shamrock, we can't keep the stuff in stock. Takes forever to get it from across the pond."

"We'd be toast without it. And I bet the McShanes keep your delivery people busy." I felt extra-virtuous as I tucked the jar into my cloth tote.

"Tell me about it," Kenya said. "Una herself popped in on Thursday, though. It was storming like crazy, and even our delivery guy wasn't out there. Said she needed more jam and rashers for Aidan O'Hearne in the morning. Can you believe that?"

"I can, actually," I said. "What time did she come in?"

Kenya shrugged. "Right at closing. Eight o'clock or so. Why?"

"Oh, no reason. Thanks."

One McShane, anyway, ruled out again for the likely time of Deirdre's murder. We'd had that lovely chat in the Smiling Shamrock's driveway around 8:30.

Not that the tiny, birdlike Una had been at the top of my suspect list. A tall person ran past Conor at Angels Hall. And my attacker was at least my height. But if Moira were somehow involved, her doting auntie hadn't been providing an assist on the scene. Being a highly unpleasant person wasn't exactly a crime. Maybe it should be.

"Give Colleen a hug for me," Kenya said.

"I will," I said. "And thanks for sending the chocolate shamrocks. She was touched."

"Always here for our best customers." Kenya waved. "Happy Paddy's."

* * *

"You're sure you still want to do this?" I asked Maeve as Zoe fitted the huge, curly red wig tighter over my daughter's head. I tucked in the last few strands of Maeve's own hair.

"It's not like I'm dancing or anything. Just helping at a stupid breakfast at the creepy ladies' house. Aargh!" Maeve half-screamed when she saw herself in the mirror. "I'm a freak!"

"It takes a little getting used to." Zoe adjusted the wide velvet headband in front of Maeve's fake sausage curls and stepped back to survey her work. "You look perfect."

"Absolutely," I agreed.

My daughter quirked an eyebrow in Chief-like manner. "So it's bad when I wear a teensy bit of eyeliner, but this is okay?" She sighed. "The Chief will have a heart attack when he sees me like this."

"It's okay for the stage, sweetie," I said.

"You look bee-yoo-tiful, Maevie." Bliz sat cross-legged on the bed with Banshee on her lap, gazing at her older sister in awe. "Like a real Irish dancer. Zoe, will you make me up too?"

Zoe glanced at the bunny clock. "Sorry. We have to be at the Smiling Shamrock by eight o'clock sharp." She stood next to Maeve in the mirror, in her matching red wig and makeup job. "We could be twins."

"Aren't you going to put on your fancy dresses?" Bliz looked disappointed.

"No, honey, they'd get all wrinkled." I picked up the garment bags from Colleen's bed. My sister was already at the Smiling Shamrock, no worse for the wear after her late-night tryst with Aidan and furious with all of us for "overreacting." "The girls will change when we get there. But you'll see the costumes at dress rehearsal, okay?"

Bliz pouted. "I wish I could go to the Blarney Breakfast."

"No, you don't." I gave her a quick hug goodbye. "You get to stay here with Gram and make corned beef and cabbage."

"Stinky cabbage, ick." Bliz wrinkled her nose. I had to agree with her on that one. But at least I knew she'd be safe at home.

Bernie had requested a more obvious cop presence this morning as a precondition for any Donnelly School members' participation. I was relieved that Frank would be posted at the front door to stand with Maeve as she greeted guests and passed out flyers.

Una and Nuala had tried to object to the extra security, claiming that guests might be intimidated or frightened. They even complained to the mayor, but Bernie and the Chief won that battle. Safety was the number one priority.

There was sure to be a crowd, especially with Aidan in his role as Grand Marshal of the Paddy's Day Parade and honored Smiling Shamrock guest. Moira would be there, of course, along with Bernie, the mayor, members of the city council and chamber of commerce, and Saint Patrick's Day committees, local politicians, and residents with special invites. I doubted there would be room for any tourists. Una couldn't have meant in her TV interview that everyone in town was welcome for breakfast. Even the Smiling Shamrock couldn't pull that off, outside of divine intervention.

I couldn't help but suspect that the McShanes were using the Blarney Breakfast more to grab publicity for the Smiling Shamrock than to honor Deirdre. They'd already reached the green tin ceiling for review shamrocks. Maybe extra shamrock leaves were being awarded now.

I wouldn't even put it past those two to promote their great-niece and her new dance academy.

Moira met us at the door. "Oh, it's you." Her smile immediately faded. "Colleen and that Darcy girl are upstairs. Go on up."

"Thanks," I said, glancing around on our way to the large, carved staircase. I'd never actually been inside the Smiling Shamrock, which was already filling with breakfast attendees. As I'd expected, it was considerably more formal than the Buckley House. The drapes were trimmed in gold, the Victorian furniture gleamed, and sparkling pieces of Waterford crystal, framed Irish paintings and photos, and Belleek china knickknacks covered every square inch of display space.

Maeve, Zoe, and I trudged up the staircase, the girls wearing Donnelly School button-up shirts with their jeans. Button-up, so they wouldn't have to pull their dresses on over those huge wigs.

They lugged the bulky garment bags, and I shouldered Zoe's dance bag stuffed with shoes and extra socks and Band-Aids and laces.

Colleen stood in the doorway of a guest bedroom—apparently the Smiling Shamrock had at least one vacancy—and Darcy, wearing a blond wig, sat across the room in an uncomfortable looking chair.

My sister didn't seem mad anymore about last night. "It's showtime!" she greeted us cheerfully, pinning a white carnation on her forest-green blazer. "Hurry and get dressed, girls, so we can get pictures. Kate, can we use your phone? Your camera's better than mine."

"Sure," I said as Maeve and Zoe headed to the other side of the room. Neither said hello to Darcy, I noticed. The girl bit her lip and looked away, clearly hurt. I'd speak to Maeve about that. No matter how loyal she felt to Zoe, or whatever the issue was between these three, I wasn't raising any mean girls.

"Good morning, Darcy," I said, walking over. "You look very nice."

"Thanks." She sounded nervous, and I couldn't help but notice her fingernails were bitten to the quick. Was she worried about her upcoming performance? Or whatever it was Zoe was so mad at her about?

"Everything okay?" I asked in a low voice. She nodded.

A knock sounded at the door, and Colleen opened it to reveal Nuala McShane frowning from the hallway. She was dressed all in gray, except for her pointy, lace-up black boots and the small spray of shamrocks and white lace handkerchief tucked in the breast-pocket of her suit jacket. "You are in the wrong room, ladies," she said.

"Sorry, my fault," Colleen said. "Can the girls finish getting ready here?"

"No," Nuala said. "New guests have just checked in, and their luggage is on its way."

We gathered up all the clothes and bags and Nuala directed us to a tiny room, half a mile down a dark hallway after two more flights of twisting stairs.

"Excuse me, where is the elevator?" I asked.

"Guests only." Nuala turned to the girls. "Dancers go on at nine o'clock. And again at eleven, after the buffet closes and before the second coffee service. Don't be late."

"I'm not dancing," Maeve said. "I'm just handing out flyers and collecting for the Deirdre Donnelly Memorial Scholarship Fund."

Nuala leveled her lizard gaze on my daughter. "You'd best get yourself properly ready and straight to work, then." She turned on her ugly boot heels and stalked off.

Maeve's mouth dropped open. I made a quick zip-it motion across my lips behind the witch's retreating back.

"I've got to get back downstairs," Colleen said. "Duty calls. And I could really use some coffee. Text me if you need anything, okay?"

Maeve finished getting ready extra-fast. "I can't believe you wear these things," she said to Zoe, touching the springy fake curls of her wig again.

"We don't wear them all the time," Zoe said. "Just for formal stuff, like shows and competitions. We're all supposed to look alike in the group numbers. But solo dancers have their own special dresses and wigs. My other wig is blond."

"I just have this one," Darcy said. "They're expensive. It was my cousin's."

I looked pointedly at Maeve. "It looks really nice on you," she told Darcy.

I adjusted the stiff velvet cape on my daughter's shoulder. "Good girl," I whispered. "Be kind."

"Wait." Zoe grabbed what looked like a roll-on deodorant bottle from her bag. "You'll need this to keep up your poodle socks."

"Poodle?" Maeve glanced down at her high white knit socks, which were covered with little white-knit bumps. "You mean, like the dog?"

"Sort of." Zoe applied some type of sticky substance to Maeve's calves, under the top edges of the socks. "This is just body glue. It comes right off with water."

"Why don't you and I head downstairs?" I asked Maeve. Hopefully that would give Zoe and Darcy a chance to resolve their issues before the performance.

Maeve handed out flyers at the door like a trouper. The plastic jug for the Deirdre Donnelly Memorial Fund was clearly visible on a nearby bench—and beside it stood my brother.

Moira hovered behind Maeve, greeting guests over my daughter's head.

"I've got this, Kate," Frank said in a low voice. "Go help Colleen and keep your eyes peeled for any funny business inside."

"Okay," I said, with a grateful smile. As I walked away, I heard a guest tell my daughter how gorgeous she looked. Another Little Miss Shamrock moment.

I circulated through the crowded rooms on the ground floor, searching for Colleen. At some point Moira deserted her welcome wagon post, and I saw her everywhere else instead. Was she following me?

No, Moira had to be looking for Aidan. Luckily for him, I spotted him first and blocked her line of sight. Wearing his colorful Grand Marshal banner diagonally across another sharp tweed jacket, he stood chatting with adoring fans by the main bar—and right next to him was Colleen.

My sister whispered something in his ear, then turned to steal a cherry from a cocktail garnish tray. She glanced back over her shoulder, and Aidan caught her eye. He winked—discreetly, but still.

Which of them was the bigger flirt? Ordinarily I wouldn't pay much attention to Colleen's love life, but in my opinion, she needed to keep plenty of dancing space between herself and Aidan O'Hearne.

She'd been furious with me when she got in from her date, refusing to even consider he could have murdered Deirdre. Then I'd asked, "That friend you ran into on the way home from Angels Hall that night—the one who gave you a ride—did he drive a Mercedes, by any chance?"

"None of your business," she'd answered. That meant yes.

I guess that definitely cleared Aidan as a suspect, time-frame-wise. Unless the two of them had worked together. Bloody heck. One thing was obvious: I couldn't protect my sister twenty-four seven.

She didn't want me to anyway. But her I-don't-care attitude was always an act.

So far, it didn't seem as if anyone had been turned away from the Blarney Breakfast. The entire downstairs of the Smiling Shamrock was filled to capacity. Where was the fire marshal? Ah, yes. Across the room behind one of the giant silver coffeepots, Una chatted his ears off and offered him a home-baked Kilpatrick's croissant. Literally buttering him up for the Smiling Shamrock's next fire inspection.

There were plenty of cops around, but I hadn't seen Chief Ryan or Surly Shirley yet. Or Garrett, not that I cared.

I shrank against the wall as Mayor Flanagan moved past, shaking hands, air-kissing ladies, slapping men hard on their backs, and laughing uproariously at his own jokes. Our gracious hostesses brought out tray after tray of scrambled eggs, bangers and rashers, fried tomatoes, white and black pudding, and brown bread. No cater-waiters for Shamrock's Martha Stewart McShanes.

Moira was in charge of the bar now, pouring mimosas and Bloody Marys from rapidly draining pitchers. Mostly she watched Aidan and Colleen and spilled half the drink glasses on the Irish lace tablecloth. There'd be plenty of laundering and ironing at the Smiling Shamrock this week.

"I'm out of flyers," Maeve announced, catching up with me in the main parlor. "Have you seen Zoe and Darcy?"

"Not yet." I winced as Una dug into my elbow with her talons.

"It's already five past the hour," she said. "Time to start the dancing." She turned her yellow eyes to Maeve.

"Wrong dancer," I said. "Zoe and Darcy are performing this morning."

"We need to keep to schedule." Una pronounced it "shed-ule" in European fashion. She pointed to her tiny gold watch and made a whiskey-sour face before giving Maeve a little push toward a section of polished floor near the grand piano, where the Oriental carpets had been removed. "Go on, now."

"Mrs. McShane, please." I kept my voice low to avoid a scene. "The other dancers will be here any second."

Una ignored me, nudging Maeve again. My daughter whirled around. "Quit touching me," she said, "or I'm calling my uncle Frank. He's a cop, and he's right out in the hall."

Una reached into her suit pocket and pulled out a small silver bell, which she rang until everyone around us stopped talking.

"Attention, guests!" She held up her bony hand. "Please give a warm Irish welcome to our young representative from the Donnelly School of Irish Dance. She'll perform for us this morning, accompanied by her mother on the piano."

What?

"Are you freaking kidding me?" Maeve whispered to me. "I can't dance."

"Don't worry, honey. We'll figure this out." I glanced around for Zoe, Darcy, or anyone else who could help. Bernie wasn't even here yet, as far as I knew. Maybe she'd decided the breakfast would be too much for her. Colleen was across the hall in the facing room, cocking her head as she listened to Aidan.

I gave her an urgent wave, but she just smiled and waved back. Hadn't she heard Una's announcement? Was she so distracted by her charming boyfriend that she didn't notice the dancing was about to start—with the wrong dancer?

Then I realized my sister probably didn't recognize Maeve in her dance costume. She looked a lot like Zoe from a distance, with her wig and makeup.

But Darcy wasn't on deck either. Theresa Meaney came up as if in answer to my thoughts. "I can't find my grandkid," she said. "Last I knew, she was with Zoe."

I sighed. "Sorry, I don't know where they are, Theresa. They must still be upstairs and lost track of time." But that wasn't like Zoe. Hopefully those two weren't fighting again.

"I checked the whole place," Theresa said. "This isn't fair, Darcy missin' her big chance. Again."

"Ladies, we're waiting," Nuala said from next to the piano. She made a shooing motion for Maeve to hit the dance floor, and another for me to take my place at the bench. Apparently she'd taken over for her sister as Grand Piano Marshal. "Did you bring your own music?" she asked me. "Where's that weedy young man with the accordion?"

"Conor had to work this morning," Maeve said. "And he's not weedy."

"The scheduled performers will be here momentarily," I said. "Five minutes."

"You'd best be starting right now," Nuala said. "Father Declan will be here soon to give a blessing. He's on a tight schedule today."

"I'm ready," Maeve called.

Everyone's attention turned to my daughter, standing squarely in the middle of the dance floor, her arms crossed. *Uh-oh.* I knew that look.

Beside me, Theresa leaned in. "Want me to play?" she asked. "I know all the music. I was gonna help Deirdre out with the show."

I stared at her. "*You* were the piano player who didn't show up the night Deirdre died?"

Theresa shrugged. "I was ticked off. She didn't give Darcy a solo."

Three impatient chords sounded from the piano. Nuala glared at me. "I'll play, thanks," I told Theresa quickly. "Go find the girls."

With an encouraging smile at Maeve and a little wave to the expectant crowd, I took my place on the bench. Where was Colleen?

I heard those judgy church voices murmuring again.

"Mom, I'm *ready*." Maeve sounded even more annoyed now.

Nuala tapped on the sheet music already in place and hissed like a tall, skinny possum. "Play," she commanded.

"Irish Wedding Dance."

The Jig Is Up

Nope, nope, nope. A brush dance would be too hard for Maeve. And way too hard for me, in the memories department. I took a calming breath and began to play the first piece that sprang to mind.

"Morrison's Jig." The one that had played endlessly on the night of Deirdre's murder.

Chapter
Twenty-Six

S tony-faced on the polished dance floor, Maeve clenched her
hands into fists at her side more tightly than they'd been
secured by Zoe's duct tape. She pointed her toes in her borrowed
soft shoes, waiting for her opening. Then she launched into a basic,
slightly awkward jig.

The steps were recognizable. A vision of Deirdre as the Faerie
Queen flashed into my brain as I continued to play the piano. The
tilted chin, the determined focus . . .

From the corner of my eye, I saw Colleen enter the room. Her
mouth dropped open, and a ragged-looking Bernie Donnelly
appeared, accompanied by Aidan. He just seemed confused. But
all the other faces in the crowd were smiling, and people began to
clap good-naturedly in time with the music.

Then Aidan jumped onto the dance floor beside Maeve. The
crowd went wild, stomping and cheering as he leaped into the air,
his feet flashing as fast as Colleen's in the driveway last night.

He danced around Maeve in a circle, as if she were the star, and
everyone cheered the King and Queen of the Dance. I wrapped up
the music in relief.

Everyone applauded. "Ladies and gentlemen, Ms. Maeve
Buckley, the newest student at the Donnelly School of Irish

Dance!" Aidan swept his arm toward Maeve. "She just started yes-terday morning, I'm told. How about that, folks?"

The crowd cheered and whistled again. Even Maeve smiled, her face red from exertion and embarrassment, as he squeezed her shoulders in a congratulatory side hug.

Had to hand it to the guy. He was smooth. But also kind. Maybe.

Now that Aidan had everyone's attention, he gave a heartfelt speech honoring his former partner Deirdre and her dear mother, then led a series of toasts until Mayor Flanagan took over.

As soon as the mayor's unusually short speech concluded, I hurried over to my daughter. "Fantastic job, sweetie," I said, giving her a huge hug. "You were amazing." I turned to Aidan. "And thanks to you too."

He grinned. "Always glad to help out a Buckley."

I let that one go.

"Maeve, that was awesome, but what happened to Zoe and Darcy?" Colleen rushed up to give her a hug as well. Behind her, Bernie was smiling, looking happy as Larry.

"We don't know," Maeve said. "Something's wrong. Zoe would never not show up, and neither would Darcy. She was really excited about dancing today."

"Theresa is looking for them," I said.

Maeve's eyes filled with tears. "Something really bad must have happened."

"Nothing bad, I'm sure, honey," I assured her quickly, praying that was true. "Look at all the cops here."

I made my daughter wait with Bernie and Aidan and rushed to grab Frank in the hallway. He, Colleen, and I ran upstairs. Half-way up, we met Theresa on her way down, looking grim. "Nuthin'. If I don't find 'em outside, I'm gettin' Chief Ryan."

The rest of us burst into the tiny room where we'd last seen Zoe and Darcy. Maybe Theresa hadn't gone all the way up. She'd probably left her granddaughter with Colleen in that first room earlier this morning.

I made a quick check. Everything looked the same: one neatly made twin bed, a maple dresser, one straight chair. Old servant quarters, I guessed. The girls' street clothes, shoes, and their dance bags lay strewn across the rag rug.

No Zoe. No Darcy.

Then we heard muffled pounding and kicking from the tiny bathroom. "Get us out of here!" a voice screamed from behind the door. Someone was trying to kick straight through it as another person sobbed.

"Oh my God." Colleen rushed to the door. "Zoe, are you all right? Is that Darcy with you?"

"Yes! Finally, someone's here. We've been kicking and screaming forever. We're locked in."

From the outside? I glanced down at the brass doorknob, which one of the girls was furiously jiggling. "It's one of those old-school locks," I said. Probably a closet once. "Hold on, girls."

"We'll take the door off the hinges," Frank said.

"There's a key," Zoe said. "We heard the person lock us in."

It took a minute of searching, but I found it in a jade-green container on top of the dresser, half-buried in a collection of odd buttons.

"I'll let Theresa know they're safe." Colleen ran to the one tiny window and tried to push it up to call to Darcy's grandmother. "Stuck," she announced. "I'll go find her, then. Be right back."

Maybe the fire marshal should do the Smiling Shamrock's fire inspection right now.

The Jig Is Up

When I let the girls out of the bathroom, with Frank standing guard behind me, Zoe's face was bright red under her stage makeup and her green-and-white-painted fingernails were broken and smudged with blood. Her hard shoes were scuffed too.

Darcy's face was streaked with tears. I gave her a hug. "I'm so sorry, girls. What happened? Who locked you in?"

"I don't know." Zoe had also been crying—tears of pure rage. "I was in there, fixing my headband, and Darcy and I were having a serious discussion—"

"Fighting," Darcy corrected. She looked at the floor. "Sort of."

"And then someone snuck up and slammed the door shut on us and locked it, totally on purpose. They didn't even say anything. Why would they do something like that?"

"They didn't want us to dance," Darcy said.

Immediately I thought of Moira and her new business endeavor. Had she wanted to make the Donnelly School dancers look like no-shows?

Zoe smoothed her dress. "Are they still waiting for us downstairs?"

"Not exactly," I said. "Maeve filled in with a jig. She did great."

"Oh." Zoe recovered quickly. "Well, that's good."

"At least someone danced for Miss Deirdre's breakfast." Darcy sighed.

"Something else good happened too." Zoe shot her a sideways glance. "Do you want to tell Ms. B?"

Darcy hesitated, biting her lip.

As a mom, I knew that response. It was something important. And private.

"Frank, I think we're okay here now," I said. "Maybe you should go back downstairs and keep an eye on things."

243

"Sure," he said, eager to make an exit. "Let me know if you need any more help." He thudded down the stairs.

"So." I smiled encouragingly at both girls. "What's going on?"

Darcy went over to the small iron bed and plopped herself down, squeaking the springs.

"I know what happened to the scholarship money," she said in a small voice.

"Oh?" I willed myself not to show any reaction.

"She didn't take it or anything," Zoe said.

I squelched my gasp so it turned into more of a hiccup. *Was Colleen the thief after all?*

I sat down on the bed next to Darcy. "It's okay," I said. "You can tell me, and we'll figure this out. Does anyone else know?"

Darcy shook her head, and the tears started again. "It was my grandmother," she blurted.

Theresa?

I cleared my throat. "Are you sure about that?"

The enormous blond wig bobbed as she nodded. The girl looked miserable.

"Ms. Meaney wanted Darcy to get the scholarship, because she really, really needs it," Zoe said. "She was afraid it would go to someone else, because Darcy never gets picked for anything. Deirdre was going to announce the winner at the show."

"Did your grandmother tell you she took the money?" I asked Darcy gently.

"No. I saw her take the jar from Miss Colleen's car. She put it in ours, in the trunk."

"And why did Miss Colleen have the money jar?"

"It was heavy, so she said she'd drive it to Miss Deirdre's house."

Exactly what Colleen had told me.

"We had a table set up in the parish hall," Zoe explained, "and Father Declan made an announcement so people could donate after Mass."

"I think my grandmother felt guilty," Darcy said. "She didn't give the money back, but she volunteered to play the piano in the show. Then she got mad again when Miss Deirdre gave Zoe the main solo, and then Miss Deirdre got . . . murdered."

"And Ms. Meaney started a rumor that Miss Colleen stole the scholarship money," Zoe finished.

"She didn't kill Miss Deirdre, though," Darcy said quickly. "My grandmother stayed with me and my little brother all that night. My mom had the late shift at work. She's an aide at Shamrock House. The nursing home."

Zoe sat down on Darcy's other side and put an arm around her shoulders. "I'm sorry I thought you took the money, Darcy," she said. "I was a jerk. Even though it sucks we got locked in the bathroom and missed the dancing, I'm glad we got a chance to talk things out. I really, really apologize."

"It's okay." Darcy traced a Celtic knot embroidered on her dress. "What do I do now? My grandma will kill me for telling. And I don't want her to get in trouble."

"I think I can help," I said. "It's okay, honey, you did the right thing. We'll figure something out."

Colleen stuck her head through the doorway. "Hey, girls, ready to dance? You're on deck."

"What?" Zoe said. Darcy sat up straighter and wiped away her tears.

"I got Aidan and Bernie and Father Declan to have a word with our hostesses," Colleen said. "They've agreed to give us time for a couple more numbers, but we have to get down there quick."

Both girls jumped off the bed and excitedly followed Colleen downstairs. "Katie, you coming?" she called back to me.

Showtime.

* * *

It was one o'clock before the Blarney Breakfast mercifully wrapped up. Zoe and Darcy were a hit, dancing in perfect unison, and Colleen gave me all the right music.

I finally spotted Garrett near the end, snagging a pastry from the dessert table. He didn't see me, but Sergeant Walker did. When our eyes met, she gave me a short nod. I nodded back.

Both were in dress uniform for the occasion, I noted. Did they know yet that two girls had been locked in a tiny room upstairs? Doubtful, because neither looked concerned. It was hard to tell with cops. But I bet nothing had been missed down on the main floor under Shirley's watch.

Frank could debrief them later. He was at the front door again, scanning each guest as they said goodbye and thanked the McShanes. I was dying to tell all three witches what I thought of them and their Blarney Breakfast, but I knew better. The scholarship fund jug was fully replenished with green bills, and everyone told Colleen how well all the girls had danced and how much they were looking forward to the show. She stood at the other side of the door, between Frank and Mr. Grand Marshal, smiling and receiving well wishes and hugs.

Theresa had hustled her granddaughter out of the Smiling Shamrock through a back exit, without a word to anyone.

As I waited for my sister and Maeve down the hall, I noticed that Moira seemed quieter than usual. Was she jealous that the Donnelly School had taken center stage this morning? Or that her sabotage plan had backfired?

The Jig Is Up

It had to have been Moira—she could have easily slipped upstairs for a few minutes without anyone noticing. It was her house, after all. Maybe it had finally dawned on her that Aidan wasn't interested in her—or her dancing, or her new dance academy—and she'd flown into a vengeful snit.

Or maybe her lack of animation was due to crushing fatigue from running up several flights of stairs to lock two teen girls in a tiny bathroom.

Ha. I doubted Moira ever ran out of energy.

The goodbyes were taking forever. I walked farther down the hall, perusing the framed photos and articles on the wall. Many featured Moira, of course, from Babies dance level through Irish Steps. Some included Deirdre, and even Colleen. Three smiling girls wearing navy and green graduation robes with "Our Lady of Angels" printed on them in gold.

Colleen and Deirdre wore their friendship heart necklaces, with the tiny birthstones in the center. Ruby and emerald.

I walked even farther down the hall, reading glowing reviews and ratings, along with glossy magazine spreads of the Smiling Shamrock. One showed Una and Nuala flanking the mayor. Other frames held faded Irish newspaper articles.

I leaned closer. Next to the large gold-framed mirror near the fancy Victorian coatrack was an ancient-looking photo from the *Irish Times*. The date had been torn off at the top edge, but the photo was sharp enough. Three teen dancers, two with black hair, one a redhead, standing on a podium.

I did a double-take. The ginger, taller than the others with a silver medal around her neck, looked exactly like Moira.

I recognized the skinny first-place dancer without even looking at the name printed below. *Bernadette Rose McFadden*. Later known as Bernadette Donnelly.

247

But the red-haired dancer who'd come in second? *Áine Moira McShane*. Future mom of Moira McShane Fake-Kelly.

I stepped back, my heart pounding. Áine died in a tragic car accident, Colleen had said, leaving Moira to the care of her great-aunts, Una and Nuala. But there was something about Áine's gaze, lasered on Bernie—it was the same look Moira had given Deirdre in the Faerie Queen video.

"Let's go, Mom," Maeve said beside me. I jumped three feet. "Aunt Colleen's waiting for us outside."

"Okay." I turned away from the McShane wall of infamy—but not before I noticed an extra-long black trench coat hanging from the coatrack. Sticking out from the pocket was a long-handled silver flashlight, just like the one I'd kicked under the seats in Great Shamrock Hall.

Bingo. I snapped a quick photo on my phone and followed Maeve out of the Smiling Shamrock.

Chapter
Twenty-Seven

The first thing I did when I got back from the Blarney Breakfast, after admiring the homemade paper shamrocks Bliz and Mom had strung in the windows and over the stair rails, was grab a sandwich. Unlike my sister and daughter, who'd hit the remnants of the Smiling Shamrock buffet, I hadn't had much appetite for the McShanes' hospitality. And I definitely needed sustenance before I talked to the Chief.

A note from Mom on the kitchen counter informed me that she and Bliz had gone to Daley's department store on the other side of town.

Perfect timing. Peanut butter and banana sandwich in hand, I went to find my dad.

He was in his usual spot in the living room, munching soda crackers and reading a thick, large-print police procedural from the Shamrock Library. "How's the book?" I asked.

"I've read better," he said, tipping up his glasses. "A lot of nonsense. The cops are all eejits."

"So, what's the latest on the investigation?" I settled myself on the floor next to his wheelchair, careful not to drop any sandwich on the carpet.

He turned down the top corner of one page to mark his place. "Maybe I should ask you that."

"I guess you heard what happened at the breakfast."

The Chief looked at me as if I were the eejit. "I did. But maybe you'd like to tell me more?"

I gave him the blow-by-blow of the morning's events, finishing with my suspicions about Moira. "She had a reason to do it, and the person had to know there was a key to that bathroom. But there's something else." I showed him the photo of the flashlight from my phone. "Same one I saw in the auditorium, after that person attacked me."

My dad closed his book, leaving it on his lap. "Circumstantial. The torch belongs to the McShanes, so any prints would be theirs. And there's a bucket full of them at Shamrock Hardware, right on the counter."

"I know. But it's something, right?" I sighed. "What do you do if you know who the murderer is, and you're really close, but you don't have solid proof?"

"That's the rub," he said with a smile. "You stick to it and find that proof. I've told you many times, good detectives have patience. They build their cases, piece by piece, and never show their true hands until it's time. The guilty party will reveal themselves eventually. But the detective has to be ready."

"What if the detective is too late?"

"Ah. Well, then she has a bit of a problem, doesn't she?" The Chief reached down to pat me on the shoulder. "You would have made a fine detective, Kathleen, if you hadn't taken up with the music and the numbers. You have the mind for it, and fine intuition to boot. Trust the facts, but also yourself. Don't overthink things. Just *do*."

Full of helpful platitudes, my dad. I hugged my knees and thought about the latest fact I knew.

"I have something that might help the case," I said. "Well, Colleen's part of it, anyway."

"Let's hear it."

I relayed what Darcy had told me about her grandmother's role in the missing scholarship money. "So if Theresa took the money, that means Colleen had less motive to kill Deirdre, right? I mean, the two of them may have had that discussion about the loan, but at least Colleen didn't steal anything from the Donnellys."

My dad nodded. "Encouraging."

"What will happen with Theresa?" I asked. "Darcy said her grandmother was home with the family the whole night Deirdre was murdered. But if she took the money . . ."

"Officially, Bernie never filed a police report," the Chief said. "But if it's confirmed that Theresa took the funds, or she admits to it, Bernie may press charges. I'll have a few discussions."

I stood up from the rug less than gracefully. "Okay. But, Dad, things may be a little tricky."

"Aren't they always?"

"Yes," I said, sighing. "But can we avoid making Darcy's life any harder? Her grandma is a tough cookie. Maybe you could hold off on those conversations, just for a bit, and we can work things out for everyone. If I—"

The Chief held up a hand. "Don't tell me any more, Katie Margaret. Make quick work of it."

I grabbed a tissue from his desk on the way out to remove the last remnants of peanut butter from my fingers.

"Keep the faith," he called after me. "Stay the course."

More platitudes. I rolled my eyes and kept on walking.

* * *

251

I found Colleen in her—our—bedroom, sitting against the bed beside a pile of old yearbooks. She'd been crying.

"Hey." I dropped down beside her. "You okay?"

She swiped at her eyes. "Yeah. It's just . . . everything."

I glanced at the open yearbook. Deirdre's senior picture. The thin, dark-haired girl, pretty in a quiet way, smiled very slightly at the camera with her lips clamped together, probably trying to hide her braces. But her eyes reflected the same determined expression that had haunted me in the dance video.

A future so full of promise, but she could never have imagined what lay ahead. And now she was gone.

"It's okay for you to grieve, Colleen Queen. You don't have to hide your feelings. If you let people around you in, they'll help you. They *want* to help you."

"I know," she said in a dull tone. "Thanks." Rain pounded at the window.

"I have good news for you. Want to hear it?"

"Sure," she said with the same level of enthusiasm.

I told her about Theresa and the scholarship money, and how I'd found out.

"Well, that makes sense, I guess. Poor Darcy."

"It's a terrible situation," I said. "But at least you're officially in the clear for stealing from the Donnelly School."

"I'll still be a person of interest, because Dee and I had that stupid fight. And it sucks for Darcy." She stared out the window. The rain was even louder now, and the sky had darkened. I scrambled to close the sash.

"Have you thought about it any more?" she asked. "Staying here in Shamrock?"

I had a bad feeling about where this might go. Maybe the Chief was right about my instinct. I turned slowly from the window.

"We have to talk about it," Colleen said.

I went over and dropped onto the bed. "Sorry, guess I haven't thought much past trying to solve this case."

"I want her back," my sister said in a small voice.

"I know," I said. "Everyone does. Deirdre didn't deserve what happened to her. I swear I'll find—"

"Katie," Colleen broke in. "I don't mean Deirdre."

Numbness crept through my body. I didn't want to hear this.

"Of course I want Dee back," Colleen said. "But that's never going to happen. I'm starting to accept that. Sort of." She twisted the little silver Claddagh ring on her pinky. "I'm talking about Bliz."

I pulled my knees tightly to my chest. I'd always known this discussion would come up between us someday. Just a matter of time. I'd probably even known when I'd gotten that mysterious text from Colleen the other night that this would be it.

I'd told myself my sister was the one stalling and avoiding since the girls and I had gotten to Shamrock. But maybe it had been both of us. "You can't have her *back*," I said, my pulse pounding in my head. "It doesn't work that way. I've been Bliz's mom her whole life."

"I know," Colleen said. "I didn't word that right. I'd never try to take her away from you or anything, I swear. Or interfere on anything. You're a great mom. I just think we should tell her. I want to be more a part of her life, Kate."

I didn't answer right away. I couldn't.

"I finally got up the guts to talk to you about it, but when you all showed up, I chickened out. Then Deirdre died, and people thought I was a murderer and . . ."

This was so overwhelming, especially right now. I fought back tears. We'd planned everything out to the last detail—or so we'd thought—almost eight years ago, before Bliz was born. How could we change The Plan now?

"We have to discuss it, at least." Colleen got up and sat next to me on the bed. "We can't keep doing things like this anymore, because the girls are getting older. We always said we'd tell them eventually. They're going to figure out the truth. And if that happens, both of them will hate us. Maybe we should have told them from the very beginning, and then it wouldn't be such a big deal now."

"Maybe." Maeve was only seven then, and she, Ian, and I were a little family of three. Maeve hadn't cared much about the details of exactly how her baby sister had joined us. Ian, on the other hand, packed his bags and left for Ireland soon after Bliz's arrival. Our marriage had already been shaky, but that was the last straw.

It was Colleen's idea for me to adopt her baby. Everyone in the family had supported us, and I'd wholeheartedly agreed. I'd never regretted it.

As far as I knew, Colleen hadn't either. At least until now.

"Maybe we could explain things to Maeve, in a year or so," I said slowly. "But Bliz wouldn't understand yet, and—"

"We should tell them now," Colleen said. "You can't just tell one and not the other. I mean, if you moved here for a while, we'd be changing their whole lives on top of everything else. And I know this whole deal is because of me in the first place, but we both owe them the truth, right?"

"Yeah, you do. So what is the truth, exactly?"

Maeve scowled from the open doorway, her narrowed eyes darting from me to Colleen.

My heart literally stopped beating. It felt like it, anyway. My sister's face drained of color, making her look almost as pale as Deirdre on the night she died.

"You two are so busted." Maeve marched into the room, slamming the door shut behind her. Tears filled her eyes. "All these big family secrets. The almost-lies and the it's-okay-sweeties and the little side comments. You think I don't notice? Nobody ever talks about anything real."

My sister and I exchanged glances.

Maeve threw up her hands. "There you go again. The looks."

Colleen looked even more stricken, and I probably did too. Maeve's truth was pretty much on target.

"Maybe I should just ask the Chief. I bet he'll tell me what's going on."

"No, no, you don't need to do that," Colleen said quickly. "Please." She turned to me, her eyes that strange cloudy-gray again, exactly like Bliz's when she got upset. "Your call, Kate."

How much of our conversation had my daughter heard? No way to tell for sure, but by her expression I had to assume . . . enough. It didn't matter. I needed to tell her the truth, and Bliz too. The longer we waited, the worse it would be.

I patted the quilt beside me and gave her a shaky smile. "Sit down, Maeve. There's something I—we—had planned to tell you soon, but we wanted you and your sister both to be—"

Maeve sat, but she looked past me, straight at Colleen. "You're Bliz's bio mom, aren't you?"

My numbness turned to painful constriction of every organ in my body. How could she possibly have figured that out? We'd been so careful.

"She looks just like you," Maeve went on, her gaze steady. "And Mrs. Donnelly said Bliz was a natural, like her mother. I saw you dancing in the driveway last night, Aunt Colleen. You're really good. And Mom is a total klutz, like me."

"Thanks," I muttered. What should I say? I had to choose my words carefully. My daughter would remember them for the rest of her life.

Colleen was quicker. "Your mom is still Bliz's real mom," she said. "But yeah, I'm her bio mom. And her aunt. But I love all of you, and I almost moved to New York so I could see you more. But then I had another idea, and I wanted to talk to your mom—well, to all of you—to see if you wanted to move here to Shamrock. So we could be together as one big family, with Gram and the Chief too. Things wouldn't change, really."

Maeve's mouth dropped so far it took her a second to reset it in order to speak. "Are you freaking kidding me? That would change everything. Like, my whole life. And Bliz's." She glared at me. "And Mom's."

I cleared my throat. "Aunt Colleen and I hadn't finished discussing the moving idea," I said. "Or any of this, really. We've had a lot to deal with this week, all of us. We need some time to take a breath and work things out."

"So okay, who is Bliz's dad, then?"

Uh-oh. Even I didn't know the answer to that one for sure. Colleen had never told a soul, as far as I knew, except maybe Deirdre. I had my suspicions, but on that question, my sister had always been mum. I had no idea why.

"I'm not going to answer that right now." If Colleen was upset, she didn't show it.

"Why not?"

"Because it isn't the right time," my sister said. "For all kinds of reasons. And one of them is, it's none of your business, kiddo."

Was it, or wasn't it? I couldn't think clearly right now.

"That's the most hypocritical thing I ever heard," Maeve said. "Another big secret." My heart broke as the giant tears escaped. "I am never speaking to either of you ever again for the rest of my life," she added in a low, even tone. Then she jumped off the bed and ran from the room.

For a moment or two, neither my sister nor I said a word. Then I sprang toward the door, but Colleen beat me to it. "Let her go," she said, blocking my way. "She's not going to talk to you right now anyway."

"She needs me," I said, trying to push Colleen aside. She had a few pounds on me, but I was determined. And older.

That last reason didn't give me much advantage anymore. Colleen held her ground. "No. She needs to breathe, Kate."

"I'm her mom. I get to decide what's best for her."

I regretted my choice of words as soon as they left my mouth. This time, it was my sister who didn't respond. "Sorry," I mumbled. "Not what I meant."

Colleen stepped away from the door and gestured for me to pass, but I stayed in place. "We shouldn't have told her," I said. "Not like this."

"The truth hurts sometimes," Colleen said. "But it's always better than lying. Trust me on that."

"Right." I stepped past her, with no idea what to do next. But I had to get away from my sister, or I might say something I'd regret forever.

"Kate?" Colleen called as I stumbled down the hall.

I turned to see her head stuck out from the doorway.

"Let me handle Theresa."

For a second, I couldn't place a single Theresa in my brain. Then I remembered, and I didn't care, at least for now. "Fine," I said.

Chapter
Twenty-Eight

I stared up at the Nest's closed trapdoor. I knew Maeve was up there.

"Honey?" I called. "Let me up, please, so we can talk."

No answer.

I hated to admit it, but my sister was right. Maeve needed some time on her own to let the information about Colleen and me and Bliz and her sink in. The details and processing would come later. Right now, she was probably so shocked, like me, she wouldn't be able to focus on anything else I said anyway. "Text me when you're ready, okay?" I called. "I love you."

My phone pinged.

Go away.

Okay, then. A subtle hint I should back off and try to figure out my own messed-up life. Oh, and solve a murder too. Even if my sister wasn't the killer, or at the top of the suspect list anymore.

Deirdre deserved justice. So did Bernie. And as far as I knew, Shirley and the Shamrock PD weren't making much progress on the case. I hoped I was wrong.

My phone vibrated as I returned it to my pocket. Another text, this time from Mom. She and Bliz were done with their shopping and heading to a matinee. *Finian's Rainbow.* That was a long movie. Good.

For once, I was really and truly alone. Off duty. And I knew exactly where I'd go.

But what if Maeve suddenly needed me, and wanted to talk?

No. She could text, and I'd come running. But right now, I needed to divert my brain from panic mode—and not with clients' tax forms.

I dashed downstairs, grabbed Mom's yellow slicker from the hook in the kitchen, and escaped out the side door.

* * *

The warmth and stale beer smell of Farrell's welcomed me again like an old friend. I wasn't much of a day drinker, usually—okay, ever—but I couldn't wait to belly up to the bar.

"Irish coffee, please, Damien," I told the barperson as I slid onto a stool and slipped my purse strap onto the old brass hat hook beneath the counter. I'd known the guy with the silver moustache and bad brown toupee since the day I'd celebrated my twenty-first. Or maybe before that, to be honest. On the jog over, I'd vowed to tell everyone, including myself, the truth about everything from now on. It was better that way. Or safer, at least. "Double whiskey," I added.

Always the pro, Damien gave a short nod and went to make my drink.

"That bad, huh?"

Garrett McGavin gave me that lopsided grin of his from the end of the bar, where the dim light revealed him behind a towering plate of Irish nachos and a half-full pint of Guinness.

Fabulous. Another blast from my past. But he was just being friendly, with no clue my life had blown up—along with those of everyone close to me. "Family stuff," I said with a sigh.

"I hear you." He took a short swig from his pint. "It's a good time to hang out here. After lunch, before the dinner crowd. Between shifts."

"Mmm." I glanced at the digital clock behind the bar. The numbers announced the exact birth date—month, day, year— after customers could legally be served. The year was obscured by a green Santa hat, drooped sadly over the corner. Stuck in the past, like me.

"Nachos?" Garrett motioned to his plate, his mouth slightly full.

I hesitated. They did look good.

"Sure. Thanks."

As I retrieved my purse and took the stool beside him, Damien placed my steaming, gold-rimmed glass of strong coffee and even stronger whiskey, topped with a stiff cloud of fresh cream, on the bar in front of me. It was too hot to drink yet, so I concentrated on the whipped cream.

Garrett pushed over his plate. "You look hungry."

I was, in fact, suddenly starving. Irish coffee and gooey, bacon-and-cheese-loaded potato chips might not be the ideal culinary combo, but after the day I'd had so far, I didn't care. "Thanks." I slid out a particularly appealing chip from the middle. "Don't mind if I do."

A semi-awkward but amiable silence settled between us as an old Chieftains song played in the background. I tried not to be haunted by the past again—our past, short as it had been. He'd joined the military straight out of high school, and I'd started seeing Ian. That turned out to be a mistake in the end, but you never knew until you'd lived it. Had it been Ian's fault? Mine? Both of ours? My money was on the last answer. Nothing was ever one person's fault.

What was the point of dwelling on the past, anyway? I knew the answer: *To learn for the future and avoid making the same mistakes.* It was the "dwelling" that was always the issue for me. "So, are you seeing anyone?" I asked, casually snagging another nacho. The pile beneath it collapsed into a soggy mess.

Colleen had said he'd been dating someone. Maggie? No, Megan.

He seemed taken aback. "Uh, no." He signaled Damien for two pints, one of them for me. "Not anymore. Why?"

My face grew warm, and not just from the coffee. I shrugged. "Just asking. That's what friends do, right?"

He swirled his glass. "Sure."

This whole line of conversation was a mistake. What was I doing? "Didn't see much of you at the Blarney Breakfast. Anything interesting on your end?"

"Nah. I heard what happened to the girls who were supposed to dance. Maeve did a good job."

"She did," I agreed, thinking of my daughter back in the Nest. Probably crying her eyes out, and here I was drinking whiskey with my old boyfriend. I half-drained my glass.

"What's wrong?" Garrett asked. "You look sad or something. Everything okay?"

"Yes. Everything's fine. Really." It sounded unconvincing, even to me. And I'd already broken my vow to always tell people the truth.

I was so pathetic right now. I realized I was literally drooping over the bar. I finished my drink and assumed a level of posture even Sister Malaria from my Angels days would approve. "Things look better for Conor and Colleen, at least."

He nodded. "The Chief told me the deal with the scholarship money."

"Of course he did," I said with a sigh. I'd hoped my dad would keep that on the down-low for a while, for Darcy's sake, but cops weren't in the business of keeping secrets among themselves, as far as case developments were concerned.

Damien brought our beers, and a glass of water for me. I didn't even have to ask. "Want to play darts?" I asked Garrett, already hopping off the stool with the beer. I knew he'd say yes.

"You've still got your Boston accent." Garrett followed me to the small, cleared area in the far corner.

"I don't have any accent," I said, opening the drawer under the dartboard to grab two sets of darts. I handed the orange ones to him and kept the green.

"Yeah, you do." He grinned. "You said 'dahts.' You can take the girl out of the city, but you can't take the Shamrock out of the girl."

"Woman." I took aim at the board with my first dart. "And you got the line wrong, that made no sense."

"Oh, I think it did." Garrett hit the bullseye with his first dart, and I muttered under my breath. "I've gotten a lot of practice while you've been gone," he said.

I don't know how long we played darts, but after a while we switched to pool, until customers started coming in for happy hour. "I've got to get home," I told Garrett. "And I think I may be a little tipsy."

"I'll walk you," he said. "Fresh air after the rain will sober you right up." Then he ordered me an Irish coffee to go. Without the whiskey.

The thought of going home and facing Maeve and Colleen and Bliz and the whole situation had already killed my buzz. Adding to my humiliation, a huge tear escaped without warning from my right eye. I dabbed at it swiftly with a dark-green cocktail napkin.

"Sure you don't want to tell me what's going on?" Garrett asked as we walked out the back door.

"It's nothing, really." I stumbled very slightly as we reached the sidewalk, and he caught my arm. "No, it's everything." The last word came out in a highly unattractive half-croak, half-sob.

"Aw, hey, Katie." He patted me gently on the back. "Don't cry. I always hated it when you bawled."

"I never bawl," I said. "I am always in complete control."

"You are," he agreed. "But you don't have to be perfect with me, okay?"

I didn't answer, except for one small hiccup.

"You're stressed out, that's all. I mean, it's not every day you come across a dead body, and it's a lot worse if you know the person. But we've got counseling services down at the station, and I can—"

"It's not Deirdre's murder. I mean, that's part of it." I blew my nose on the crumpled stack of extra napkins he handed me from his pocket. "It's . . . everything. My crazy family, and the case, and now everything's changing, and I can't stop it."

"Change is change," he said. "It isn't good or bad. Just . . . change. No one can stop it. And you can't really control it either, no matter what you think. All you can control is your own attitude and how you react to whatever happens."

I sniffed and nodded.

"That's life, right? Ups and downs. You gotta roll with the punches, Katie. And maybe punch back every once in a while."

I smiled through my tears, which were dripping everywhere now. "Thanks. Sorry. I'm a freaking mess."

"No problem." Garrett pushed a damp strand of hair from my cheek. "Come on, take another chug of coffee and let's keep walking. If you don't show up for dinner, your dad will have me officially demoted to whatever is lower than rookie detective."

"It's only five o'clock," I protested.

"Six."

"I'm a full-grown adult," I said. "It's not like I have a curfew or anything."

"Keep walking," he said cheerfully.

In no time, Garrett escorted me up the steps of the Buckley House. Even though it was mid-March, the early darkness screamed December, thanks to yet another brewing storm. "Maybe I should just ring the bell and run," he said.

"You don't need to wait around." My hand was already fumbling with the doorknob. He reached past me for the assist, and I fell back slightly. "I think maybe I do," he said, steadying me again.

"It's all the sugar and caffeine from that coffee."

"Right." His hand stayed on my shoulder. "This was fun. We should do it again sometime. Text me if you need me, okay? I mean it."

"Okay." This close, he smelled of Irish Spring soap and water, with a shot of Guinness. Clean as a whistle. I closed my eyes, waiting for the brush of familiar lips.

He kissed me, hard, and I kissed him back, throwing my arms around his neck as he pulled me against him.

Instantly, the porch lights came on—then just as abruptly, turned off. And on again. The Chief's old signal code. The warning kind.

The moment was gone. "I can't believe him." I extricated myself, mortified. "What were you saying about change? My dad never changes."

"Maybe that's a good thing." Garrett grinned as he stepped away too, but not as quickly. "Night, Katie. Drink lots of water." He started down the porch, hands jammed in the pockets of his police windbreaker.

The Jig Is Up

I stood there for a moment, watching him walk away, until a chattering group of Buckley House guests turned down Galway Court from the corner. Uh-oh. Time to go in.

"Ups and downs," I reminded myself as I stepped through the front door. Mostly downs, lately.

Except, maybe, the last couple of hours.

Chapter
Twenty-Nine

Luckily, Mom was so busy directing me and Colleen in last-minute family dinner prep and serving drinks to the guests that she didn't seem to notice I was a little fuddled. No one else did either.

Our mom also failed to comment when Maeve didn't appear in the kitchen for dinner. "We'll make her a tray," was all she said.

"I filled her in," Colleen whispered as she passed me the bowl of green beans with prefab fried onions.

Bliz chattered nonstop about the movie, and the new dance skirt and black turtleneck leotard she'd wear to match the other girls in her show number. I smiled and nodded, wondering how I could possibly tell my youngest daughter that her aunt was her bio mommy. Bliz was just starting to ask more specific growing-up questions she'd gathered thanks to the internet, older kids, and movies other than *Finian's Rainbow*.

It was time, I knew. But some things would probably still go right over her head for now.

I had no idea what Colleen was thinking beside me, but on the surface everything seemed right as rain. Mom kept things moving by passing extra platters of food and asking my sister and me to check on the guests in the parlor more frequently than usual. That killed any buzz I'd felt earlier. Maybe I'd imagined it.

"And guess what?" Bliz said excitedly. "Brogan and Ginger and Fiona have a foster dog at their house. His name is Rover, and he's staying with them 'til he gets adopted, but Aunt Colleen said maybe he could come and visit us while me and Maeve and Mommy are in Shamrock."

I almost choked on my water.

"She said that, did she?" The Chief arched an eyebrow at my sister, then turned back to Bliz. "Taking care of an animal is a big responsibility."

"I know." Bliz nodded. "The triplets walk him and feed him and help clean up when he has an accident." She looked pleadingly at me. "Can he come for a sleepover, Mommy?"

"I don't think that's a good idea," I said. "What about Banshee? He and Rover might not be friends." *Bet on it.*

Mom rose from the table and picked up her apron from the back of the chair. "You can talk with your mother about that later, Mary Elizabeth. Weren't we going to roll your hair in socks tonight?" She looked at me and Colleen. "You two clean up, please, and see if the guests need anything else for the evening. And don't forget Maeve's dinner and a pack-up for Bernie Donnelly."

I whirled toward Colleen as soon as we were alone. "Seriously? You're bribing Bliz with a *dog*?"

"Not a bribe. It was her idea. I didn't discourage her, that's all, because I didn't know what you'd say."

"Oh, I think you did."

We worked in silence around the kitchen, and Colleen checked on the guests. None of them wanted anything other than tea and the living room TV tuned to a twenty-four-hour marathon of *The Quiet Man*. One guest multitasked by knitting a sweater that looked as if it might fit the Jolly Green Giant.

"I'm checking on Maeve." I squeezed out the dish sponge and gave the dishwasher a light kick after I'd set it to run. Sometimes that helped get it going.

"I'll go with you." Colleen grabbed the guest tray from the ledge and heaped a plate with shepherd's pie and two huge, fluffy biscuits from the still-warm oven.

I almost told her I wanted to deal with my daughter on my own, but I didn't because that wasn't really true. My head was already beginning to throb, either from the Irish coffee or the prospect of the conversation.

The stairs to the Nest were still folded. Colleen handed me the tray and pulled on the chain, then carefully lowered the ladder.

"Maeve, it's me," I called.

"And Aunt Colleen," my sister added.

Silence.

"Just take the food up," Colleen whispered. "She has to eat sometime. She never turns down food."

Don't think, do. How many times had the Chief told me that in my life? I took a deep breath and started up the ladder.

The attic was dark, with Maeve nearly invisible under the bed quilt. "Go away. I told you, I'm not talking to you guys."

Colleen took that as her signal to pull herself up and into the room beside me.

"Come on, honey," I said to Maeve. "It's shepherd's pie, yum. And Gram's biscuits."

"I don't care." Her voice was muffled.

My sister took the tray from me, placed it on the nightstand, and sat at the end of the bed. "Come on, kiddo. We have to talk.

All three of us. And the mashed potatoes on top will turn into a gross lump of paste if you don't eat the shepherd's pie now."

Maeve threw the quilt back and sat up, taking the tray. "Why didn't you tell me the truth?"

"I'm sorry," I said. "We should have—*I* should have—but at the time we thought it was the best way to handle things."

"You thought wrong."

"We meant well," Colleen said. "The important thing is your mom is the best mom you and Bliz could ever have." She smiled at me.

I smiled back. That was sweet, and I hoped it was true. Was I a good mom? Sometimes I wasn't so sure. I made a ton of mistakes every day. But I tried.

"Was that why you gave up dancing, Aunt Colleen? Because you were going to have Bliz?"

My sister looked startled. "What? No. I didn't join Irish Steps because I just wanted to dance for myself. For fun. I never liked to compete, like Deirdre and Moira. And I wasn't really into shows either, to be honest—except for the dresses and all the attention, maybe. I only tried out for Irish Steps because Deirdre did. We were going to live together in New York and travel the world. Except I don't like to travel. I'm happy here in Shamrock."

Now it was my turn to stay silent. I'd never known any of that about my sister. Not really.

"You're an amazing dancer," Maeve said. "I told you, I saw you dancing in the driveway. You're even better than Deirdre was, I bet."

"Nah." Colleen gave a small laugh.

Maeve had put together a lot more pieces than I'd realized. She wanted to know whether I'd officially adopted Bliz—yes—and how she had missed that I hadn't been pregnant. She'd been around

Bliz's age at the time, and she remembered when Aunt Colleen lived with us in New York for a while, but she hadn't noticed anything different about her.

We'd sent Maeve to spend that summer at Emerald Lake with Mom and the Chief. She'd been so excited about the cabin and swimming and playing with all the other kids. And when she returned to the city, she had a new baby sister. And no more Daddy, but that was a different story.

"When are you going to tell Bliz?" Maeve twisted back to me, her eyes still puffy and red. It killed me to see her like this and know that I was responsible. If I'd explained things earlier, maybe we wouldn't be in this situation. But it was impossible to know that for sure.

"I'm not sure, honey," I said honestly. "We really haven't figured that out yet. Soon, I promise."

Maeve was quiet again for a moment. "If you're still Bliz's mom, am I still her sister?" she asked finally. "Or just her cousin?"

My heart broke. "Oh, sweetie, of course you're sisters. One hundred percent. And that won't ever change. Sisters are forever." I smiled at Colleen.

"And you're cousins too," she added. "Pretty cool, huh?"

Way to spoil a beautiful sisterly moment. I almost bopped her with a throw pillow.

Maeve scraped the whipped cream off the top of her banana pudding with her finger. "So who's Bliz's bio dad, then?"

Colleen bounced off the bed and started toward the trapdoor. "I told you already. That, missy, is none of your business."

Missy? Maeve threw her the same scowl my sister gave the Chief when he called her that.

"Wait a second," Maeve said after Colleen disappeared down the ladder. "Did Dad leave because you adopted Bliz?"

"Absolutely not," I said. "That had *nothing* to do with you or Bliz. We'll talk about that some other time, okay? I think we've had enough discussion for one night."

"Okay." Maeve seemed tired of talking too.

I kept my fingers crossed until I hit the hallway. There were some little green lies it was better to hold on to.

* * *

I was so exhausted, I went to bed at the same time as Bliz. But thanks to the day's events, and too much Irish coffee, I lay wide awake with my brain buzzing. So. Many. Things.

Usually I dealt with multiple problems by separating them into individual mental files. Like a hallway of doors, with a problem behind each one. My rule was, I could only open one door at a time. I'd deal with that issue, then close the door and open another.

Usually the hall was short, with a Work door, a Money door, and a Personal-slash-Family door. Now it felt like a really long corridor with way too many doors. That Doors of Dublin poster again, come to life in a less charming version.

In my mind, I closed the Personal door and crossed the hall to the Investigation door, where I was confronted by even more doors. One for Moira, another for Aidan, and a smaller door marked "Theresa." There was even a fourth, much smaller door scrawled with "McShane Witches."

I'd already eliminated Una due to her build and the likely time frame of Deirdre's murder. She had motive—removing the main obstacle to Moira's new dance academy—but that was about it.

271

And Nuala, who shared that motive, was tall, but I had to eliminate her from the running too, for the same reason: timing. I'd seen her in the Smiling Shamrock's window that night, spying on us. Too bad just being evil didn't qualify anyone as a killer.

This hall of doors was a crazy-house nightmare. What was I missing?

Chapter Thirty

Bliz's dancing didn't wake me up the next morning, even though she was step-hopping all over the bedroom. The bagpipes did. Their long, steady tones came from the front steps of Our Lady of Angels Church, which held a special Mass before the Paddy's Day Parade kicked off at noon. I wouldn't be in attendance, although I could stand to offer a prayer or two.

Officially, Saint Patrick's Day wasn't until tomorrow. Holding the parade a day early meant that more police officers, firefighters, and EMTs, who made up a fair number of the marchers, could be available for duty on the actual holiday.

Bounce, bounce, bounce. I pulled my pillow over my aching head. We should have nicknamed her Tigger instead of Bliz.

My younger daughter was already dressed for the parade. She might have slept in her Donnelly School parade outfit because it looked a little rumpled.

"You'll need to wear that T-shirt over your Irish sweater," I said.

Bliz stopped dancing to pout. "But, Mommy, I'll look all bulky."

We had the same discussion every Halloween about Bliz's costumes. "At least you'll be warm. It's freezing out there, even if it's

273

sunny." To prove my point, the early spring wind rattled the branches of the maples outside the window.

She gave an exaggerated sigh. "Okay. Why isn't Maeve marching in the parade?"

I checked my phone to find out my family's status. Colleen was already at the start of the parade route. Mom had gone to Mass and would meet us later. Maeve was . . . not going.

"She's very tired this morning." I motioned Bliz over so I could readjust her headband. "But I'll be waving when you pass the police station, and I'll be at the gazebo when you finish. They give you green bagels for being in the parade."

"I'd rather have ice cream."

"Ice cream isn't Irish," I reminded her. Neither were green bagels, but the real estate office sponsoring the free handouts weren't sticklers. "We'll stop by PJ Scoops on the way and get you a hot chocolate."

I threw on jeans, a turtleneck, sneakers, and the first green thing I could find of Colleen's: a sweatshirt that said *Everyone Loves a Shamrock Girl*.

"Aunt Colleen is all dressed up," Bliz said as I wound my hair into a messy bun on top of my head.

"Well, she's marching," I said. "I'm cheering everyone on."

I guided Bliz away from the already rowdy throngs headed toward Our Lady of Angels, clad in every shade of green and plaid and Irish knitwear. Hopefully they were skipping coffees from PJ's and moving straight on to green beer.

The place was nearly empty. Conor leaned against the counter, sipping his own coffee and reading his phone. "Hey," he greeted us as the "When Irish Eyes Are Smiling" chime ended.

"Do you ever get sick of that song?" Bliz pressed her nose against the glass over the ice cream. I shooed her away from it and handed her a wet wipe.

"Part of the job. How come you're not at the big parade yet? My sisters left an hour ago."

"We're on our way," I said. "Could we get one hot chocolate and a nonfat cappuccino to go, please? And an oatmeal cookie, warmed up."

"The one with the icing," Bliz said.

"Sure." He headed to the espresso machine. With Bliz admiring the colorful ice creams again, this time from a safer distance, I followed him down the counter. "Did Zoe tell you about the Blarney Breakfast?" I asked.

"Yeah," he said. "Crazy stuff. She's still mad about being locked in the bathroom with Darcy. At least they're friends now. But some of the kids aren't coming to the dress rehearsal tonight. Did Miss Colleen tell you? Their parents said it was too dangerous."

Who could blame them? I was surprised there'd be a dress rehearsal at all, or even a show. "Are they dropping out of the show too?"

He shrugged. "Dunno. Maybe. Mayor Flanagan said he'd personally be at the rehearsal to show everyone how safe it was, but the cops told him no."

I bet the Chief hadn't had to intervene on that one. All the PD needed was a clueless, attention-seeking town dignitary they'd have to babysit.

Conor gave me my drink, then prepared Bliz's hot chocolate. I resisted a shudder as he sprinkled green sugar over the whipped cream into an approximate shamrock shape. "There you go," he said, handing it to her over the counter. "Do a good job in the parade today."

"I will." Bliz beamed. Amazing how a little green flower could brighten a day.

We made it to the start of the parade route in plenty of time. They were having trouble inflating the giant shamrock balloon. "Remember to smile," I told Bliz. She nodded and rushed off to join the Donnelly School group.

Mom stepped onto the curb beside me in front of the Shamrock PD. "You made it," I said.

"I've never missed a year," she said, pulling her scarf tighter. The wind had picked up again, but at least it was still sunny. The only person frowning was Detective Sergeant Surly Shirley, standing stiffly in her dark suit a couple yards away. She wasn't marching today. Just watching the crowd.

It seemed as if every resident of Shamrock other than Mom and me was marching in the parade.

The parade kicked off to the solemn sound of bagpipes, followed by dueling Irish music piped out by floats crowded with parade committee members and town officials headed toward the reviewing stand. All three McShanes had finagled themselves into that group. I was shocked that the Smiling Shamrock didn't have its very own overbloated float.

The Grand Marshal and his entourage were next, walking and waving to a rousing medley from Irish Steps played by the Shamrock High School marching band. The crowd cheered in waves as a rosy-cheeked Aidan passed, doffing his cap to old dears and blowing kisses to thrilled young fans. Every so often, he executed a quick set of dance steps without losing a beat, to more applause.

Next, I spotted the Chief riding toward us, waving to the crowd beside Chief Ryan from the back of an open black Caddy driven by Frank. The vehicle was sandwiched front and back by two highly polished Shamrock PD cruisers with their lights on. Frank hit the horn as he passed us.

To my surprise, Maeve squeezed in between me and Mom just in time to cheer for her grandfather.

"Good girl," Mom said, with a side wink at me. "You're feeling better."

"Oh, honey, I'm so glad you changed your mind." I tried not to sound overly pleased and relieved as I gave Maeve a quick hug.

"Sort of. Did I miss the Donnelly School?"

"No," I said. "And look, I have something for you. I know how much you loved the one Zoe brought you." I rummaged in my bag and pulled out a bagel. Shrink-wrapped, glutened, and green this time. "I snagged it from a table near the parade start. They had a bunch of them in baskets."

"Thanks." Maeve poked at the bagel with her finger. "Hard as a rock. They must bring out the same ones every year."

"Probably," I agreed.

My daughter gave me her signature eye roll, but at least she was speaking to me. A promising start.

We stood and clapped and cheered for what felt like forever until the Donnelly School marchers appeared. Not as many as in past years, but a good turnout. Their performance in front of the reviewing stand would close out the parade, but the dancers— from the smallest to the tallest—were already drawing a huge crowd response. People with cell phones pushed and shoved around us, angling for the best video position.

The Murphy triplets carried the green-and-gold-felt Donnelly School banner, struggling slightly. Poles could get heavy on a long parade route. Natalie ran ahead from her group to provide an assist on one side, and Garrett, who walked beside them, grabbed the other end.

Every inch the cop in his starched white shirt, green tie, and dress uniform, he stared straight ahead as he marched down

Centre Street. I knew he was watching his nieces from under the brim of his hat, as well as the crowd in both directions.

Behind them, Bernie rode in a dark-green antique car, waving from the open back window to more cheers. I didn't recognize the driver, but I was surprised to see who was wrangling the dancers, marching beside them and yelling at them to keep in line.

Theresa Meaney.

Had Colleen spoken with her yet? Did Bernie have any idea that Theresa had stolen the scholarship money?

Zoe and Darcy came next, pulling the new scholarship fund jug in a decorated wagon with Deirdre's photo. The jug was almost completely filled to the top with cash. A few people ran up to stick bills through the slot in the lid.

I could sense Sergeant Walker was about to have a heart attack. "Step away from the marchers!" she shouted. "You can donate at the finish."

We still hadn't seen Bliz, but there she was, bringing up the rear with Colleen. She held my sister's hand as she waved to the crowd, looking ecstatic.

"Isn't she adorable?" someone said behind me. "I have to get a picture."

Colleen had opted for boots and a fitted navy suit with a green cashmere sweater and a print silk scarf threaded in gold. I was pretty sure she'd gotten most of the outfit from Mom's closet, but it was perfect. She wore her wavy ponytail tied to one side with a Kelly-green bow.

My sister was smiling, but she wasn't waving to the crowd. In her other hand was a green-and-orange leash, and at the end of it was Rover, wearing green shamrock feelers and green doggy goggles.

"Hi, Mommy!" Bliz called. "Hi, Maevie! Hi, Gram!"

My own mom leaned closer to me. "Is that the sleepover dog?" she asked in a low voice as we all waved back. "He's enormous."

"That's the one," I said, still waving. "Don't say it."

"Saints preserve us," Mom said.

* * *

That afternoon, I took a nap with Bliz up in the Nest. There were only a few hours left until we needed to be at Great Shamrock Hall for the dress rehearsal, and I was exhausted. After we'd all made it back from the parade—without Rover, for now—there was work to do at the Buckley House. I'd helped Mom and Colleen with housekeeping and laundry and hand-washing the gold-rimmed china for the special guest buffet table set up in the living room. The corned beef and green cupcakes were ready to go for tomorrow, covered in plastic and jamming every space in the fridge. All we had to add was the tea.

Hopefully the guests would think the fairies had readied everything for Paddy's Day in their absence.

I lay on top of the quilt, feeling distinctly unfairylike. I was about to set my phone alarm when I noticed something sticking out of Bliz's bag across the room. Another dance magazine, a newer one. Someone must have given it to her.

It had to be recent because Deirdre's face stared out at me from the cover. The head storyline read, "Deirdre Donnelly: Death of a Dynasty."

Bliz didn't need to read that garbage. I swung my feet to the floor, taking care not to wake her, and crept over to the bag.

When I pulled out the whole magazine, I saw a smaller photo of Bernie in the lower right of the cover. A young Bernie in her

279

champion sash, looking a lot like Deirdre. There was another, much older photo beside it—Bernadette's mother, also wearing a sash and holding an enormous bouquet of flowers.

I flipped through the pages to the feature article, reading in the fading light from the Nest window. The story was short, mostly photos, and very sad. With Deirdre's death, her long family lines of champions—maternal and paternal—had come to an end.

As if the loss of Deirdre herself wasn't awful enough. I rolled up the magazine, intending to tell Bliz I'd get her her very own subscription to a more kid-appropriate Irish dance magazine. But then I had another disturbing thought.

The McShane family had suffered a tragic loss too, when Áine was killed with her husband in that terrible car crash in Ireland. At least she'd left little Moira behind to carry on their own family dancing dynasty. But there was no mention of any McShanes in the magazine.

Their only legacy, Moira, had never won a world title, or even a national one. She'd been let go from Irish Steps. Her dance school in New York was a failure.

That had to be disappointing for the McShanes. Moira was probably devastated she'd let her aunts down. But enough to permanently remove the person she considered her big competition?

As I looked over at my sleeping daughter and her blond curls strewn across the pillow, I couldn't help thinking there was something more to the story. A tiny missing jigsaw piece. And studying the nearly-identical Donnelly family photos again, I had a sudden suspicion of what it might be.

Only one person could help me. A glance at the clock told me I had two hours left before we had to leave for rehearsal. If I hustled, I could make it back from Bernie's in time.

I'd bring her a plate of Mom's corned beef.

Chapter
Thirty-One

"Ms. Buckley, are we up soon?" I felt a tug on my sweater as I stood in the wings off the stage at Great Shamrock Hall. One of Conor's little sisters, the blonde, looked up at me hopefully.

I consulted my dress rehearsal clipboard. Actually, it was Maeve's clipboard now. She'd been delighted to trade in her dancing spots for the stage manager duties of a mom whose kid dropped out. I was just filling in until my daughter got back from the bathroom. Conor was busy with the sound guy and monitoring the playlist from his computer, so I had a nice long stretch before I'd need to return to the piano.

"No, Brogan," I said. "Maeve will tell you before it's time for the ceili reel, okay? I promise. But don't go anywhere," I called as she zipped away. "Stay with your group in the seats."

Judging by the number of cops and adults around the hall, security today was extra-tight. The kids had to stay in their seats at the front until they were called so there'd be no running around backstage or downstairs. No one was taking any extra chances.

I peeked out again to check on Una and Moira. Maybe in return for Deirdre's Blarney Breakfast, Bernie had graciously invited them to attend, along with Nuala, who'd chosen not to

281

stick around for long. Too bad, because after talking to Bernie tonight, I wanted to keep a sharp eye on all the McShanes. Bernie was staying home to recover from the day and save her energy for tomorrow, she'd said. I left her with the plate of corned beef and a steaming pot of Barry's tea.

Moira had probably shown up hoping for an opportunity to bug Aidan again. My sister had convinced him to make a special appearance in the show. Why Una was sticking around, I had no clue. Maybe just to make the kids nervous.

Theresa circulated through the auditorium, selling tickets for tomorrow's fifty-fifty raffle—hopefully without pocketing any proceeds.

Most of the dancers were watching the action onstage as Zoe ran through her solo without the music, under Colleen's watchful eye. To close the show, Zoe and Aidan would perform a popular number from Irish Steps, with Zoe dancing Deirdre's old part.

Sad, but a lovely tribute to Deirdre. Colleen had come up with the idea after Maeve and Aidan's impromptu breakfast performance.

All heads swiveled when the King of the Dance himself made his way down the center aisle. He waved to the captive audience, tossing his latest tweed jacket over the back of an empty seat but leaving on his cap and scarf. Moira eagerly half-rose, but he ignored her and ascended the stage to join my sister.

I could tell Moira was embarrassed. She exited the row anyway, clambering over parents, guardians, and babysitters—and bounded straight toward me on the other side of the stage.

"Hi, Kate." Tonight she was dolled up in multiple shades of purple, from nubby coat to chiffon scarf to sparkly shoes. A grape nightmare. "Need any help?"

I threw her a Colleen smile. "Gosh, Moira, thanks, but everything's under control."

She looked disappointed. "Oh, okay."

"Too bad your auntie Nuala had to leave," I said. "Is she coming back?"

"No." Moira glanced over her shoulder at Aidan and Colleen. "She needed to be at the Smiling Shamrock for when the guests get back. You know, St. Paddy's Eve and all."

"Right."

"Thanks, Mom, I've got it from here." Maeve took the clipboard from me, and Moira made a hasty retreat to her seat.

"Okay," I said. "Watch for uncorralled kiddos and give a holler if there are any issues."

"Yup." Her eyes didn't leave the clipboard.

Conor was still with the sound guy in the lower balcony at the back of the auditorium. On the near-empty stage, Colleen, Zoe, and Aidan were engrossed in blocking out dance moves. Maybe I should make a quick trip to the downstairs ladies' room before I returned to my bench. I'd been drinking a ton of tea.

First, I texted Garrett to see if he was here at the rehearsal—and if not, whether he could low-key swing by the Smiling Shamrock to check for Nuala.

Maybe I was being overly cautious, but I didn't trust her, especially after my convo with Bernie. Deirdre's mom had told me a few stories and confirmed that Nuala had always been jealous and unpleasant. Being a nasty witch didn't make anyone a murderer, of course, but it was part of the skill set for the job.

Plus, I'd realized something else. I may have made a huge mistake when the girls and I arrived in Shamrock on the rainy night of Deirdre's murder.

Nuala and her great-niece shared the same build and facial features, if you got past Nuala's lizardy qualities and Moira's Jokeresque cosmetic skills. What if it was Moira, not Nuala, I'd seen in the Smiling Shamrock's window? It was dark, with all that lightning and the neon-green glow from the sign. Moira had checked Aidan into the Shamrock that evening, with a time-stamped selfie to prove it. Nuala had no alibi, as far as I knew, if the person spying from behind the lace curtain was actually Moira. I'd been tired. Could I have screwed up which witch as I looked back at the house from the driveway? Yes.

No answer from Garrett. I texted the same request to the Chief, just in case. He'd drive by the McShanes' in a heartbeat, no questions asked. Until later.

It was dark at the back of the huge stage, but I spotted the door to the stairs just under the Exit sign. I hesitated, remembering the night Colleen and I had found Deirdre, and considered making a one-eighty toward the ladies' room in the front lobby. But that reminded me of when I'd been assaulted near the doors. Downstairs would be quicker. I had my phone with the flashlight app— and 911 at my fingertips.

I heard a half-muted clank high above my head to the left. Someone was up on the bridge.

Probably one of the light guys. But they'd already done a run-through with Conor this afternoon, without the kids.

I gazed up at the darkened steel walkway. Was it my jumpy imagination, or had I glimpsed a small, shifting beam of light in the cavernous gloom?

Now a flash of silver. Nuala, with her trusty torch. I was sure of it. I reached for my phone in my back pocket, ready to make the call.

Irish Steps music blasted through the sound system. Way, way too loud, at least back here.

Was I overreacting? What if I caused a panic for nothing? The show would be canceled for good.

Nuala was elderly, but also tough and in decent shape. And if she'd knocked out Deirdre with that flashlight, and half-suffocated me with her hands, she'd proven she could be pretty effective without a real weapon. Well, I'd be ready for her this time. I just needed to see what she was up to. And while I didn't see any cops right now, there were plenty of them on hand.

Don't think, do.

I found the steps leading up to the catwalk.

Great Shamrock Hall was built in the early 1900s, and the backstage area had never seen much in the way of updating. The catwalk stairs were curving slats of rusted iron.

At least I wasn't afraid of heights. Cell phone in hand, I made my way carefully up the stairs and took a cautious step or two onto the walk. There was a simple railing along the outer edge, but it didn't seem steady, and the wide gaps between the lighting mounts made me nervous.

Thanks to a sole, fading fluorescent light from the pipe grid above, I could see just enough to edge slowly along the walk, which sagged and wiggled with each step I took. I ducked to avoid the low-hanging air ducts but kept my gaze ahead.

No more flashlight beams, and I couldn't hear any clanks now over the blasting show music anyway. I squinted to make out a narrow wooden workman's platform against the far wall, littered with debris: boxes, bolts, nails, screws—even a stray hammer. Looked as if stuff had been left out on the catwalk too—even a bucket. Jeez. Anyone could trip and fall, or knock something off the ledge and injure someone below.

I needed to be more careful. This was a stupid idea. I'd head back down to the stage level and get help.

The catwalk lurched, and I grabbed for the railing.

"Don't move, girlie."

She'd snuck up on me after all. I whirled to meet the glare from Nuala's yellow eyes—and another old-school fluorescent light tube in her gloved hand, broken at one end and pointed directly at my chest. I drew back, keeping one hand tightly on the rail.

"I said don't move." Nuala pointed the jagged tube closer to my throat.

"P-put that down," I choked out. "There's mercury in that thing. It'll hurt you too." I had no idea if that was true. It sounded scientific. And hopefully scary.

Nuala's thin lips turned up at the corners. She lowered the tube slightly and nodded down the catwalk. "Now you can move. Start walking. Go."

I shouted as loud as I could, but no one could hear me over the pounding music. It would stop when the show number came to an end. Or Zoe made a mistake. I just needed to buy time.

Keeping my eyes on Nuala, I tried to dial 911, but she lunged with her makeshift light saber, swiping the air an inch from my hand. My phone fell to the metal grate below my feet, and she kicked it farther down the catwalk.

I had to get it back. I edged away from Nuala toward the phone, holding on to the shaky railing for as long as possible before I'd be forced to let go for the wide gap around the light. I lost my balance and steadied myself on the back of the black metal box, slicing my leg through my jeans on a jutting corner.

"Ouch!" I squeezed my eyes shut against the pain. The metal was probably rusted. If I survived impalement and mercury poisoning, I'd get tetanus. This woman was a fiend. A freak of nature.

And Zoe was still dancing like one, because the music kept playing. Irish Steps was known for their long production numbers.

"Don't be a whinger," Nuala said. "It doesn't suit you."

I glanced behind me as I kept edging back, hoping to catch her off balance as she navigated the same light box. Unfortunately, Nuala was a lot more agile—graceful, even—than I'd expected as she practically leaped around the box. All that girlhood dance training, maybe. And zero fear.

That's when I spotted the black harness straps, barely visible against Nuala's dark raincoat, and the silver chain fastened into the edge of the railing behind her. She was working with a virtual safety net.

"Move along." She sounded more impatient now.

This time I refused. Time for a different tack.

"The cops know you killed Deirdre," I lied, shouting over the infernal music. "I've told them everything I found out about you. You won't get away with whatever you're doing up here either. They're waiting for you below. For both of us."

Nuala didn't flinch. Instead, she moved closer. "Poppycock. That girl had a terrible accident. She fell down the stairs and hit her head. So sad."

"A witness saw you in Angels Hall that night." No need to mention Conor hadn't actually identified the person as Nuala McShane.

She weighed that information. "I went to talk some sense into the girl. She turned down the chance to work with our Moira, the worst mistake she ever made."

And the last one. "You knocked Deirdre out with that flashlight." I nodded at the hardware store torch tucked into the belt of her harness strap. "The same one you stuck in my back the other night to make me think it was a gun."

"Nonsense."

"But knocking Deirdre out wasn't enough for you. You wanted to make sure she was dead. You dragged her backstage when she was unconscious, or disoriented, and threw her down the stairs."

"Rubbish," Nuala said, but I saw a nervous flicker in her eyes. She made another close jab with the jagged tube. "Two more steps should do it."

Do what? I glanced down at the stage where Zoe was dancing, with Colleen demonstrating in front of her. Aidan stood at the side, frowning in concentration as the full-orchestra jig grew faster and louder.

No one would see us up here, with the light mounts. Unless they were already looking.

Make a mistake, Zoe. Please, for once in your life. Stop the music.

Nuala made another lunge. I jumped back—just short of that metal bucket left on the edge of the catwalk.

As I caught my balance, I saw that the bucket wasn't empty. It held an open bag of nails and what looked like a solid ball of cement. If the bucket fell to the stage, anyone in or near its path could be badly hurt. Or worse.

If I stood my ground, I wouldn't hit the bucket—and allow Nuala to escape in the chaos. Plus, people might even think I'd set this evil plan up myself and fallen by accident.

Colleen and Aidan were dancing now, with Zoe behind them, shadowing my sister's moves. The three moved closer to the catwalk. This was the finale, where all the dancers would assemble on the stage in front of them and take their bows.

"Look out!" I screamed down as loudly as I could, frantically waving my arms. "Stop!"

There was a quick ripping sound, as the light tube split the arm of Colleen's leather jacket. Thank heavens I'd kept it on due to

Mayor Flanagan's cheapness with the heating bill for Great Shamrock Hall.

"Do that again, and it will be your neck," Nuala practically spat.

Now or never. *Just do.* "You weren't jealous of Deirdre because of Moira," I said. "It was all about your daughter, wasn't it? Áine."

I saw the bile hue drain from Nuala's face, even in the dark. "Áine was my niece, you wagon."

"No, she wasn't," I said. "You and Una came here to the States before she was born. You two passed her off as your niece. But your dancing career was over."

The witch was finally speechless.

"Áine was your pride and joy. She became a top Irish dancer, just like you. But she never beat Bernadette Rose McFadden—now Donnelly—did she? I had a little chat with Bernie a couple of hours ago. She always kept your big secret. Instead of being grateful, you murdered her daughter."

Nuala tightened her grip on the light tube. "Stop."

"Bernie retired to marry her sweetheart. Áine wanted to quit too, but you pushed her to keep competing. Instead she eloped with a fellow dancer she hardly knew and had Moira."

"My Áine did no such thing."

"That's right," I said. "*Your* Áine. And then, years later, Bernie's daughter beat Moira in every championship and got all the attention. Moira didn't headline in Irish Steps with Aidan—Deirdre did. Moira got fired. Then her dance school in New York failed, and you wanted her to come home to Shamrock and start over. But Deirdre was in the way again."

"Ridiculous." Nuala's voice came out in a hiss.

"You wanted Deirdre and Moira to be business partners to save face, because you knew Moira's new dance academy couldn't compete against the Donnelly School," I went on, still praying for the music to end. "But Deirdre said no to Moira, and you went to Angels Hall and hit her with your flashlight. Then you dragged her to the stairs and pushed her in a fit of rage."

"Hold your tongue, you impudent little missy."

"You thought you'd solved everything, didn't you? As a bonus, what better way to get back at Bernie after all these years than by making her feel the loss you did, the loss of an only daughter—and destroy her school too? The end of an Irish dance dynasty."

"Aren't you clever?" Nuala sneered. "Just like all the Buckleys."

"But you didn't expect Colleen to take Deirdre's place running the show, did you? The sad thing is, Moira didn't even want to have a dance school anymore. That was just a backup plan. She wanted to join Aidan's new show, since he couldn't have Deirdre. She still wanted to be a star."

"Enough!" Nuala waved the light tube over her head and took another swipe at me. I twisted and it sliced air. "Aidan didn't want Deirdre for his show. He wanted your hussy sister. He's always wanted her, you stupid girl."

What? My head spun. It was true, I realized, with a rush of horror. And Colleen was Nuala's next target.

"You Buckleys will be sorry for your meddling when you're both lying dead on that stage."

"Don't think so." I saw my chance and grabbed the flashlight from her safety harness strap. Nuala brought down the jagged tube, but she was too close, and it missed again. I switched on the flashlight, blinding her.

Disoriented, she slipped from the catwalk, but the harness held her weight. She flailed the tube around as she grabbed the chain and tried to pull herself up with her other hand. She wasn't strong enough, but the catwalk swayed from her frantic motion. I grabbed for the bucket to keep it from going over the catwalk as well, but couldn't quite grasp it. I'd nudged it directly to the edge.

I swept the flashlight beam from the stage floor to Nuala and back.

The music stopped. *Finally.*

"Mom!" Maeve called, her voice shrill and terrified.

Colleen looked up just as the bucket slipped from the catwalk. She dashed toward Zoe and shoved the startled girl from its path like a defensive back knocking a receiver out of bounds. They rolled to safety as the bucket slammed to the floor, spraying nails in every direction. Fortunately, everyone else had already run, and the stage was empty.

"Freeze!" Frank shouted to Nuala, his gun pointed straight at her. "Do not drop that weapon!"

She glowered down from her safety harness. For a moment, I thought she might throw the broken tube at him, but she didn't, thank heavens. She looked defeated.

Then I felt Garrett's strong arms around me, pulling me down the catwalk. "I'm fine," I said as Sergeant Walker barked directions below. The fire department had already arrived with a net in case Nuala's harness failed, and paramedics rushed into the auditorium.

Garrett released me as soon as we made it down to the stage. "Katie, what—?"

"Don't even start, please. I'll get the lecture from the Chief later."

"Okay." He put his hands up in surrender. "But maybe you should stick to dumpster diving. It's a lot safer."

He meant to keep things light, but I heard the catch in his voice. I didn't have a chance to reply as Maeve and Colleen ran to hug me. Behind them, Aidan held a trembling, wide-eyed Bliz in his arms, and he handed her to me. Zoe stared up at us from the floor, still stunned. "Everything's fine," I told them all. "No one's hurt. It's over."

Colleen held back tears. "You were so brave up there," she said, giving me another python squeeze. "You're always my hero."

"You saved Zoe," I said. "You're a hero too."

I glanced over my shoulder. Sergeant Walker, all-business as usual, guided a cuffed and silent Nuala out the back of the auditorium, accompanied by Frank and another officer. Moira and Una scurried to follow them.

If Nuala was lucky, maybe she'd be served a special Saint Patrick's Day breakfast in Cloverhill County Jail.

Chapter
Thirty-Two

The Paddy's Day show was a huge success, despite the tragic way things had started in Angels Hall—and almost ended at the dress rehearsal. With Nuala McShane safely in custody for Deirdre Donnelly's murder and her lesser attempted shenanigans, every dancer participated, and Great Shamrock Hall was packed to capacity.

The crowd gave all the dancers a standing ovation, the music was a hit, and Bliz and the Murphy triplets brought flowers onstage to Colleen and Bernie. The loudest applause came as Bernie named Darcy as the recipient of the first annual Deirdre Donnelly Memorial Scholarship, and Theresa burst into tears. Then Aidan took the stage again to announce that his new Irish dance show, Crossroad Dreams with Aidan O'Hearne, would be based each summer in Shamrock, with free town performances. Mayor Flanagan was so ecstatic, his "Find Gold in Shamrock" button burst off his tuxedo lapel.

After the show, all the performers and guardians and the entire Saint Patrick's Day committee—half the town—gathered for an informal reception thrown by the Our Lady of Angels Rosary Society. I stood in the doorway, surveying the huge, elegant ball-room decked with streamers, balloons, and tissue-paper flowers in green, white, and orange. The only residents missing, it seemed, were those affiliated with the Smiling Shamrock.

From all reports, Moira and Una were in complete shock and denial over the recent turn of events regarding Nuala. They kept an unusually low profile, and their B and B guests checked out faster than the media checked in on the lawn.

Nuala claimed innocence, of course, but she'd crack eventually, under Sergeant Walker's questioning. Her flashlight was taken into evidence—not to mention the security footage from the new cameras at Great Shamrock Hall. Bernie had insisted on them after I'd been attacked that first time in the auditorium, and the mayor took full credit.

There wasn't a dry eye in the house when Colleen turned out the lights and everyone lit the candles Zoe had saved from Deirdre's rained-out vigil. Bernie was clearly touched, bringing out her shamrock handkerchief again as Mom patted her arm.

When the lights came back on, Theresa handed out memorial cards and the rosary members served homemade desserts. The adults celebrated with a toast of fizzy green champagne to Deirdre, Bernie, and Colleen. Aidan and my sister had a fabulous time uncorking bottles onto the ornate ceiling and adding green food coloring to refill glasses at the ready.

Maeve, Conor, and Zoe tried to corral their younger siblings, who ran through the crowded ballroom like oversugared gerbils in a timed maze trial. Bliz and the Murphy triplets searched for Mikey under the linen-skirted tables as he and Theresa's grandson snickered from behind an enormous woman with a plate piled with fancy tea sandwiches.

We Buckleys had a long road ahead of us, I knew. There would be a lot of talking and compromising and probably tears as we navigated our new family journey. So far, all we'd decided for sure was that the girls and I would stay through Easter, and I'd handle the Buckley House taxes. We'd return in June, when Maeve and Bliz finished school, and spend the summer in Shamrock. Our lease was up in September, so I'd decide by then whether we'd stay for longer. And, of course, Colleen and I would need to work through some tough issues. First item on the agenda: the big talk with Bliz.

That was a lot. But I felt ready for the challenge, and my sister did too. I smiled as I watched her now, laughing and working the crowd and accepting congratulations from everyone on the show—and becoming Bernie's partner at the Donnelly School. The two would have help from Theresa, who'd returned the scholarship money she'd stolen and volunteered her assistance. I hadn't seen my sister this happy in a long time.

Was I happy, with the celebrations going on around me in my ever-green hometown and Deirdre's alleged killer safely in custody?

Yes. Somehow I felt lighter than I had in ages. I snagged an extra-full champagne glass from the table, then retreated to my spot by the door. My sister raised her own glass to me, flashing her dimple.

"Hey, I hear you'll be around this summer." Garrett stepped toward me from the other side of the doorway. "Maybe we can take a cooler out to Emerald Lake, like old times."

"Aren't you a cop?" I asked. "No alcohol allowed at the lake."

He shrugged. "Well, yeah, but there's always the cabins . . ."

"In your dreams," I told him, with a Colleen smile. "I'll have the kids, remember?"

"And a dog." Siobhan joined us, carrying a plate of tarts. "Rover is really looking forward to his extended stay. Have to say, your sister made a persuasive case."

"Can't wait," I said.

"So are we going to have that girls' night soon?" Siobhan pretended to knock her brother out of the way. "We deserve one, don't you think? Just us, *no* family members."

I helped myself to a tart. "I completely agree."

* * *

Later that night, after the rest of the family and happy guests had gone to bed and the Buckley House was finally quiet, I tiptoed into the darkened living room and turned on the vintage hobnob lamp near the old piano. The police scanner was crackling, as always, but I ignored it. I was off duty again.

I slipped onto the bench and softly touched one ivory key.

"Play us a tune, Katie," the Chief said from his usual spot.

I jumped. "Whoa, I didn't see you there."

"Couldn't sleep. Happens sometimes." He reached over and—another Saint Patrick's Day miracle—turned off the scanner himself. "Go ahead, Katie. I'll just rest my eyes."

"Okay, Dad." I took a deep breath and played the first song that came to mind.

Not that fateful jig this time. But I didn't need the sheet music in front of me to play this one either.

"Irish Wedding Dance."

My dad relaxed against the back of his wheelchair, tapping its arm. And somewhere, somehow, I felt Deirdre Donnelly smile.

Acknowledgments

It took a village to bring Shamrock and its residents to life, and I'd like to express my love and gratitude to all who inspired and supported me in writing *The Jig Is Up*. First, thanks to my own Irish dancers (and one dance mom): Stephanie, Rory, Alison, Eleanor, and Kim. Fionn and Margaux, you're next! A huge shout-out to the Buckley (no relation) School of Irish Dance in Windsor Terrace and Bay Ridge, Brooklyn, for bringing neighborhood kids like mine confidence, community, and an understanding of ups and downs, as well as a joy for dance. A wave also to my birthday twin, Bliz.

I can't thank enough my wonderful editor, Terri Bischoff, and my amazing agent, Stephany Evans of Ayesha Pande Literary, who believed in me and this little Irish series from the start, and the entire team at Crooked Lane. From the mystery author community, a chirp, chirp, hooray to my dear friends and fellow blogmates at Chicks on the Case: Ellen Byron, Jennifer J. Chow, Becky Clark, Vickie Fee, Leslie Karst, Cynthia Kuhn, and Kathleen Valenti. Undying appreciation also to my three fellow members of our Fearless Foursome, Gigi Pandian, Ellen Byron, and Diane Vallere, both for your spot-on insights and for always holding my hand. Profuse thanks to my earliest readers, Chicks Emeritae Marla

Acknowledgments

Cooper and Kellye Garrett, my fabulous beta reader and friend, Lori Roberts Herbst, and the ever-supportive Tammy Barker, Ruth Koeppel, Mary Monnin, Dru Ann Love of Dru's Book Musing, and the organization Sisters in Crime (join us!). A special thanks also to Samantha Gallo and the Fuller Public Library in Hillsborough, New Hampshire.

Finally, much love to my extended Irish family, and most especially to my non-Irish husband, whom my sister calls "Saint Rich." A fitting name, for sure. May the road rise to meet you all.